W9-COG-718

Perfect Pleasures

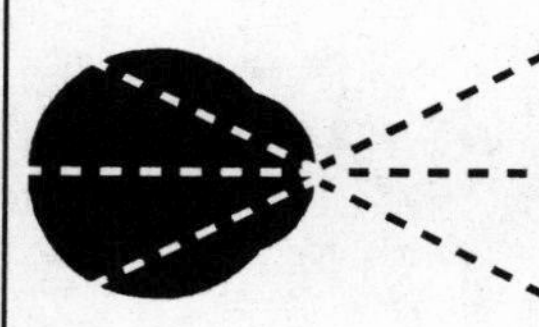

This Large Print Book carries the Seal of Approval of N.A.V.H.

Perfect Pleasures

Deborah Fletcher Mello

THORNDIKE PRESS
A part of Gale, Cengage Learning

GALE
CENGAGE Learning

Farmington Hills, Mich • San Francisco • New York • Waterville, Maine
Meriden, Conn • Mason, Ohio • Chicago

Thorndike Press® Large Print African-American.
The text of this Large Print edition is unabridged.
Other aspects of the book may vary from the original edition.
Set in 16 pt. Plantin.

LIBRARY OF CONGRESS CATALOGING-IN-PUBLICATION DATA

Names: Mello, Deborah Fletcher, author.
Title: Perfect pleasures / Deborah Fletcher Mello.
Description: Large print edition. | Waterville, Maine : Thorndike Press, 2017. | Series: Bad boys of Boulder ; 2 | Series: Thorndike Press large print African-American
Identifiers: LCCN 2016045167| ISBN 9781410495266 (hardback) | ISBN 1410495264 (hardcover)
Subjects: LCSH: African Americans—Fiction. | Large type books. | BISAC: FICTION / Contemporary Women.
Classification: LCC PS3613.E448 P47 2017 | DDC 813/.6—dc23
LC record available at https://lccn.loc.gov/2016045167

Published in 2017 by arrangement with Dafina Books, an imprint of Kensington Publishing Corp.

Printed in Mexico
1 2 3 4 5 6 7 21 20 19 18 17

To Johnnie Cool, my all-time favorite Bad Boy,
You have my heart now and always!

ACKNOWLEDGMENTS

Gratitude, first and foremost, to my Lord and Savior, for without His many blessings, none of this would be possible. I owe everything to a generous and loving God, and I am grateful beyond measure.

I am immensely blessed. Loving what I do and calling it work is my dream come true. Breathing life into my characters and fleshing out a great story just makes my heart sing. My sincerest appreciation to all those who have traveled this road with me. To the family and friends who keep me lifted in prayer and the readers and fans who buy my books and share my stories. I value each and every one of you. I have much love for you all!

Chapter One

Kenzie Monroe had arrived just in time for the rainy season, that period between July and October when rain came daily in short, intense bursts. The downpour outside pulled her from a deep sleep, the soft lull from earlier replaced by the harsh rattle of water hitting the tin underlay of the thatched roof. Kenzie had been in Phuket, Thailand, for forty-eight hours. She'd slept forty of them away, jet lag kicking her backside big-time. And now it was raining.

She stretched her lithe body up and out, her back arched toward the ceiling as she tried to ease the tightness out of her muscles. She still felt funky but knew the discomfort had nothing to do with the dull hunger pangs in the pit of her stomach and everything to do with snagging the biggest story of her journalistic career.

A freelance writer for *Sports Illustrated International,* she'd been on the job for less than a year when she'd pitched an interview and feature on UFC heavyweight champion Zachary Barrett and his twin brother, former NBA phenom Alexander Barrett. The brothers were superstars in their respective fields, and both owned and operated major athletic facilities, Alexander directing Champs in Boulder, Colorado, and Zachary running Revolution in Phuket. They were the poster children for everything right in the sports industry.

After Zachary Barrett's last successful title fight and with the sporting world touting the elite training program he and his brother had developed together, her proposal had been green-lighted, the okay coming with a respectable budget for expenses. Kenzie had been elated, feeling like she'd won the journalism lottery. Now she was scared to death that she might not get it right. She blew a soft sigh past her full lips as she considered the best way for her to approach the article that would eventually carry her byline.

She reached for her cell phone, noting the missed calls and text messages that had come in as she slumbered. Only one number had been repeated multiple times, the caller apparently anxious to get in touch with her. She pushed the REDIAL button and waited as the call connected on the other end.

Stephanie Guy, Kenzie's agent and best friend, answered on the third ring. "Hello?"

"Do you miss me?" Kenzie questioned.

"Like a fungus," Stephanie answered.

"So much love!"

Her friend laughed. "What happened to you? I've been trying to reach you for days now. Why didn't you call?"

"Jet lag. I've been asleep damn near since I got here."

"That's because you spent all of last week stressing instead of getting some rest. You should have known better."

"So did you call just to lecture me?"

"I called to see if you've made contact yet with the Barrett brothers."

There was a moment of pause as Kenzie reflected back on her run-in with Alexander and Zachary Barrett. It had been during her check-in at Revolution, both men standing in the office like two chocolate bodybuilders, buff and hard-bodied, their dark complexions glistening like expensive candy. When she arrived, she had already been out of sorts; the bald, toothless guy who had tried to grope her on the plane had left her feeling some kind of way. Had she been able to carry her Taser, she would have jolted the man; instead she'd left him cringing from an elbow drop to his crotch. Then, seconds after her arrival, the two brothers had her salivating and tongue-tied. It had been a lot to handle!

There had been no missing the amusement that had danced across Zachary's face as she'd shared the details of her experience, babbling nonsensically. His laugh had been deep, rising from someplace in his midsection. His very rock hard, six-packed midsection. She'd eyed him warily, trying to contain the perspiration that had suddenly begun to run between her cleavage, and then she'd introduced herself.

"Congratulations on your win, Mr. Barrett. It was an impressive fight. And it's nice to meet you as well," she had said, shooting a look at Alexander.

Zachary had nodded, his head bowing ever so slightly. "Thank you." He had extended his hand to shake hers. "And you are?"

"Kenzie Monroe. I'm with *Sports Illustrated International.*"

"Kenzie is here to do the article on you and Alex," Sarai Montri-Barrett, Alexander's wife, had interjected.

Zachary's gaze had shifted between the two women, then settled back on the newcomer. He had looked her up and down, the gleam in his eye practically stripping her naked where she stood. His stare had stirred something deep in her feminine spirit, igniting a slow-burning flame between her thighs.

"Where are you from, Ms. Monroe?" he'd asked.

"Please, call me Kenzie. And I was born here in Thailand, in Bangkok. But I was raised in New York."

"So your mother is Thai?"

"No, my father," she'd said, her eyes fastened tight to his. "My mother is black."

Zachary had stared at her intently, his expression shifting into something Kenzie couldn't quite discern. It was almost like a moment of recognition had flashed in his eyes. But although she had never formally met him before, his face had become flushed with color, his eyes wide as he stared at her, looking like he'd just seen a ghost. Then things had suddenly turned awkward. It got really uncomfortable when his sister-in-law had asked him to help her with her luggage.

He had turned, giving Sarai a look. "Find Sing. Have him take care of it," he'd said gruffly.

When Sarai had tried to interject, he'd snapped. Rudely. He'd spoken in Thai, the exchange meant to be between the two of them. "Get Sing. Then call that magazine and tell them this isn't going to work. I have something I need to handle."

Kenzie had watched as he suddenly turned and stormed from the room, his family embarrassed by his bad behavior. But she had been thoroughly entertained. Because she spoke Thai and had understood every foul word he'd muttered. As he'd raged, his brother following to calm him down, she'd sworn that she had heard him call her beautiful.

She shook the memory, her mouth pulled into a slight smile as she returned back to the conversation. "I met them both the day I arrived."

"Well, you must have made quite an impression because one of them called the magazine to request another writer. It appears that Zachary Barrett has some reservations about you working on this story."

Kenzie's eyes widened. "He barely spoke to me!" she said, her voice rising to just an octave below a shout. "Do not tell me the magazine is pulling me!"

"No. I saved the day. That, and a Mrs. Barrett called back to say there had been some kind of misunderstanding and that they were fine with you doing the interview."

"That had to be Alexander's wife, Sarai.

She seems cool."

"So, really, what did you do to the man? Because he is too damn fine for you to be alienating him on your first day there."

"He ain't all that," Kenzie muttered, punctuating each word slowly. She paused, thinking about the man. Zachary Barrett was the epitome of good-looking. He was a solid six feet plus a few inches tall, with a strong athletic build, a dark chocolate complexion, chiseled features, and eyes the color of gray steel. The man was orgasmic eye candy. *Damn fine* didn't begin to describe him, she mused to herself. And Stephanie knew her well enough to hear the hint of denial in her tone.

Her friend laughed. "If you say so, but I have seen photos of him. He looks like all that *and* a bag of chips to me."

"That was so cheesy!" Kenzie said, laughing along with Stephanie.

"Maybe it was, but you get what I'm saying. So what's your schedule?"

"I was just trying to figure that out. Obviously, I'll talk to both brothers, but I also want to talk to the people who work for and train with them. I want to get a sense of who they are from what others have to say about the duo."

"As long as you have a plan. Just keep in

touch. And send me your expenses, please, so I can keep track, because I know you won't, and I don't want the magazine to get any surprises we can't explain."

"Yeah, yeah," Kenzie answered with a slight eye roll.

"And one last thing," Stephanie added before disconnecting the call. "Don't piss off the man. Pissed-off men don't give good interviews!"

Kenzie chuckled as she dropped her cell phone back onto the tabletop. She and Stephanie had met in college. They'd been roommates for three of the four years they'd been at Seton Hall University in South Orange, New Jersey. Stephanie knew all of her dirty little secrets, and there was nothing the two wouldn't do for each other. They often joked that when one called asking for help burying a body, the other would just bring the shovel, a rose bush, and never once ask any questions. Stephanie was like a sister, and she'd been watching over Kenzie since they'd both chosen their respective career paths.

Rising from the bed, Kenzie threw open the door of her less-than-luxurious accommodations. She'd been housed in one of the larger guest bungalows at Revolution, the MMA training camp owned by Zachary

Barrett. With a reputation for being a premier destination for Muay Thai, MMA, and fitness training, the facility had been featured in many a documentary and travel show, but nothing had prepared her for the extraordinary property. She had often read about Zachary boasting that this property was his dream come true, and now she understood why — it was one of the prettiest places she'd ever visited.

The entire property was surrounded by coconut palms and banana trees on one side and beach front on the other. A gravel road lined with lush foliage greeted visitors; the thick, verdant vegetation looked like a postcard pictorial. About a mile in, the road opened onto a clearing that gave way to all things Revolution. On the left side of the property was an extensive open-air gym. The space hosted multiple fight rings and was equipped with training bags, free weights, isolation machines, and other assorted gym equipment. The entire area was covered with a high thatched roof that allowed the breeze to flow through from the beach area that bordered the property.

On the right side of the facility, there was a fully equipped indoor gym, rooms for dance and yoga training, and an on-site cafeteria. There were twelve additional bungalows to accommodate paying guests, and just a few steps behind where she was staying was Zachary's private residence. Despite the early-morning hour and the rain that was coming in a heavy downpour, there were dozens of people already working out, a team of devoted and hardworking trainers putting them through their paces.

Kenzie wrapped her arms around her torso, hugging herself tightly. It still amazed her that she was actually back in Thailand. It had been twenty-six years since her last visit. She'd barely been four years old when her mother had come back one last time, hoping to connect them both with her father. Knowing nothing about her paternal parent was why Kenzie had embraced all things Thai, desperate to connect to that half of her bloodline. She'd learned the language and the traditions, had studied the history, and considered herself as Thai as anyone else born and raised there. But she still knew nothing about her paternal lineage, and she fully intended to spend every spare moment she could find discovering her father's people, praying that she might actually find her father as well.

She inhaled deeply, the earthy scent of the rain on dry earth and the pungent sweetness of the flora filling her lungs. She closed the door, leaving the damp air and rain outside.

Stepping back into her space, she took in the view, seeing it in the daylight hours with a clear head for the first time. The structure in its entirety was teak, with an insulated thatched roof. The tropical hardwood was brownish red, everything about the natural striations warm and inviting. The interior of the room was sparse, just a full-sized bed dressed in white bedding, a nightstand, one lamp, and a chair. Attached, there was a small bathroom with a shower. If it was nothing else, it was comfortable.

Kenzie moved into the bathroom, leaving a trail of clothes behind her. After pulling her tank top over her head, she stepped out of her lace G-string and right into a heated shower. The warming waters felt blissful against her skin as she turned in a slow circle beneath the massaging spray. It was minutes before she was done, the water beginning to cool substantially when she finally stepped out. She grabbed a plush white towel to wrap herself in, then kicked her dirty clothes out of her way as she moved back into the living space. After moisturizing her skin with a rich emollient of coconut cream and vitamin E oil, Kenzie tossed on a pair of athletic shorts and a Bob

Marley T-shirt. She took time to pull a wide-toothed comb through her voluminous curls, then twisted the thick tresses into two Pocahontas braids that fell down the length of her back. Slipping her feet into a pair of high-top Converse sneakers, she grabbed her digital recorder, her notepad, and an ink pen and headed out the door.

Zachary Barrett should have been paying attention to his opponent. He should have been focused on throwing punches and blocking blows. Instead, he hesitated, finding himself staring across the yard at Kenzie Monroe. Her complexion was like honey, a deep, rich, sweet coloration that paid homage to her African heritage. But her features were Asian — almond-shaped eyes, forest-thick lashes, and chiseled cheekbones. Her hair was a definite melding of the two cultures — thick, curly hair that fell well past her shoulders and was now braided neatly into two plaits. Her body was a contradiction, her petite stature boasting voluptuous curves. She was a perfect figure eight with a full, lush bustline, a rail-thin waist, and a bubble-shaped ass that had him wondering what it might feel like in the palm of his hand.

Zachary was so distracted by her presence

that it had him feeling off sides, and he was staring unabashedly. Kenzie Monroe had been out of sight and almost out of mind since her abrupt arrival at his renowned athletic facility. The journalist who'd come to do a magazine article on him and his twin brother had arrived like a storm wind — loud, abrasive, and wanting to be noticed. After discovering who she was, he had wished her away, cursing her presence in his personal space. Then, just as quickly, she couldn't be found. She'd disappeared. Nothing left but the barest breeze of memory and the decadent scent of her perfume lingering in the tropical air. That's when he suddenly found himself wanting her to return. It was crazy and out of character for him, and he had no one to blame, so he blamed her.

And now she was back, intruding in his space, everyone else acting as if she belonged there. Zachary stared, and suddenly Kenzie was staring back, her large eyes keyed in on him, her entire face pulled into a bright smile. He abruptly snatched his gaze from hers, and in that same instant, his brother nailed him in the chest with an easy right cross, the blow knocking the wind out of his sails.

"Humph," Zachary gasped, the guttural

sound rising from deep in his midsection.

Alexander laughed as he stepped back. He shook his head as he pulled off his boxing gloves. "You're not going to win any fights like that."

Zachary sputtered. "It's . . . a good . . . thing . . . I . . . already won . . . the fight . . . I needed to win." He gulped air, filling his lungs and then blowing his breath out slowly.

The current heavyweight MMA champion had successfully defended his title just weeks earlier. He had his brother to thank for getting him fight-ready. The two men had been estranged for many years, and it had taken some serious intervention from Zachary's best friend, Sarai, who was now his brother's wife, to bring them back together. The duo was once again back in sync — A to Z, the bad boys of Boulder, Colorado, looking to conquer the world side by side. Together they were a childhood dream come true and then some.

"Do you want to talk about it?" Alexander asked as the two exited the fight ring. "What's going on with you? You're not usually so distracted."

Zachary shrugged his broad shoulders, shifting his gaze back to Kenzie, who was standing in conversation with his friend and manager, Gamon Montri. Gamon, who was usually stone-faced, was smiling at her eagerly, seeming to enjoy whatever was being said. "It's nothing," he answered, shifting his silver-gray eyes back to meet his twin brother's bright blue stare.

"Like hell it's nothing! You've been acting funny for a few days now."

Zachary gave his brother a slight shrug. "I've just got a lot on my mind, a million things to do, and I'm trying to get back into a routine that makes sense."

Alexander stood staring at his brother. The two were as close as any two siblings could possibly be, but it hadn't always been that way. For too many years, there had been a bitter rift between them, based on their fight over a woman who hadn't been worth either's energy. Back then, they'd vowed to never speak another word to the other. That had been a lifetime ago, and now the two were grateful that things had changed for the better, unable to fathom any kind of life without each other.

Alexander persisted. "You're holding something back, and you and I both know that's not a good thing, Z," he said, calling his brother by the nickname that only they used for each other.

"I'm good, A. Just leave me alone."

"And you know that's not going to happen, so you might as well tell me what the problem is so I can help you solve it."

Zachary shifted his gaze back to Kenzie again, hesitating for a brief second as he watched her jot notes into her notebook. Alexander's eyes followed his twin's, turning to see what Zachary was so focused on. When he turned his attention back to his brother, Zachary was shaking his head at him.

"I said to let it go."

"Let what go?" Sarai Montri-Barrett asked, suddenly interjecting herself into their conversation. "What are you two talking about?"

The twins both jumped.

"Where'd you come from?" Alexander asked as he looped an arm around his wife's waist and kissed her cheek.

The woman grinned as she bumped her hip slightly against his. Sarai laughed. "That's not important. What are you two whispering about?"

Alexander shot his brother a quick look, his twin exchanging eye contact with him. A little white lie spilled out of his mouth. "We were just talking about this interview. Zachary's not feeling it, but he didn't want to say anything to you."

"Why? What did Kenzie do?" Sarai glanced to where her father and the young journalist were in deep conversation. "Because I know you called the magazine trying to get her fired!" she added.

Zachary rolled his eyes skyward. "I wasn't trying to get her fired! And who said Kenzie did something? She didn't do anything. Why does this have to be about her? I've just changed my mind about the damn interview is all!" His tone was terse, just a breath shy of being hostile. "Can't a man change his mind?"

Sarai and Alexander exchanged a look, both trying to make sense of the situation.

Zachary changed the subject abruptly. "I need a shower. I'll talk to you two later," he said. He turned to scurry off in the opposite direction.

"Zachary, wait!" Sarai called after him, stalling his steps.

"What?"

"Family dinner tonight. Don't be late!"

Zachary narrowed his gaze, a gust of air blowing past his full lips. "What time?"

"Seven o'clock. We're eating at Sam's," Sarai said referring to the popular grilled steak restaurant in Patong.

Nodding his head, Zachary turned back

around and disappeared across the court-yard.

"What's going on with him?" Sarai asked, turning her attention back to her husband.

Alexander laughed. "I don't have a clue." He shifted his gaze across the courtyard, staring after Kenzie, who was headed into the main building. "But something tells me it might be about her."

Sarai frowned, concern twisting her expression as she watched her husband watching the other woman. "You need to talk to him. I don't know if I like her."

"You don't have to like her. Besides, I don't think you like any woman Zachary is interested in. You're worse than our mother is."

"I just want your brother to be happy."

Alexander grinned. "He would be," he said as he winked an eye at her. "Even if it was only for one night."

Shaking her head, Sarai gave her husband a look. She rose up on her toes to kiss his mouth, the gesture short and sweet as she tossed a look over her shoulder to insure no one was paying them any attention.

"You have jokes," she said as Alexander grabbed her hand, leading her across the compound toward the offices. "But your brother needs to settle down and find what we have. Then he'll be very happy!"

Kenzie gestured toward the young man behind the desk. He was slight in build, looking like he was barely out of his teens and far too young to be handling business behind a reception desk. He eyed her warily before giving her a nod, a wide grin pulling full and bright across his face.

"How I help you?" he asked, his broken English broken just good enough to be understood.

"Hi! Do you by chance know where I can find Mr. Barrett?"

The young man looked confused, eyeing her with wide eyes and a furrowed brow as he visibly struggled to decipher her Brooklyn accent.

She sighed softly. "Zachary Barrett? Do you know where he is?"

The bright smile widened, his head bobbing up and down eagerly. "Mr. Zachary, he say he gone for the day. Be back tomorrow."

Kenzie nodded. "Thank you," she said as she turned, moving in the direction of the cafeteria.

Frustration painted her expression as she hurried toward the other end of the building. She had tried earlier to catch up with the man, hoping to catch him off guard, but each time she'd gotten within reach, he'd disappeared out a side door, slipping past her as if he didn't want to be found. It wasn't rocket science for Kenzie to know that Zachary was purposely avoiding her. Sooner or later she was going to find out why.

Not paying attention, she took the corner at the end of the hallway at lightning speed and abruptly collided with Zachary, the two slamming into each other harshly. Instinctively, he reached out his arms and grabbed her by the shoulders, pulling her into his chest to prevent them both from falling to the floor.

The moment was suddenly surreal as Kenzie fell against his broad body, his large hands drawing her close. As recognition swept between them, a wave of heat followed, the eruption feeling volcanic. The intensity of it surprised them both.

Kenzie cussed. Loudly. The expletive echoed through the space. Zachary frowned as he took a quick step back, snatching his hands down to his sides. She was the last person he had wanted to see. He mumbled an apology, the words barely audible. Both were stunned into silence, eyeing each other reservedly.

He took a deep breath and held it briefly before blowing it out. "Are you okay?" he finally asked, his eyes sifting back and forth to avoid hers.

"No!" Kenzie exclaimed, rubbing a soft palm against her shoulder. She snapped. "You really need to look where you're going!"

"Me? Do you think maybe *you* need to pay more attention? I wasn't the one running down the hallway!"

"Running?"

Zachary ranted. "That's what I said! This isn't a playground, Ms. Monroe. For safety reasons we don't allow *running* in the hallways! We have a track outside for that. If you can't get it together, we will ask you to leave!"

Kenzie bristled, her hands falling to the line of her lean hips. She clutched the waistband of her shorts with a tightened fist. Before she could fix her mouth to tell him what she thought, he pushed abruptly past her and headed toward the building's front door. Minutes later, Kenzie was still standing with her mouth open, completely dumbfounded by the exchange.

Chapter Two

The outdoor shower was just warm enough. With high temperatures permeating the deep blue sky, the flow of moisture over Zachary's shoulders was a welcome relief.

He found himself in a bad mood and unable to explain it if his life depended on it. He was angry at no one, bitter about nothing, and surly for no reason. He bit back the rancor that twisted his heart, his chest feeling as if he were choking on stagnant bile. Kenzie Monroe had his emotions twisted, and he was feeling some kind of way. But there was no explanation that made any kind of sense.

The last time he'd felt so discombobulated was when his marriage was falling apart, his now ex-wife purposely riding roughshod across his heart. Felicia Wells Barrett had been his brother Alexander's college sweetheart. Back then the two had planned to spend forever together. The day Zachary and Felicia had been introduced, all that changed, and the direction of all their lives took a serious nosedive.

Sibling rivalry had often pitted one brother against the other, but being highly competitive reached a whole other level with Felicia deep in the mix. In the beginning, Zachary hadn't taken the young woman seriously. She wasn't the first girl the two had fought over, and back then he'd imagined she wasn't going to be the last.

But Felicia fell hard for Zachary's bad-boy personality. Zachary was more laid-back and impetuous than his brother; trouble followed him everywhere he turned. Alexander was the more conservative twin, rarely willing to take any unnecessary risk. His no-nonsense demeanor could be a touch rigid, and he second-guessed each step. Zachary would act on impulse, rarely considering the consequences of his actions. And he hadn't been thinking when he fell for his brother's girlfriend seducing him.

Before he could get a handle on what was happening, Felicia had them engaged, and right after graduation, she was dragging him down the matrimonial aisle. The day he and Felicia exchanged vows had been the last day his brother would talk to him. Months later, the newlyweds moved from Colorado to Thailand so that Zachary could pursue his business and athletic dreams, which would eventually make him a household name in the sporting world.

The honeymoon had been over before they landed. Felicia had been a viper in high heels and too-tight dresses. She'd been manipulative, condescending, a habitual liar, and a cheat. The lie that had hurt him most was when he believed he was going to be a father, only to discover that she'd been having an affair with her gynecologist and both had lied to his face. There had been a host of red flags that had given him fair warning about the kind of woman Felicia was. He'd closed both eyes to her deceit, and his relationship with his family had suffered the brunt of it. Then one day he'd come home to find Felicia gone, his house and bank accounts empty. She had charmed one of his clients, a wealthy expat from England, into whisking her away to a whole other life that didn't include him. Through all of it, the chasm between him and his brother had been voluminous.

It had taken an act of nature to fix what had been broken. Hurricane Sarai drew the two brothers together, twisting and turning them about until letting go of each other was no longer an option. Reconnecting with

Alexander had given Zachary a new lease on life, his twin brother's support a much-needed lifeline. The past few months had been the best he'd had in years, everything falling into place and fitting neatly. And now he was suddenly feeling out of sorts and blaming another woman for causing his angst.

But Zachary knew that finding fault with Kenzie made no sense to anyone but him. She was a stunning woman, and it seemed as if she was exceptionally professional. She hadn't done or said anything to offend him because he hadn't given her any opportunity to. He understood that from the outside looking in, most would assume that he knew absolutely nothing about her except what he'd learned the first time they'd been introduced. She had told them all that she'd been born in Bangkok to a black American mother and a Thai father but had been raised in New York. That initial conversation hadn't been enough for him to form any kind of character assessment. But he knew things about Kenzie that she herself probably had no awareness of. Things he'd been sworn to keep to himself. A promise that he had no plans to break.

Those secrets had him on edge. So much on edge that he could barely find himself within ten feet of the woman without his emotions getting away from him. Desperate to maintain control, he'd been avoiding her like the plague despite her efforts to engage him in conversation. And just like that he'd barked at her about running.

Zachary shook his head from side to side. He was suddenly feeling foolish and embarrassed, hoping that the way he had acted would be dismissed without prejudice, that Kenzie would not hold it against him that he had acted like someone had stolen his candy. An air of contrition suddenly washed over his spirit. His family had often admonished him about acting impulsively and allowing his emotions to sway his actions. He had honestly never seen it himself, nor believed it, earlier. Now, he was completely convinced that he needed to do better. He had no doubt that Kenzie Monroe would probably agree.

He stepped out of the shower and reached for one of the plush white towels monogrammed with the Revolution name. He swiped the moisture from his skin, the soft cotton gently massaging his body. There were only a few remaining bruises from his last MMA title bout, the flesh barely tinged black and blue beneath the pattern of tattoos that decorated his body. He was in the best physical condition of his life, every sinewy muscle a hardened line of rock-solid steel. It had been months of pre-fight preparation, a stringent diet, and the emotional support of those he loved most that had gotten him to this point. He worked extremely hard to be in shape, and he was determined to lead by example those who sought him out for training. He also knew that there was a host of young men and boys wanting to one day steal his belt from him, and he had no intentions of letting that happen easily.

He imagined that his last fight would probably be one of few that remained, so he was grateful that it had been memorable, going down in the record books as one of the best in history. Truth be told, he was tired, physically and mentally, and he knew that it was only a matter of time before he would have to announce his retirement. The fighters gunning for him now were getting younger and younger, some as young as half his thirty years, and had twice his stamina. Right now he was riding a winner's high, enjoying the luxury of being number one in the game. He didn't look forward to the day when a win might come only after a lucky punch. Because luck had never been his friend.

Moving into his bedroom, he threw his large body across the bed, drawing his arm up over his eyes. He had a few hours before anyone would be looking for him, and he was grateful for the time. As he relaxed, he found himself reflecting back on his career and the people who had contributed to his success, and then he thought of Kenzie Monroe, and his mood suddenly shifted back to brooding.

Kenzie Monroe being there in the flesh wasn't a good thing, and there was no way he could say so without exposing his hand and another man's secret. Kenzie's connection to his past was why he was bothered in the present. And as he lay there reflecting on the wealth of it, he couldn't even begin to imagine what it might mean for his future.

When Zachary entered the restaurant, his brother and sister-in-law were already seated across the table from Kenzie Monroe. He came to an abrupt halt. Sarai had said family dinner, he mused. *When had Kenzie become family?*

He was just about to turn on his heels and head for the door when a loud cheer erupted through the room. All the staff and some of the patrons came to their feet to salute him, the applause heartwarming. He lifted a hand to wave, a slight smile pulling at his full lips. The restaurant's owner rushed to his side to greet him.

From where she sat, Kenzie watched as Zachary paused to sign a few autographs and pose for a selfie or two with fans. He was well loved in Phuket, and it was obvious he didn't let the accolades go to his head. He genuinely appreciated the love and support, and for a brief moment she detected an air of shyness about him.

"He's really not fond of all the attention," Sarai suddenly interjected. Kenzie shifted her gaze to meet the look the other woman was giving her. She continued, "Zachary's a great showman for the sport, but on his own time he really likes to keep to himself."

"I never got that impression about him," Kenzie said.

"Neither did I," Alexander added with a soft chuckle.

Sarai cut an eye in her husband's direction. "Zachary is very sensitive."

Alexander laughed heartily. "My wife is very protective of my brother. Almost to a fault."

"I am not!" Sarai chimed.

The man nodded his head. "You really are, baby! Because there is nothing sensitive about my twin."

His wife rolled her eyes skyward.

Kenzie laughed. "So, you and Zachary were good friends before you met Alexander. But you married Alexander? Is that right?"

"Zachary and I were like brother and sister. He was my best friend. When I met this one here," she nudged her husband, ". . . well . . . he was hard to resist," she said with a sly smile.

Alexander grabbed his wife's hand and gave it a squeeze. Kenzie sensed he wanted to lean in and give Sarai a kiss, but he hesitated, his eyes skating around the room as he resisted the urge to press his mouth to hers. Kenzie was fully aware of the cultural attitudes about public displays of affection, and although she didn't quite understand all the nuances, she respected those that chose to respect what she thought was an antiquated attitude.

They changed the subject as Zachary continued to make his way around the room. "So what made you want to be a journalist?" Alexander asked.

Kenzie took a slow sip of her Singha beer, then swallowed before answering. "I fell into it by accident. My last year of college, I had a grueling load, but I needed one more class in order to keep all of my financial aid money. So I signed up for a mass communications class that required me to work on the student newspaper. I thought it would be an easy course that I could fly right through. But it wasn't! I actually had to work, and I absolutely loved it! Before that, I was planning on being an attorney."

"We were all impressed by your credentials," Sarai noted. "You've had a stellar career."

Kenzie smiled. "Thank you. I appreciate that."

The conversation was interrupted as Zachary finally made it to the booth where they all sat. He dropped down beside her, into the only vacant seat. As he did, his leg brushed against hers. The touch was heated, igniting the faintest hint of fireworks between them. They both shifted at the same time, the abrupt gesture almost comical for anyone who might have noticed. And Sarai and Alexander did, shooting each other a look as they held back their laughter.

Zachary muttered under his breath. "Sorry."

"No problem," Kenzie mumbled back as she shot him a quick look. She brushed a hand against the skin that had been touched, the gesture meant to stall the rise of heat but failing.

"I thought this was a *family* dinner?" Zachary said. He cut an eye in Kenzie's direction, the question meant to incite a reaction.

Sarai shook her head. "It is. Kenzie wanted to sit down with us all together. A family dinner was the best way to make that happen."

Zachary grunted.

Alexander shook his head. "Kenzie, I wish you'd had a chance to meet our parents before they flew back to Colorado last week. I'm sure they would have had a lot to tell you about the two of us!"

Kenzie smiled. "I'm sorry I missed them, too. Hopefully when I stop in Colorado on my way back to New York, they'll be able to make some time for me."

"You're going to Colorado?" Zachary questioned, shifting in his seat to stare at her.

She nodded. "That's the plan."

There was an awkward silence as the two locked gazes and held on. The corner of Kenzie's mouth lifted in the faintest smile, her whole face brightening. "I do believe this is the first time that you haven't been snarling at me like some trapped animal, Mr. Barrett."

Zachary's eyes widened, bristling with a hint of attitude. "Excuse me?"

"Something wrong with your hearing? You heard me." Bemusement skipped across her face, her eyes still dancing a two-step with his.

Zachary smirked, his head waving slightly. There had only been one other woman in his life bold enough to call him on his crap, and she had married his brother. His eyes shifted toward Sarai, who was eying them both curiously.

Alexander laughed, and in no time at all, the entire table was laughing together.

"You owe me an apology," Kenzie said as she slid a bite of chicken satay into her mouth.

Zachary rolled his eyes toward the ceiling. "Sounds like you have a personal problem to me. I'd think in your line of business you'd have tougher skin. Not everyone you're interested in writing about is interested in telling their story."

"No, they're not, but the apology you owe me has nothing to do with my interview."

Zachary sat back in his seat. "No?"

"No. You practically bowled me down in the hallway earlier. It felt like you dislocated my shoulder, you hit me so hard. That wasn't cool."

"Please!" He shot her a look. "Next time, remember you're inside and not outside, and don't run in the halls. When you run in the halls, accidents happen. You don't have anyone else to blame but yourself. Besides, I think you fractured my thumb, and I make a living with these hands. But you don't see me complaining." He held out his left hand, his palm upright as he flicked his thumb back and forth.

Kenzie's expression was incredulous as she dropped her fork onto her plate, shifting her full attention in his direction. She shook her head as she cupped her hand beneath his, folding her finger around the appendage. She drew the fingers of her other hand across his palm, the gesture teasing. "Poor baby!" she cooed.

Zachary suddenly felt himself blush. Her touch had ignited a firestorm, an erection threatening to pull full and taut in his slacks. He pulled his hand from hers and shifted forward in his seat. Reaching for his glass, he took a gulp of his Thai iced tea. The bright orange drink was a mix of sugar, coconut milk, tamarind, orange blossom water, star anise, cinnamon, and other spices. The sweet brew was one of Zachary's favorites, but in that moment he found himself wishing for something stronger. He gestured toward the waiter and ordered a bourbon.

"You drink? For some reason, I imagined you to be a die-hard health nut," Kenzie said, a hint of surprise in her question. She gently spun her own drink glass between the palms of her hands.

Zachary shrugged. "That would be my brother. I've never been quite so committed."

"Do you have any other vices that my readers would be interested in?"

He levied a narrowed gaze at her. "Vices?"

"You drink alcohol. Some in the sports world might consider that a vice."

"They would be the ones who need to stay out of my business," he countered. He pointed at the waiter, then tapped his empty glass for a refill.

"Are you always so pleasant to be around?"

"Excuse me?"

"I didn't steal your puppy, so I'm not sure why you've been so hostile."

Zachary laughed. "That's a bit dramatic, don't you think? Just because I'm not fawning all over you, Ms. Monroe, doesn't mean I'm being hostile."

"I didn't ask you to fawn, Mr. Barrett, but it wouldn't hurt you to simply be polite."

Sarai interjected. "He's just been under a lot of stress lately, with the big fight and . . . ," she started.

"I can speak for myself, thank you," Zachary snapped.

Alexander bristled. He sat straighter in his seat. He and his brother locked gazes, the two seeming to have a silent conversation.

The two women looked from one to the other, their eyes skating back and forth as they waited to see who would jump first. The tension was palpable, everyone suddenly feeling on edge.

Alexander broke the uncomfortable silence that had descended over the table. "Since this is family dinner, now is as good a time as any to tell you that we're going to be going back home at the end of the week."

Kenzie shot Zachary a look, eyeing him curiously to see how he reacted to the news.

He lifted his head to stare at his brother. "You and Sarai are leaving?" he said, looking from Alexander to his sister-in-law and back.

His twin nodded. "Yeah, Z, I need to check on my own business, and it really is just time for us to go home. You know that we've stayed longer than we planned."

Zachary sighed, the weight of his growing emotion touching them all. He suddenly moved onto his feet, his eyes glazed. He reached into his pocket for his billfold, tossing money onto the table to cover the bill. He avoided catching any of their eyes. "I need to run," he said, his tone dropping to a loud whisper. "I have some paper work to finish." He finally lifted his eyes to meet his brother's stare. "I'll catch up with you later."

He gave Kenzie a quick glance and a nod. "Good night, Ms. Monroe," he said, and then he turned on his heels and disappeared out the door.

Watching him leave so suddenly had Kenzie in her own feelings. There was no missing that his brother's news had knocked Zachary off sides. With Alexander and Sarai leaving Thailand, she imagined that getting the story she needed from Zachary was going to be difficult at best, if not completely impossible.

Lifting her gaze, she found Alexander and Sarai both staring at her, seeming to read her mind.

"He's just being a little sensitive," Alexander said. "He'll get over it. I promise."

Sarai laughed, tossing up both her hands. "How come when I say he's sensitive, you always shut me down?"

Alexander grinned. "Because I can say it. I'm his brother. Don't you know how weird it sounds to have my wife say my twin brother is a little *sensitive*?"

They all laughed, but despite their assurances, Kenzie wasn't sure she believed them.

Days later, Sarai and Kenzie sat alone in a corner of the cafeteria. It was Kenzie's last opportunity to interview the other woman before she and her husband would leave Phuket to return to the United States. The two were staring out the window toward the open gym, their gazes following Alexander and Zachary, who were working out together in one of the fight rings.

"They're very close, aren't they?" Kenzie asked.

Sarai nodded. "Yes, they are. They're sometimes lost without each other. I know that's why Zachary isn't feeling good about us leaving. They just reconnected after years of being apart, and he doesn't want to lose that."

"You also have a very *special* relationship with Zachary. Do things ever get awkward with him and your husband because of it?"

Sarai eyed her with a raised brow. "Why would it get awkward?"

Kenzie shrugged. "I don't know. I was just asking."

Sarai stared at her for a moment before

speaking. "Zachary and I were friends, *best* friends, before I met his brother. He was a blessing to my father and me when we needed it most. You do know that Gamon is my father, right?"

Kenzie nodded her head yes as Sarai continued.

"When I met Alexander, it was love at first sight. He captured my heart. The love they have for each other and the bond they share allows me to have the two most favorite people in my life without it being an issue for either of them. So no, it doesn't get awkward."

Kenzie dropped her ink pen to the table. Her eyes shifted back out the window. "He seems very sad sometimes," she said softly. She dropped her chin into her hand, her elbow propped against the table.

"He's suffered a lot of loss. Maybe he'll tell you about it and you'll understand him better," Sarai whispered back.

Kenzie shot her a look, a wave of understanding seeming to waft between the two of them. Their conversation continued for another hour, the two women getting to know each other better. Without realizing it, most of her questions centered on Zachary and his accomplishments, hoping Sarai's answers would help when she next got a chance to talk to him directly.

Zachary Barrett fascinated her. He was somewhat of an anomaly, unlike most of the men she'd ever known. She'd watched how focused he was when training clients and running his business. She had no doubt that he was wholeheartedly dedicated to his family, friends, and employees. From everything his staff and friends and business associates had to say about him, he was well-respected and much loved. But something was missing. Something that kept his smile at bay. Something that he hid with his bravado and his swagger. His public persona was boastful and audacious, but more often than not, when it was just him and he thought no one was watching, unhappiness would settle against his shoulders and weigh down his spirit. It was then that Kenzie sensed his vulnerability, an air of insecurity that he didn't want anyone to know.

"He really isn't interested in talking to me, is he?" Kenzie asked, refocusing her attention back on Sarai.

Sarai shook her head, tossing the length of her hair over her shoulders. "I don't know why, but he doesn't trust the process."

"You mean he doesn't trust me."

There was a moment of hesitation. "I'm sorry, but I don't know why he has issues with you. I wish I did."

"But you agree that he has issues with me?"

Sarai smiled, her mouth bending slowly upward. "Well, there's something about you that has him all riled up!"

Kenzie laughed. "I have that effect on men," she said jokingly.

They turned back to stare out the window, watching as the two brothers laughed heartily about something they found funny. Watching them together made the women smile. After a few minutes, Sarai rose from her seat, gathering the remnants of her lunch from the table. She hesitated for a brief moment as she carefully chose her last words.

"Don't hurt him," she said as she looked Kenzie in the eyes. "He can't handle being hurt again. If this is some kind of game for you, then you need to leave. Don't play with his emotions. If you do, you'll live to regret it."

Kenzie's brow lifted in surprise. "I'm not . . . I . . ."

"I know, you're just here to do a story. But I see how you look at him, and I see how he looks at you. Neither one of you is ready to admit that there is something going on with you, and since I'm not sure that whatever that is will be good for Zachary, I'm giving you fair warning."

"So are you threatening me?"

Sarai shook her head. "Not at all. Just warning you that my husband won't take kindly to anyone who attacks his brother or hurts his heart. And neither will I." And with that, Sarai headed for the door and out of the building.

Kenzie blew a soft sigh past her full lips. She didn't say it out loud, the words feeling foreign to her, but she instinctively knew exactly what Sarai had been thinking. And she found herself suddenly feeling the same way, wanting to protect Zachary from pain of any kind.

Chapter Three

The ride back from the airport had been bittersweet. Zachary had hated to see his brother and his best friend leave him, but he was excited for them and the future he imagined them having. As he'd watched their plane taxi down the runway, he'd whispered a quiet Thai prayer that Sarai had taught him, wishing for protection and guidance to lead them on their journey.

He turned onto the property and drove his jeep down to the main building. Sarai's father, Gamon, spoke for the first time since kissing his daughter and new son-in-law good-bye. "That reporter woman would like to ask you questions today. Sarai told her you are free this afternoon."

"Tell her I'm not available, please. Today's not a good day."

Gamon gave him a stern look, the man's expression scolding. "She is a nice girl. And she will be good for the business. You must talk to her."

Zachary cut an eye at his old friend. "Please, don't do that. I know Alexander and Sarai put you up to it. Don't do it!"

"Don't do what? I'm not doing anything."

Zachary rolled his eyes skyward, just imagining the conversation the trio had had about him. He'd gotten a lecture from his brother, advice from Sarai, and now Gamon was wanting to tell him what a nice girl Kenzie was. How the woman had managed to hoodwink the three of them into thinking she was somehow God's gift to their establishment was beyond his comprehension. But somehow, some way, Kenzie had bewitched the entire compound.

It had taken her no time at all to befriend most of the staff and at least half of his clients. She'd been quite the social butterfly, flitting from point A to point B, making conversation as she asked questions about him and his brother. He understood she was doing her job, and she was doing it well, but her presence was more of a thorn in his side than he wanted to admit.

Kenzie Monroe had gotten under his skin, and it surprised him. She was extraordinarily beautiful, and under different circumstances he would have been tripping over himself to know her better. He would have wined and dined her and used every bad pickup line that he could think of to get her attention. Once he'd bedded her, he would have let go and moved on to his next conquest.

Too often since her arrival, he'd gotten himself lost in daydreaming about her, imagining what it might be like to kiss her sumptuous lips, to taste her, his mouth exploring every inch of her luscious body. He thought about his palms against her curves, trailing his thick fingers into places his hands had no business being. After dreaming about taking her in every position imaginable, he'd allowed himself to go a step further and envision the impossible, wondering if it were even conceivable to see a relationship between them grow and bloom into something wondrous.

He couldn't help but wonder about a relationship with any woman that didn't end after a single night of passion! Speculating what it might be like to open his heart again and find love that didn't feel dark and depressing. What if he could have that and more with her? What if she were the one? No one had ever accused him of not dreaming big, he suddenly thought. But Kenzie wasn't a luxury he could afford to allow himself, and he needed to let his musings about the woman go. It didn't serve him, or her, well at all.

He shook his head as he kicked himself back into reality. "Whatever. I'm not available. Not today. Maybe tomorrow."

Gamon sat staring at him, and the pain his deep gaze stirred in Zachary was excruciating. Gamon was like a second father to him, and he held the man in high regard. Ignoring his request only served to increase Zachary's angst because there was nothing he wouldn't have done for the old man. But he wasn't ready to sit down across a table with Kenzie Monroe.

"What should I know?" the patriarch finally asked, reading him like no one else, other than his brother, could do. "Who is this woman?"

There was a moment of pause as Zachary pondered the question. "It's not important," he finally said as he shook his head. "It's not important at all. Just tell her not today. But I promise you, I'll talk to her tomorrow. Please!"

The two men sat staring at each other, Zachary's gaze pleading, and then Gamon nodded his agreement. He exited the car without uttering another word, leaving Zachary to stew alone.

Zachary swiped a large hand over his face.

He wished he could have answered the question Gamon threw at him, but revealing what he thought he knew about Kenzie Monroe would only have opened a whole host of problems that he wasn't ready to deal with. Tomorrow he would talk with her, answer her questions, and pray that when they were done, she'd be gone from Phuket as quickly as she'd come. He blew out a heavy sigh. And then he prayed that he wouldn't miss having her around.

Kenzie had slept longer than she planned. After Zachary had canceled their scheduled interview, not even bothering to speak to her himself, she had come back to her room to sulk. Then the rain had come, and there had been nothing left to do but nap. Her planned thirty-minute power siesta had lasted for almost four hours. It was now dark and dank, the entire afternoon having passed her by.

She blew out a soft sigh as she pondered her next move. She had already transcribed the notes from her interviews with Zachary's family and the staff at Revolution, and the outline of her article was well under way. What she'd initially written had taken a turn, the original direction she'd proposed no longer feeling right. There was still much work that she needed to do before it would be finished, and getting Zachary to answer some questions was just the beginning.

She moved toward the sliding glass door to peer outside. Lights from the larger house behind her flickered, the rear yard lit up like it was Christmas. Kenzie knew that Zachary lived in that bungalow, just steps away from the small patio that bordered the rear wall where she was staying.

Music echoed over the gated wall. It was soft and seductive, the ambience reminding her of a smoky jazz club. She stood listening, her eyes closed, her body swaying gently to the beat. It seemed like a good idea when she slipped her feet into a pair of flip-flops and headed in the direction of the music. And then she was standing at the back gate of Zachary's patio and pool, knowing she should turn around and run. Instead, she approached in stealth mode, crouching low and tiptoeing closer to see without being seen.

Zachary lay in his soaking pool, his torso reclined back, his legs extended outward. His eyes were closed, and he looked relaxed, not an ounce of concern creasing his brow. Kenzie's eyes danced over his face, across his torso, flitting past his rippled abs to where the water line shadowed his trunks.

She imagined his muscles were as hard and tight as they looked. She clenched both fists at the thought of what he might feel like against her fingertips.

Something, or someone, inside the home drew his attention, his eyes flying open as he turned his head in that direction. He suddenly stood up, and Kenzie's eyes widened. Naked, Zachary stood in full glory, exceptionally endowed, his male prowess moving her to actually salivate. He had the body of an Adonis — brick hard, marble slick, and too pretty for words. He was as perfect as any man she had ever romanticized about, and there had been plenty she'd fantasized about. She gasped, loudly, slapping her hand over her mouth as he suddenly looked in her direction. She dropped down lower behind the fence, the plants and bushes shadowing her frame, her heart racing as she prayed that he didn't come her way to inspect. His eyes skated across the landscape for a quick minute before he grabbed his towel, wrapped it around his waist, and headed inside the house.

Kenzie blew out a sigh of relief as she tiptoed back down the path that had brought her there and into her bungalow. Clutching the front of her T-shirt as she calmed her nerves, she giggled. And Kenzie was not a giggler. She suddenly felt foolish, as though she was a teenager who'd seen a naked man for the first time. Invading Zachary's privacy had not been her intent. Seeing him butt-ass-naked had been unexpected, a pleasant surprise that still had her panting. And now she suddenly didn't have a clue what to do with herself.

Before she could formulate a plan in her mind, a to-do list that would turn her thoughts from him to something else, there was a knock on her door, the harsh rap meant to get her attention. She moved to answer it and was stunned to see Zachary standing on the other side. He was still bare-chested, but he'd pulled on a pair of sweatpants that sagged low against his hips.

"Did you need something?" he asked, his low tone too seductive to be any good for anyone.

Kenzie stammered. "I . . . what . . . it . . ."

Zachary grinned, his look telling. He shook his head. "I have some time right now if you want to talk."

Kenzie was still struggling to find her voice. "Talk?"

"Ask questions. Start your interview. Unless you have other plans. I guess I should have asked if you were busy, but I figured since you were peeking over my fence, you needed something to do with your time."

She pretended to be shocked. "Me? Peeking? I didn't . . ."

He held up his hand, his index finger pointed to stall her comment. "I looked at the security tape. I have cameras all over the property, and you tripped the alarm. Besides, not even that bush could hide that backside of yours."

Kenzie's eyes widened, astonishment melting into embarrassment at being caught red-handed. She blushed profusely, her cheeks heating with color. "It's not what it looked like," she said as she crossed her arms over her chest. "I was just out walking and . . ."

"And you tripped at my gate?"

She rolled her eyes skyward. Zachary laughed, a deep chortle that had her laughing with him.

He swiped at the tear that had spilled past his lashes, his amusement gut deep. "You're welcome to come over if you want. There's some food they brought up earlier, and I have beer."

Kenzie smiled, her expression wary. "I appreciate that, but why are you being nice to me?"

A smug smirk pulled at his full lips. "I can

be mean if you want!"

"Don't do anything different on my account," she said facetiously.

There was a moment of pause as they stood staring at each other, each reflecting on how the tide had changed. She broke the silence. "I just need to change first."

Zachary eyed her, his gaze noting the grass stains at her knees and the mud splattered on her bare feet. He shook his head one last time. "I'll leave the front door open," he said as he turned and headed off in the opposite direction.

Kenzie was freshly showered and perfumed when she knocked on Zachary's front door before pushing it open to let herself inside. She called out his name once, and then again. He answered from the rear patio just as she was starting to get nervous.

Moving through the space, she was surprised by how stark and sparse the home was, the décor as minimalistic as one could get. There was little about his home that spoke to his personality or gave any insight to his spirit. None of his trophies or awards were displayed, and his title belt was nowhere to be seen.

A punching bag hung from the ceiling in the corner of the modest living room.

Leather boxing gloves rested in a chair that sat off to the side. There was a small sofa in an unassuming shade of gray and a black wooden coffee table in the center of the room. One magazine rested on the table. Kenzie realized it was the issue of *Sports Illustrated International* that carried her first cover story, a feature on American gymnast Simone Biles, the teenage sensation who had taken the summer Olympics by storm.

There was a wall of bookcases filled corner-to-corner with books, the only thing that was outstanding in the room. Kenzie paused for a quick moment to read some of the titles, continuing on only when Zachary called to ask if she was okay. She followed his voice, and when she stepped through the glass doors to the outside, Zachary was reclining on a lounge chair, a hardcover novel resting in his lap.

"You clean up nice," he said as he gestured for her to join him.

She had changed into a simple denim shift dress. Her legs were bare, and beaded sandals adorned her feet. She'd pulled her hair into a high topknot, ringlets framing her face. Mascara, eyeliner, and lip gloss defined her delicate features. *She was stunning in a fresh-faced, girl-next-door kind of way,* he thought.

Kenzie moved to take the seat beside him, taking the bottled brew he offered from his hand. "Thank you."

"You're welcome. Are you hungry?" he asked. "There's some chicken pad Thai in the wok on the stove and a kale and blood orange salad in the refrigerator."

Kenzie shook her head. "Not really, but thank you for the offer."

An awkward silence suddenly filled the space between them. Kenzie's eyes skated back and forth, trying to take it all in. She broke the uncomfortable quiet with a question.

"Do you have another home? Because this place doesn't feel like you." She shifted her eyes to his.

"No," Zachary answered. He looked around and shrugged. "How can you say this doesn't feel like me?"

"It's not what I expected. It . . . well . . . the inside is too bland and stark. It's more business-like than personal. It doesn't feel very homey."

He paused for a moment as he pondered her comment. "How does *homey* feel?"

"Like an extension of your personality and the things you love most. You don't have anything with color, no pictures, and where are all your trophies? Where's your belt?"

He hesitated for a brief moment as if he were searching for an answer. When he finally responded, there was something in his tone that sounded like he wasn't being wholeheartedly straightforward. "It's all in storage."

"You keep your fight memorabilia in storage? Even the title belt that you just won is already put away?"

Zachary shrugged, suddenly uncomfortable with her questions. Despite Sarai's admonishments, he hadn't thought about decorating the space since his ex-wife had left. She had taken everything — the pretty pictures, colorful throws, and all else that had given this home some personality. All she had left him was his books, and since then he hadn't worried about what his house looked like, since he rarely spent time in any of the rooms besides his bedroom.

"So, are you planning to write about my skills as an interior designer or what I've accomplished in the fight ring?"

"You don't have any design skills, so there is definitely no story there." She lifted her legs onto the lounge chair and adjusted the back until she was comfortable. She took a swig from the bottle in her hand. "So, what are you reading?" she asked.

He gestured toward his book. "James

Baldwin."

"Classic."

"I think so."

"I was impressed by your book collection. It's diverse, sometimes intellectual, some classics, first books, just a very wide range of titles. I was intrigued."

"Thank you. Are you a reader?"

She nodded. "I tend to lose myself in mysteries and suspense thrillers. Maybe the occasional romance novel."

"I've never read a romance novel."

"Why not?"

I don't believe in it," he said matter-of-factly "Romance, that is. Happily-ever-after is for story books." For a split second he thought about his brother and Sarai, honestly believing they might be the exception. He didn't bother to say so.

Kenzie nodded in agreement. "I hate to say it, but I actually agree with you. I read them every now and again because I need one when I get hopeful, so I can remember that it's all just a fairy tale."

He smiled. "Who broke your heart?"

Kenzie took another swig of her drink. "I haven't met him yet. I've never let anyone get that close."

Zachary nodded. "Hopefully you never will. You don't deserve to have your heart broken," he said softly.

She let that sink in for a moment before she spoke again. "Do you think you'll ever get over your ex-wife?" Kenzie suddenly questioned. She cut an eye in his direction.

The harsh look he shot back was chilling. He didn't respond. Instead, he guzzled his own drink, finishing it off. Rising, he moved back into the house, returning a minute later with two more bottles of beer. He passed one bottle to Kenzie as he sat back down.

"So, do you have some questions to ask me?" he asked.

She persisted. "You didn't answer my last one."

He shot her another look. "So, maybe, you should move onto something else," he said.

Kenzie gave him a slight nod. "Fair enough. Are you involved with anyone? Do you have a girlfriend?"

"Why are you so hung up on my personal life?"

"Inquiring minds want to know. Besides, you're one of only a few professional athletes who isn't hugged up with some beautiful woman in all of his photos. I just wondered why."

Zachary took a deep breath. He stole a line from Kenzie's playbook. "I guess I haven't met her yet!"

Kenzie smiled. "So what do you want me to tell readers about you, Zachary Barrett?"

He paused for a moment, then he shrugged. "Does it matter? Most of it's just smoke and mirrors. More readers than not are going to think it's just a load of crap anyway. No one's going to believe half of it."

Kenzie folded her hands in her lap. "People are going to believe *all* of it. I hope to show them a side of you they've never seen before. If I'm good at what I do, I'll paint a very honest assessment of the man you are. People will know you. Men will see you as their best friend or the guy they'd give anything to hang out with. For women, you'll be the lover they hope to have — the man they want to father their children."

"Except you really don't know me. I may not be any of those things."

He and Kenzie exchanged a look, Zachary eyeing her intently. She nodded. "I know enough to know that I'm on the right track. And I hope to discover more," she finally said softly. "I hope that you'll trust me enough to let me know you."

Zachary nodded, shrugging his shoulders ever so slightly. He changed the subject. "So, can I ask you a question?"

Kenzie smiled. "Sure, ask me anything!"

"How long have you been a peeping Tom?"

Kenzie laughed, the wealth of it rising from her core and spreading outward like a growing vine. It was thick and rich, and it made him smile.

"I am not a peeping Tom," she said, her singsong tone like a breath of fresh air. "Not by a long shot!"

"I couldn't tell with the way you were crouched down in those bushes," he replied, a smirk across his face. "Trying to be all stealth-like!" He chucked heartily.

"You didn't see me in the bushes!"

"No, not until I played back the security tape. And trust me when I tell you the camera caught you at the perfect angle!" The memory of her ample backside on the screen had him grinning from ear to ear.

Kenzie's face was flush with color, her cheeks warm with embarrassment. "You have me on video?"

He nodded his head as he took a sip of his beer. "I do. In fact, I've already made a few copies to share with family and friends. Would you like one?"

She sat forward in her seat. "That really isn't funny!"

He laughed heartily. "Oh, it's actually

quite hilarious!"

Kenzie smiled, her head waving from side to side. The light danced across his chiseled features. He was a beautiful man, almost too pretty, with his dimpled cheeks and full lips. She found herself staring at his mouth, wondering what it might feel like pressed to hers. Imagining herself tasting him suddenly had her heated, perspiration rising with a vengeance to trickle into her creases. They suddenly locked eyes, studying each other intently, and then she snatched her gaze away, fearing that he might read her mind.

She gulped her own drink to shake the thoughts from her head, and then she changed the subject. "So tell me your most embarrassing moment." She sat back in her seat.

There was a quiet pause as he pondered her question. "Before I answer that, was hiding in my bushes your most embarrassing moment?"

Kenzie giggled. "No. A few years ago I had an interview with a national publication. I'd gotten to the third round of interviews, and I was feeling pretty confident that I'd gotten the job. I bought new shoes to wear to the interview. The cutest pair of stilettos. As I'm walking into the room to meet the publisher and his executive staff, my feet slipped out from under me and I landed on my ass. Hard. To add insult to injury, when I went to stand up my slacks split and I didn't have on any underwear. It was not one of my finest moments."

"No underpants?" he grinned.

She rolled her eyes skyward. "It was that kind of day."

"So you like to go commando?" he said, amusement seeping from his eyes as he imagined what might be missing beneath the dress she was wearing.

As if she were reading his mind, she pulled at the hem of her garment and crossed her ankles tightly. They locked gazes a second time.

Zachary's eyebrows were raised curiously, his expression wanting an answer to his question. "Do you?"

She licked her lips slowly as she leaned forward in her seat. Her look was sultry and teasing. "Panties are so overrated, don't you think?"

Zachary didn't know how long they'd talked. He only knew that he thoroughly enjoyed the conversation. Kenzie was funny, quick with the one-liners, and she had him thinking about things he'd never considered before. They had talked sports, politics, books, and food. He discovered her penchant for exotic islands, large dogs, and Greek pastries. She had talked, and he enjoyed listening.

By early morning, he had grown so comfortable with her that he found himself opening up about things he had never before discussed with anyone. Not even Alexander or Sarai. They talked about his brother, his childhood, the memories he had of his biological mother, who had passed from breast cancer when the twins had been four years old. And he shared all the ugly that had happened between him and the ex-Mrs. Barrett. It was only when he realized there were tears dampening his cheeks, his emotions running high, that he withdrew from the conversation, abruptly calling an end to their night.

He had jumped from his seat, practically racing into the house. Kenzie had called after him, asking if everything was okay. Assuring her that he just needed a bathroom break, he had cracked a joke about his age and small bladder. But the truth had been quite different. He had suddenly felt vulnerable, and weak, and that was not the man he had wanted her to know.

He blamed his behavior on the alcohol. One beer too had many clouded his judgement. But if he were honest with himself, he simply liked that she seemed eager to listen. Kenzie had been earnestly interested in getting to know who he was, and it hadn't felt like he was being interviewed or judged. It had felt good not to close himself off, to be open and honest about things that had happened in his life, that had impacted who he was and how he thought. And he liked that she didn't seem to hold any of it against him.

He genuinely *liked* Kenzie. There was something very special about the woman. She had what some would have called a blessed spirit, the ancestors diligently watching over her. It surprised him that he actually felt he could trust her, because Zachary didn't trust any woman.

By the time he'd regained his composure, moving back outside, Kenzie had fallen into a deep sleep, curled in a fetal position in her lounge chair. He stood watching her, lulled by the soft inhalation of her breath and the soft whistle at the end of each exhale. She looked angelic, and he found himself imagining what it might be like to wrap her in his arms and hold her tightly.

For a brief moment, he thought about waking her, but she was sleeping so peacefully that he couldn't bring himself to do it.

Instead he fetched a blanket from his linen closet and laid it gently over her. After whispering a soft good night, he left her there.

When Kenzie opened her eyes, the sun was shining brightly. The air was scented from the perfumed flora that bordered the patio, and the morning temperature was rising swiftly. She sat upright, startled when she remembered where she was and everything that had happened last night. She suddenly smiled as she thought about the prelude to the evening, which had started with Zachary in the pool and her peeking through the slats in his fence.

She called out his name as she stretched her limbs up and out, elongating her body to ease the tension out of her tightened muscles. When she got no answer, she called out a second time. Rising from the chair, she realized she was alone, as Zachary was nowhere to be found. For a brief moment, a wave of sadness actually flooded her spirit.

Curiosity pulled her to the other rooms in the home, all of them as empty as the living room. And when she opened his bedroom door, the interior actually surprised her. His bedroom was a cluttered mess of clothes and sneakers, with file folders and papers strewn from the bed to the floor. This was where he spent much of his time when he was home, she mused. It also spoke to a side of Zachary she hadn't expected, belying his meticulously controlled, well-ordered persona. Clearly there was nothing neat or tidy about him, she thought as she tiptoed over the trash on the floor.

Moving to the dresser, she pulled open a drawer. Boxer briefs and T-shirts were folded and lined neatly in a row. She was expecting a continuation of the mess and clutter, so it surprised her that it was as organized as it was. Shock registered on her face when she opened the bottom drawer. She hadn't known what to expect, but she hadn't expected to find his last championship title belt stuffed in the bottom of the drawer beneath a pile of sweatpants. She ran her fingers over the engraved metal and leather, marveling at the beauty of it. She couldn't help but question why he kept it hidden and why he had blatantly lied about it. She wondered how she could ask and not give herself away. She closed the dresser drawer and looked around the room.

Beside the bed, framed photos rested on the nightstand, and she stepped over his dirty T-shirts and a pair of briefs to spy some more. There were three photos. The first was an old family photo of him and his brother, their father, and the woman she assumed was their stepmother. The parents were seated, the boys at either side of them, wearing ill-fitting suits, and a Christmas tree sparkling behind them. It looked like one of those shots families used for holiday cards. The second was of Zachary and his brother after his last fight win, the image that had graced multiple sports articles. But it was the last photo that made her gasp suddenly and had her heart racing.

Kenzie had never seen the photo before. Even with the many that she'd found when she'd first researched the two Barrett brothers, this picture was new. It was an image taken after one of Zachary's very first title fights. She knew that because he and his team were sporting the logo of the first gym he'd been affiliated with — Galaxy Sports. It had been the only other training center that he'd actually competed for. He'd lost that belt, but he'd won the respect of everyone in the industry with his showmanship. He was shaking hands with the winner, a man most didn't remember anymore. And behind Zachary stood the infamous Kai Tamura.

Kai Tamura was a legend in the Thai boxing community. He held records that still hadn't been broken by the men who'd come after him. After a phenomenal fight career of his own, Kai had trained the best in the business. Zachary had been his protégé, and he had influenced every aspect of Zachary's burgeoning career until the day he had disappeared. In earlier interviews, Zachary had often praised Kai's teachings, acknowledging his mentor for all that he did. And starting the day Kai was gone, Zachary had never publically mentioned the man again.

Kenzie realized her hand was shaking as she studied every detail of that photo. Because here it was in black and white. Proof that there had been a connection between the two men. Evidence that Zachary Barrett had known her father.

Chapter Four

Zachary stood outside the fight ring, shouting out pointers to a tall Latino who actually looked afraid of his opponent. His sparring partner was two feet shorter and almost forty pounds lighter, but he was fast on his feet and packed a powerful punch. The duo were dancing in circles around each other, the tall Latino ducking and dodging blows.

He cut a quick eye in Kenzie's direction when she suddenly moved to his side, motioning for his attention. Her presence was startling, causing a wealth of emotion that hit him like a tidal wave. His body reacted of its own volition, and the rising desire had him feeling completely out of sorts.

"Do you have a minute?" she asked, her smile bright and unassuming.

"Now's really not a good time," he quipped, his tone dismissive as he struggled with the urge to kiss her. "Maybe later."

She persisted. "I just have a quick question."

He cut another eye in her direction, hesitating briefly. He lifted his hand and gestured for Gamon to come take his place. Stepping off to the side, he gestured for her to follow him. When they were out of earshot from the staff and patrons, he turned to face her. He stood close, towering above her as she twisted her hands together anxiously. "What's up?" he asked, eyeing her curiously.

"Are you still in contact with Kai Tamura?"

"Excuse me?" he bristled, the gesture visible as every one of his muscles tightened.

"Kai Tamura. I'd like to interview him about his time training you. I was hoping you might know how I can reach him."

Zachary suddenly looked like a dark cloud had dropped down over his head, the pall dulling the luster that had been in his eyes just moments earlier. "I don't," he finally muttered. He turned abruptly, and she called after him.

"Do you know anyone who might be able to put me in touch with him?"

Zachary hesitated for a brief moment. "Look, we really need to get this project of yours done. You're starting to interfere with my business, and I can't have that. Kai can't tell you anything about me that I haven't already told you. I don't know what other questions you have, but he can't help you."

Kenzie recoiled ever so slightly. "You don't know that."

"Trust me. I do."

"Why are you trying to sabotage my article?" She was suddenly indignant, both hands clutching her hips in anger.

"Sabotage? That's a little dramatic, don't you think? It really isn't that deep."

"I would think you'd be more concerned with how I present you."

Zachary smirked. "You act like I actually *care* about your little story."

"You should!"

He shrugged again, his broad shoulders jutting toward the sky. "Ms. Monroe, if I had a dime for everything in my life I *should* have cared about, I'd be a very wealthy man. Now your interview here is over. It's really time for you to let it go," he said, his tone abrasive, and then he turned, moving swiftly in the opposite direction.

She called after him, yelling his name, her voice thundering with attitude.

Zachary hesitated. "What?"

"You really are a prick!"

For just a split second, Zachary thought

about snapping back, but he caught himself. If only she could have left well enough alone. Bringing up his old friend Kai was as good as poking a hornet's nest as far as he was concerned. The dynamics of that relationship had changed substantially, and he couldn't begin to explain to her or anyone else why. As he met her gaze, the expression on her face was suddenly pulling at his heartstrings. Tears misted her eyes, but he knew they were tears of anger and frustration. Her bottom lip quivered, and he suddenly imagined himself kissing that tremble away. He went from wanting to argue with her to wanting to wrap her in his arms. If he could have told her that everything was going to be okay he would have, but in that moment he didn't have the words. And he definitely couldn't tell her what she wanted to hear. No one had ever accused him of being a really nice guy, and there was no reason to start now.

He shrugged his broad shoulders. "Old news," he quipped and then he turned, moving as far away from her as he could get.

Zachary stood with his head in his hands, trying to make sense of the information he was getting. His day was not starting well, and lack of sleep had him on emotional overload. Yesterday, after getting into it with Kenzie, his afternoon and evening had gone right to hell. Discerning how to fix it had kept him up most of the night. Now Gamon was upset, his friend ranting in Thai. It was moments like these that reminded Zachary what he least liked about having his own business.

"It's a big problem!" Gamon finally exclaimed, throwing his hands in the air, frustration painting his expression.

"Yeah, it is," Zachary agreed, still unsure how to handle what he didn't want to be bothered with.

For a few weeks they'd seen a decline in their clientele, registered guests just not showing up. He expected people to change their minds, but not at a rate where their bottom line would be affected. Sarai had been hammering him to demand a nonrefundable deposit from those who wanted to train with him, and he just hadn't bothered with the logistics of it, trusting that those who went out of their way to make it to Thailand, and Revolution, really wanted to be there.

Now they were learning that their registered customers were being shanghaied at the airport. Another fight team and training camp was scooping up unsuspecting patrons and getting them checked in at their facilities before they suspected something was amiss. By the time they realized they were checked into the wrong property, their credit cards had been charged, and there was little they could do. It was a classic game of bait and switch, the likes of which would make the best grifter proud.

Zachary blew a soft sigh. “Call Sarai. Ask her who did the graphics on the jeep. I think they were out of Bangkok. Then order us a bus specifically for airport pickups, and get our logo on it.”

“Small bus. You don’t need a big bus,” Gamon noted.

Zachary nodded. “That’s fine, just something that we can put our name all over. And tell that place in Bangkok that I want our name and my picture as big as they can get it. I don’t want it to be missed.”

“You need to do deposit. Make people pay up front.”

“I’ll get to work on that,” Zachary said, a checklist of things to do lining up in his head.

“What are you doing now?” Gamon questioned, his brow raised.

“Right now I’m driving over to that gym to let them know I’m aware of what they’re up to, and it had better stop. Then I'm going to try and get our customers back without them losing their money to those crooks. And while I'm at it, I think I'll pay a visit to all the other gyms in the area to let them know not to fuck with me."

"Don't get into a fight. It would not be good."

Zachary rolled his eyes. "I didn't throw this punch. They did. But I do plan to hit them back. And hard."

Gamon shook his head. "What are you going to do about her?" he questioned, gesturing across the way.

Zachary didn't need to look to know who Gamon was talking about. After their time together two nights ago and their confrontation the previous day, he hadn't been able to get Kenzie off his mind. But he turned anyway, spying her as she was crossing the grassy knoll in their direction. She waved a hand and called his name.

Zachary shook his head. "Nothing," he said. "I can't deal with her right now." And then he jumped into the jeep, gunned the engine, and pulled away.

By the time Kenzie reached Gamon's side, Zachary was pulling out of the driveway. Frustration furrowed her brow, knowing that he had ignored her calling out his name. She dropped both hands to her hips as a gush of air blew past her lips.

"Mr. Montri, good morning."

The older man nodded, a warm smile lifting his mouth. "Good morning, Miss Kenzie."

"I really needed to speak with him. Do you know when he'll be back?" Her eyes followed the car, watching as it disappeared past the line of trees.

Gamon took a deep breath, holding it for a brief second before sending it back into the warm day's air. "Zachary has a busy day today. I'm not sure when we will see him again."

Kenzie fought the wave of emotion that crossed her expression. "He's avoiding me again. What's his problem now?"

Gamon didn't answer, the slight smile across his face locking into place.

She shook her head, her lush curls waving against her shoulders. "Fine," she huffed. "I'll just wait for him to get back. But let him know I'm not going away," she professed.

Kenzie turned to leave, then hesitated, spinning back around. "Mr. Montri, did you know Kai Tamura?" she asked.

The man's eyes narrowed ever so slightly.

"Everyone here knows Kai Tamura. He is a national hero. The Thai people are very proud of his accomplishments."

"But did you *know* him. Were you two friends when he was training Zachary? Or did you come after? Do you know where I can find my father?"

Gamon's head snapped in her direction, shock wafting from his eyes. "Kai Tamura is your father?"

Kenzie nodded, tears suddenly misting her eyes. "Yes. He is. And I can't find him."

Gamon stared at her for a brief moment; then his eyes skated off into the distance as he seemed to fall into thought. It felt like an eternity before he returned his attention back to her. "I am sorry. I did not know him," he finally said. He turned in an about-face and started to walk away.

Kenzie persisted. "But Zachary knew him, right? Zachary trained with him, so Zachary might know where he is?"

Gamon gave her one last look, and then just like the wind, he blew out of her sight, not bothering to answer her questions.

Driving around Phuket had always given Zachary much joy. Despite his love for and connection to Boulder, Colorado, he considered Phuket home. Thailand was unlike any place he had ever been before. Phuket was the country's largest island, and it drew an international crowd of water sport enthusiasts. Beach lovers, deep-sea divers, and those just wanting to get wet and say they did it in the Asian country were drawn to the Andaman Sea. Even in the rainy season, the atmosphere was dreamlike and the people welcoming. It was paradise, and if he were Adam, all he needed was his own Eve to make it perfection.

Just as the thought hit him, memories of Kenzie and the evening they shared struck a chord, inciting every nerve ending in his body. He still couldn't believe he'd opened up so unabashedly, sharing far more than he ever imagined himself sharing. Now he wondered just how much of it would become fodder for her article. He suddenly imagined himself the butt of every joke, his photos becoming memes for others to cackle over thanks to her and her story.

He shook his head. If every dirty detail was suddenly printed for the world to read, he would only have himself to blame. But he knew himself well enough to know that he would hold her solely responsible, and his anger at himself would land as though there were a target on her back. That wasn't anything that he wanted for either of them.

When he'd gone back to his room after their talk, he had wanted her, imaging the two of them lost in the most intimate connection. Fantasy fueled the sweetest dreams as he'd drifted off to sleep. When he woke up the next morning, he had wanted her even more, his desire so intense that it actually frightened him. Knowing that she was just on the other side of the wall, sleeping peacefully, had only served to exacerbate the problem. And Kenzie Monroe was one more problem he didn't need to deal with.

He needed her gone, to be done and finished with her questions and as far from his longing as he could muster. There was something in her eyes that told him Kenzie Monroe was there for more than his life story. If he were a betting man, he'd lay dollar to a dime that what she truly wanted was more about her own life than his. But that was nothing he could help her with. He needed her gone, because trying to ignore her was becoming an art form, and he wasn't an artist. And truth be told, getting caught up in his feelings for any woman wasn't something he was willing to do. Not purposely. And not without a fight.

After his last stop, his conversation with the gym owner intense and direct, he wasn't ready to head back to Revolution. There was too much racing through his head. Instead he headed up to the west coast, starting at Naithon Beach. Parking, he jumped out of the jeep and walked the sand, grateful for the peace and quiet that came with the seclusion. When he tired of that, he hopped back in the jeep and drove on route 4018, parallel to the beach, the ride showcasing the magnificent coastline. The trip took him south, past Bang Tao Beach, Banana Beach, and a resort whose name he didn't know. He turned onto Layan Soi toward Layan Beach, then finally came to a stop at the north-end entrance to Laguna Phuket resort, where there was a cluster of beach-front restaurants.

Taking a seat on the patio outside one of the little mom-and-pop shops, Zachary savored a chilled bottle of beer, a bowl of fried rice, the blue lagoon that kissed the damp sand in the distance, and the salmon sunset that filled the darkening sky. He sat in the moment, thinking about the many blessings that filled his life — his family, his friends, and his success. He wanted for nothing. He was loved, and he was respected. But even with all of that, he suddenly realized that although he had no problems being alone, this was the first time he could admit to feeling lonely.

He blew a soft sigh. He missed his brother's wife. And he missed his twin brother. He and Sarai had been best friends for so long that she could read his moods and motivate him without him ever saying a word. With Alexander, there was little that he couldn't tell his twin, and he really could have used him right then to bounce his emotions off of. During moments like this, he wished they were still here, still keeping him grounded and focused. Because in that moment he couldn't think straight — thoughts of Kenzie kept spinning through his head.

Frustration had turned to anger. Kenzie had been sitting in front of Zachary's home for most of the evening. She had questions, and she was hopeful that he had the answers. But he hadn't bothered to come back, and he wasn't answering his cell phone. So there was nothing left for her to do but wait. And now she was angry because patience was not one of her virtues. She stood up and began to pace for the umpteenth time.

She would have sworn on everything she held sacred that she and Zachary had made a connection the previous night. Being with him had felt like the most natural thing in the world to do. There had been little that they hadn't talked about. And she'd been amazed at how easily the conversation had come. She thought back to him talking about his brother and the time they'd been estranged. Even in the darkness of that, he'd found something to joke about.

"So one day, I suddenly get this pain in my leg. It was unbearable," Zachary said as he started to tell the story. "Two doctors later, no one could tell me what was wrong with me. It really started to mess with my head. I was sure my career was over." He took a deep breath as he continued.

"Weeks go by, I can't get any relief, and then one day my mother calls to check on me. I tell her the problem I'm having, and she says, 'Isn't that the funniest thing? Alexander broke his leg in a game a few weeks ago. His leg is hurting him too!' " Zachary mimicked his mother, adding in the head and hand gestures. The movements were exaggerated and comical. "And just like that the pain went away. It was like grade school all over again. One of us would get hurt and the other would feel it. Back then, I swore he broke his leg on purpose to get even with me for breaking his heart."

Kenzie had laughed. "So what happens now when you fight? Do the punches you take hurt Alexander?"

"No, it's like that crap only works one way!" he said with a deep chuckle. "Some kind of prophetic karma."

He had made her laugh and had seemed comfortable enough in her presence to tease her playfully. The time they'd spent together had felt all kinds of right, and she'd been hoping for more of him when she opened her eyes that morning. Instead, he'd been gone when she woke from the night's rest. By the time she'd caught up with him, he had gone back to being cold and distant, completely ignoring her, and that made her even angrier.

It had been a good long while since Kenzie had allowed her emotions to get caught up over any man. The men she usually allowed into her inner circle were never more than casual friends; some were just dick-on-command if she needed an itch scratched. They were convenient arm candy, and none were allowed to pull her into any emotional foolery. Those connections worked when she wanted them to work, and when she didn't, letting them go was as easy as breathing. So she didn't have a whole lot of experience with relationships because she'd never been willing to invest the time or the energy it took to maintain one. Compromise was a dirty word in her vocabulary because she was always determined to have things her way or not at all. But Zachary had her wondering what it might look like to be with a man who made her laugh the way he did. A man who appreciated her quirks and seemed to be a nice balance to her personality. She liked him, and although she fully intended to maintain that professional line with him until her story went to press, she couldn't help but consider what might be when that was done and finished.

And even as she contemplated the possibilities, she found herself angry all over again. *How dare he ignore her?* she mused. No man had ever been so dismissive toward her; most fell all over themselves for her attention. Zachary was nonchalant where she was concerned, almost to the point of disinterest. He was seemingly unmoved by her presence, and that irritated her beyond comprehension.

Kenzie suddenly realized that being angry wouldn't serve her well. Especially if she hoped to discover more about the relationship between Zachary and her father. She needed to maintain her composure, and that was going to be difficult to do if she was harboring a grudge because her ego was bruised. It also wasn't going to win her any cool points if she hoped to capture his attention for longer than a few hours.

She took a deep inhale of air and then a second, practicing one of the many breathing exercises that she'd learned in a mandatory anger-management course that she'd been made to take a few years back. The technique was the only good thing that had come from her punching a blind date in the face in a public place when he'd rubbed her the wrong way, trying to force his tongue down her throat and his hand up her skirt. He'd called for police backup; both had been arrested, and she'd gotten off lightly, that six-week course her only consequence for flying off the handle. Her date had suffered a broken nose and a fractured jaw, and had received a conviction for sexual battery. She blew that breath slowly past her full lips and took another until she felt her nerves begin to calm. She stole a glance down at her wristwatch. It was almost midnight, and Kenzie realized that Zachary was probably gone for the night.

She made a slow stroll back to her own unit, closing and locking the door behind herself. As she stripped out of her clothes and settled down for the night, Kenzie couldn't begin to imagine where Zachary might be. Then suddenly she found herself pondering just *who* he might be with. Was there a woman in his personal life that he was committed to? Had he evaded her questions about his relationship status because there was something he didn't want her to know? Was he with *that* woman at that very moment, making her laugh, holding her hand, loving her with the best of himself? And if he was, then what about her and them and the couple she imagined the two of them being? But they weren't a couple, and Zachary had never given her any reason to think that such a thing was a possibility. As all her thoughts spun like a bad storm in her head, Kenzie suddenly realized she had gotten caught up emotionally and was feeling out of control. As she reflected on that disaster, she realized she was raging all over again, angry that Zachary Barrett had her feeling some kind of way.

Chapter Five

The way his staff was acting, Zachary would have thought he'd been gone for two years and not two days. But he had desperately needed time to himself to work through the feelings that had galvanized him. Now that he was back and feeling more like himself, he felt better able to handle whatever might be thrown at him.

He had just finished reviewing the mountain of paperwork on his desk, signing the last check to pay the bills, when his cell phone rang. His brother's face popped up on the digital screen. Zachary was grinning broadly as he answered the call.

"Hey, A!" he exclaimed, calling his brother by their favored nickname. "What's up, family?"

"Just calling to check on you, Z. How's it going?"

"It's all good. I was just here in the office trying to get some business done. But I have no complaints."

"Glad to hear it. So how's it going with Kenzie?"

Zachary hesitated for a quick minute. "Why are you asking me about Kenzie?"

"She called Sarai to postpone her trip to Colorado. Kenzie said she needed to stay in Thailand a while longer. I thought maybe you two . . . well . . . you know . . ."

Zachary laughed. "No, bro! There is nothing like that going on between me and that woman. I can't tell you why she's delaying her trip. I haven't talked to her."

"So you still aren't talking to Kenzie?"

"I mean . . . well . . . we . . . I . . ." Zachary was suddenly stammering. He paused as he gathered his thoughts. He extended his legs and lifted them to rest on top of the desk. "Man, let me tell you . . . ," he started.

Minutes later he'd filled his brother in on everything that had happened since Alexander and Sarai had gone back to the United States. He told his brother about Kenzie peeping through his fence and the evening they'd shared together. Then he opened up about how he'd been feeling. "So, I've been gone the last two days," he concluded. "I needed some time to think. I haven't seen her since I got back, so I'm not sure why she changed her plans."

Alexander laughed. "Sounds like you dropped into some drama," he said.

"You know damn well that is not my style. I'm not playing games with that woman," he said with a deep chuckle.

"I don't think she's interested in playing games with you either."

"Maybe not, but all I'm interested in doing is finishing this interview and getting back to business. I'm already getting fight requests, so it's just a matter of time before I'm going to have to defend my belt again. I need to stay focused."

"Why are you afraid to care about this woman?" Alexander asked, the question feeling like it had come out of left field. "Any woman for that matter? You can't spend the rest of your life mastering those one-night stands. That's just not cool, Z!"

Zachary took a deep breath and held it as he reflected on the question. His ex-wife had left him bruised and battered to a point where he hardly recognized himself. She had come into their lives and had devastated Alexander first, before turning her wrath on him. Zachary had owned up to his part in the hurt that had ravaged his twin — his decision to marry the woman breaking his brother's heart. Alexander coming back from that had taken years, and it was only when Sarai had broken down his barriers to get to his heart that he and his brother had been able to turn things around between them. Until he'd experienced that exact pain himself, Zachary had thought such a hurt unimaginable. But now he was standing in his twin's size thirteen shoes, still whirling from the storm. He didn't know if was ready to tear his walls away. He was still holding tight to the bricks that fortified his heart.

His twin seemed to read his thoughts, understanding wafting between them. Alexander answered his own question. "I get it. I really do, and you know it. Trust me when I tell you that it doesn't always have to be this way. But you have to be willing to let yourself love again. She's special, Zachary. Kenzie is a beautiful woman. She's smart and has a great sense of humor and a beautiful spirit. She seems very genuine. And you like her. I know you do. Being afraid that you'll get hurt again isn't going to serve you well, and I speak from experience. If I hadn't taken a chance with Sarai, I would have missed out on the most incredible woman God put on this earth."

The two brothers continued to talk for another hour. Their conversation was intense as they shared their feelings about the women who had come into their lives and left, and the women still there holding on. Zachary found himself wishing he had called his brother days earlier, and he said so.

Alexander grinned into the receiver. "Hey, that's what family is for, right?"

Zachary nodded his head as if his twin could see him. Before he could respond, Gamon suddenly poked his head into the room, waving a hand in his friend's direction. Zachary gestured for him to come inside and take a seat.

"A, it's been good talking to you, but I've got to run. Your father-in-law needs me to get back to work!"

"Tell Gamon I said hello," Alexander directed. "And think about what I said, please."

"I will. I love you, man! Kiss my girl for me, and give her a hug from her old man."

"I love you, too, Z! We'll talk again soon!"

Disconnecting the call, Zachary felt so much better as he met Gamon's stare.

"Mr. Montri, to what do I owe the pleasure of your company?"

"You have sparring class in a few minutes."

Zachary nodded. "I didn't forget. I was just about to head in that direction."

Gamon nodded. He stared intently, his

stoic expression suddenly making Zachary nervous.

"What? Why are you looking at me like that?"

Gamon responded in Thai, narrowing his gaze. His tone was curt, bristling with indignation as he chastised Zachary for his behavior.

Zachary cringed. "I know. I know," he hissed between clenched teeth.

Gamon shook a finger at him. "You must do better. You cannot be an example for the young men here when you are behaving badly."

The young man nodded. "I agree, and I promise I'll do better."

Gamon tilted his head at him. "Did you know she is Kai Tamura's daughter?"

Zachary met the older man's deep stare, their gazes locking. They sat like they were about to go head to head, the air in the room becoming thick and stagnant. Zachary's good mood was like a balloon losing air, deflating quickly as it slapped back and forth around the room. He snatched his eyes away, turning to stare out the window at the beachfront outside. He blew out the breath he'd been holding, suddenly realizing that he hadn't inhaled since Gamon's question. "Did she tell you that?"

Gamon nodded his head. "Yes, and she says she is looking for her father. She had questions that I couldn't answer for her."

Zachary blew out another breath. "Well, we can't help her."

Gamon shrugged. "If it were me, I would want to know my daughter. And curse the man who kept her from me."

"That's you. But I made a promise that I have to keep. Kai trusted me, and I will not betray his trust. I owe him that and much more, and you know it."

"Well, I made no such promises," Gamon snapped.

Zachary's gaze narrowed, and his jaw tightened, but he didn't bother to acknowledge the comment, knowing that Gamon would never betray *his* trust.

"You need to do what's right," Gamon said matter-of-factly.

Zachary moved onto his feet. Tears misted his gaze, the emotion not missed by the old man "I'm trying, Gamon. I really am."

The older man nodded his head as the two stood staring at each other a moment longer. "It's time to work," he finally said softly, and then he turned, leading the way out the door.

Zachary enjoyed sparring. Students would

spend time with his team of trainers, getting help with their techniques and then be afforded an opportunity to practice those techniques with him. The clients who came to Revolution to be trained ranged from aspiring MMA fighters to bored housewives wanting to try something new. Some had been as young as seventeen. And his favorite client, who was also one of the oldest, had been pushing ninety-two years of age. There had been students, doctors, an astronaut, and a pastry chef. But what they all had in common was a love for the sport and enthusiasm to see how far they could push their own bodies. And then there was Kenzie.

Zachary couldn't begin to imagine what her motivations were as she climbed into the fight ring with him. He struggled to keep from smiling, surprise and joy shining in his gray eyes.

She wore a sports bra beneath a loose tank top, oversized running shorts cinched at the waist, and the mandatory safety equipment. Her thick curls hung from the bottom edge of the cushioned helmet. Her hands had been wrapped, and she clapped the leather boxing gloves together harshly. Her feet were bare, her toes painted a pale shade of pink, and she had declined the mouthpiece.

Zachary couldn't stop the grin from pulling full and wide across his face. He made the mistake of dropping his hands. "What are you doing?" he asked.

Kenzie threw a punch that nailed him hard in the chest. "Sparring," she snapped as he bent forward, sucking in air as he fought to catch his breath. "What are *you* doing?"

Zachary took two steps back. "So it's like that?" he gasped as he lifted his hands to block the second punch she threw. He stood defensively.

"Like what?" She connected with a left, right, left hook combo, then ducked as he threw his own round of punches back.

"This is ridiculous!" Zachary exclaimed as he danced back and forth on his toes to avoid her connecting.

"I don't think so. What I think is that you're an asshole," she said as she suddenly slapped him with a roundhouse kick that actually stung.

"Stop cussing," Zachary scolded, still dodging back and forth. "You cuss like a sailor."

"Fuck you. I don't know any sailors," she replied. "Just an asshole who thinks he can do whatever he wants, and to hell with how it might affect everyone else."

"I'm not doing this with you, Kenzie,"

Zachary said as he deflected a series of combinations that she'd been taught. He read her body language easily, amused by the frustration that painted her expression when she missed.

"Why is that?" she questioned. "Scared? Think I might get the best of you? Or that you might actually have to show me an ounce of respect and kindness?" Her right hook hit him in the arm.

"I've been nothing *but* respectful. Your problem is you expected me to just drop everything because you said so. You're full of yourself, and I didn't fall for it. I don't have any need to give you any attention."

He danced from one side of the ring to the other, and she chased him, her frustration beginning to get the better of her.

"Your problem is that you're egotistical! And you're arrogant!" She threw a hard punch that blew past him like a cool breeze. "And I plan to make sure everyone knows what an ass you are!"

"You say that like I give a damn!" he said as he threw his own punch, aiming for the air beside her head. The swoosh of his fist rushing in her direction struck a nerve, her eyes widening as she spun left to avoid a strike of any kind.

Amusement lifted the edges of his full lips.

"No need to duck. Trust me, if I had wanted to land that punch, I would have."

"So you really would have hit me?" She threw a right hook, then spun a fast side kick that connected with his upper thigh.

"You stepped into this ring. I didn't ask you to come. In fact, you act like I *want* you here, but I don't remember extending an invitation! So don't get it twisted! You really don't mean anything to me!"

Kenzie looked at him for a moment with an unreadable expression, and then she suddenly lashed out with surprising venom: "You're a coward! And a dick! I can't believe Kai Tamura ever considered you his friend!"

Zachary bristled. Her words were like a bolt of lightning hitting its target. He suddenly swept her feet out from beneath her. "I said I'm not doing this with you," he hissed between clenched teeth.

Kenzie hit the mat with a loud thud. The impact knocked the air from her lungs. Stunned, she lay flat on her back, panting as she sucked in oxygen.

Zachary stood above her, one of the trainers pulling his gloves from his hands. He was shaking his head, frustration furrowing his brow. But there was no missing the contrition that seeped like mist from his eyes. He reached out a bare hand to help her up.

Still trying to shake the fog from her head, her eyes fluttered open, her lengthy lashes batting rapidly. "Now you want to be nice?" she sputtered, tears brimming at the edges of her dark eyes. She swatted his hand away.

Gamon and one of the younger sparring partners rushed to the center of the ring to help her to her feet. Gamon cut an eye in his direction, and Zachary shrugged his broad shoulders. He shifted his gaze toward Kenzie. She was flush with color, embarrassment flooding her cheeks.

"I'm fine," she said as she brushed the dust from her clothes.

She shot him a look, her eyes narrowed as the two locked gazes for just a brief moment. With nothing else to say, Zachary turned on his heels and left her standing there. As she watched him storm off, tears clouded Kenzie's vision. She was suddenly feeling like she'd ignited a bomb that had decimated everything around her, the damage too much to ever come back from.

"Well, *that* was unprofessional!" Stephanie said. "What made you get into the ring with the heavyweight MMA champ and throw a punch at him? Have you lost your mind?"

"I got caught up in the moment." Kenzie could just imagine her friend shaking her head, the look in her eyes scolding. She got defensive. "But he put me on my ass and that wasn't cool!"

"You threatened him!"

"I didn't threaten him!"

"Yes, you did! The minute you made that comment about making sure everyone knew what an ass he was, you threatened to use your influence with your article to discredit him. I know that's how *I* would have taken it."

Kenzie sighed. "Did I tell you he put me on my ass? And it hurt?"

"You took the class. I'm sure you're not the first student he's knocked down, and you probably won't be the last. So now tell me what's really going on with you and that man?"

Kenzie suddenly got misty-eyed. Because she didn't have an answer that made any sense. For two days, trainers had put her through her paces as she'd totally immersed herself in the sport, wanting to experience Revolution the way other clients experienced the facility. For two days, trainers had knocked her down, picked her up, and taught her how to not get hit. Zachary knocking her off her feet had been nothing none of the others hadn't already done, but for some reason, coming from Zachary, it had her in her feelings.

"I don't think he likes me," she finally said, nothing else coming to her.

Stephanie was in full agent mode. "Does he need to *like* you? You were hired to write an article about him, which is due in the next few weeks, by the way. So why is it necessary for him to *like* you for you to do that?"

"It's not, but . . ."

"But nothing. You can't afford to be unprofessional, Kenzie. This is your reputation and your career that we're talking about."

Kenzie blew another loud sigh, a part of her wishing she hadn't called Stephanie to complain.

The other young woman shifted into friend mode. "There must be something really special about this guy. I can't wait to meet him."

"Why would you say that?"

"Because you like him. And you don't like any man!"

Kenzie laughed. "That is so not true!"

"Yes, it is. The men in your life have always been disposable. But it sounds to me like you might want to keep this one around for a while. Which is cool and all, but, girlfriend, you really need to get out of your own way before you sabotage yourself and any hope that you might have."

"That's exactly what I'm doing, isn't it?"

"Yeah! So let's try to figure out why."

"I really like him, Steph! He has this commanding presence. He's intelligent and funny and even a little snarky, like I can be sometimes. And girl, he is sexy as hell! And I mean well-endowed, from the top of his head to the bottom of his very large, sexy feet!"

"So he isn't one of your scratch that itch and get gone kind of guys?"

"Hell no! He's the kind of guy you desperately want your parents to like. The kind you get excited about taking home to meet your father." Her voice dropped an octave. "If you have a father," she muttered.

This time Stephanie sighed. "You really need some serious counseling, and I say that from a place of love."

"Thank you. I appreciate that."

"I'm serious, Kenzie. You really have some issues you need to work through. Between your mother and your father, you are all screwed up, and I can't fix all your stuff."

"Well, don't worry about fixing all my stuff. Just help me figure out what I need to do now!"

Zachary needed to fix what was broken, but he didn't know where to even begin. Kenzie was a spitfire when she was angry, and clearly she was angry with him. He rubbed the bruise on his chin where the top of her foot had connected with his head. He smiled at the memory.

He stood in the shower, washing away the sweat from the workout he'd just put in. He and Kenzie needed to talk, and he needed to initiate the conversation. He'd put the wall up between them, not allowing Kenzie into his personal space, despite her efforts to engage him. And when he had let his guard down, the moment brief, the ensuing emotion had knocked him off sides, surprising him. So he'd pushed her away, but closing himself off hadn't been fair to her. He needed to say that and apologize. But Zachary wasn't good at saying that he was sorry. It wasn't something he had ever practiced.

He thought about Kenzie. He'd actually been impressed by her chutzpah. Stepping into the ring had taken a lot of nerve. He'd been pleasantly surprised to learn that she had spent all the time he'd been away taking classes and working with the trainers.

She'd taken an active interest in what he loved to do, and a part of him wanted to think that she'd made the effort for him and not necessarily for the article she was supposed to be writing. He questioned her motives, but he wanted to imagine that maybe Kenzie was actually feeling something for him. Because if he were honest with himself, he was feeling something for her.

He swiped a soapy palm across the erection that had swelled full and thick between his legs. His dick had been heavy with wanting since he'd laid eyes on the exquisite woman stepping into the fight ring. Hiding his desire had been close to impossible, and so he had to run. Now he was thankful for the cold shower, the spray of chilled water dousing the nerve endings that were screaming for attention. Leaning against the tiled wall, Zachary didn't have a clue how he was going to start the conversation he and Kenzie needed to have. But as he stroked his male member, he realized that was the least of his concerns.

Kenzie was throwing her clothes into the Samsonite carry-on bag that she had tossed into the corner when she arrived. The harsh knock on the front door was unexpected, and when she threw it open to find Zachary standing sheepishly on the other side, she was completely knocked off guard.

"Can we talk?" he asked as he stepped inside, bogarting his way past her. He stopped short as he took note of her packing. He spun back around to face her. "Where are you going?"

Kenzie rolled her eyes skyward. "I'm going home. I'm finished here."

"Why?"

"You know why."

"I really don't. So humor me." He moved to the side of the bed as he stared down into her open luggage. He reached for a lace and satin tank top that rested on top, the garment sliding against his fingers.

Kenzie moved brusquely to his side, snatching the lace from his hands and slinging it back into the suitcase before slamming the lid closed. "What do you want, Zachary? I really don't have time for this."

"So who's not being kind and respectful now?"

The look she gave him was icy, her large eyes half-moon slivers. She stood with her arms crossed harshly over her chest. She closed her eyes for a split second to stall her rising emotion. When she inhaled, taking a deep breath of air, his cologne wafted up her nostrils, the aroma reminding her of something sweet and decadent. Nervous energy raced up her spine and deep into the pit of her stomach. She gasped, the sensation completely unexpected.

Her eyes snapped open as Zachary took a step toward her, closing the space between them. He trailed a large hand down her arm. "We need to talk," he said. "Take a minute and come on over to my place. Please. If you want to leave after that, then so be it."

She took another deep breath. "And what if I don't want to?"

"Then don't. But I did say please. That should count for something."

Kenzie watched as he moved back to the door. He tossed her a look over his shoulder, his gaze smoldering. "If you don't mind, plan on staying long enough to have dinner with me," he said. He paused for a moment before continuing. "After that, if you still want to leave, I'll have Gamon take you wherever you want to go." And then he closed the door easily behind him. It was only then that Kenzie realized she was shaking, moisture suddenly puddling in her most intimate places.

CHAPTER SIX

Kenzie had been sitting in the dark for over an hour trying to decide what she wanted to do if she did anything at all. Nothing about her day had gone as she had hoped. From the moment she'd heard the staff whispering about the champion being back, it had taken a downhill slide.

First, she had wished for Zachary to seek her out, but he hadn't. She'd even gone to his door hoping to find him home, but he hadn't been there, the doors and gate locked tight. She had searched him out, but he had been like a magician, disappearing to parts unknown.

Joining the sparring class had been a last-minute decision. By the time she stepped into the ring, her nerves were on edge. Her frustration had been acute, and then she'd thrown that first punch.

She had read one of Zachary's previous interviews where he talked about boxing being therapeutic, a balm of sorts to ease a fractured soul. He talked about how you released hurt and pain with each punch, feeling renewed when you'd let it all go. And for a brief moment, she had understood. But when he'd turned his back on her and had walked away, she'd been angry and frustrated all over again.

The decision to pack and leave had come after little thought and much emotion. She found herself feeling fragile and needing to put some distance between them. Her friend Stephanie had been on point about her being in her own way and sabotaging herself. When it came to relationships, she was notorious for getting it all wrong, which was why Kenzie didn't bother to do them at all.

Now Zachary wanted to talk. He'd shown up smelling like the aftermath of a fresh spring rain, new car leather, and sin on Sunday. And that look he'd given her! His steel-gray stare had been everything but cold. His gaze had been heated, stripping her naked and burning like a hot massage in an ice storm, and she had melted. The way her body had reacted had been cataclysmic, unlike anything she'd ever experienced before. She hadn't known how to handle it. Now she was sitting in the dark, not having a clue what she should do.

Another thirty minutes passed before Kenzie finally moved. She was hungry, and Zachary had promised food. If hearing him out included a good meal, it would be worth the effort. She'd feel foolish about her behavior in the morning.

Zachary closed the cover to his book. It had only taken him six months to finish the three-hundred-plus pages. He'd started the suspense thriller just weeks before flying to Boulder, returning home for the first time in years. Then training had gotten in the way, leaving him no time to sit back and just relax. He'd finally been able to get through the last two-thirds of the novel over the past few days and was ready to start on another before something or someone got in his way.

He glanced at his watch, then moved to the window to stare outside. *Kenzie wasn't coming,* he thought, his mind racing as he tried to fathom how things had turned so far left with the two of them. For a brief moment, he thought about going back to her door to try and wrangle her over, to implore her to give him a chance. And then he second-guessed himself, changing his mind. *If she wanted to come she would,* he thought.

He moved into his kitchen, staring at the pans of food resting on the stove top. He'd been ready to eat hours earlier but had waited, hopeful that he wouldn't be eating alone. He was just about ready to give up that hope when he heard the faintest knock on his front door. A wave of excitement suddenly swept through his spirit. Kenzie hadn't let him down.

He hurried to the door and threw it open, the gesture just a hair shy of being too abrupt. Kenzie hesitated for a split second as he stepped aside to let her by. Neither said a word, greeting each other with their eyes. She paused in the front foyer, her hands pushed deep into the pockets of her low-slung denim jeans as she waited for Zachary to take the lead.

"I was afraid you weren't going to come," he said softly as he closed the door.

Kenzie shrugged. "I almost didn't. But I'm hungry, and the cafeteria has closed."

Zachary smiled. "I'll take that." He turned and moved back toward the kitchen. "Come in so I can feed you."

As she moved into the dining area behind him, Kenzie came to an abrupt halt. There had been a marked change in the space from the last time that she'd been there.

He'd actually set the table, and she was impressed by his good china, polished silverware, and the fresh flowers adorning the table. Zachary pulled out a seat for her, and as she sat down, he trailed his fingers across her bare shoulder. His touch was heated, and she felt herself jump. He disappeared into the kitchen as she tried to regain her composure.

Conversation between them was minimal, with little to nothing being said. The ease and comfort they'd felt the last time they were in his home was non-existent, and both felt off balance. There was no place for casual chatter, and neither was ready for the serious talk they knew would come.

Minutes later, he'd given her a bowl of shrimp tom yum soup, and filled her plate with spicy beef salad and chicken red curry and rice. It was all too good, and they ate in silence, quietly savoring the moment.

Zachary's second plate was empty when he moved from the table to the fridge to grab them both another beer. "If you're done, we can drink these out on the patio while we talk," he said, eyeing her hesitantly.

Kenzie met his stare and nodded. "I'm fine with that," she said, rising from where she sat. She picked up both their plates and dropped them into the kitchen sink before following after him.

Outside, they sat across from each other. Soft jazz billowed from the stereo speakers. Kenzie sipped her bottle of Singha slowly, hoping to stall the moment when things blew up between them. She was hoping for the best but expecting the worse.

Kenzie's rising anxiety had incited Zachary's. He broke the quiet that had settled over them. "I'm sorry," he said. He shifted forward in his seat, clasping both hands together in front of himself.

Kenzie cut an eye in his direction. "You hurt my feelings," she said, the words slipping out of her mouth before she could catch them. The comment actually surprised her because she wasn't used to putting commentary to her emotions.

Zachary nodded. He stood up, moving to the seat beside her. His leg brushed against hers, the touch teasing. He took a deep breath and then a second before he spoke. "I didn't mean to. I really . . . I don't know . . . I've just had a hard time with you being here and opening doors I had hoped to keep closed."

She took her own deep breath, her nerves vibrating intensely. "You need to understand that I'm not usually so sensitive. I wasn't expecting you to roll out the red carpet for me, but I thought we'd at least gotten to a point where we could be civil with each other. I thought the dinner we had with your brother and sister-in-law let us get to know each other, and then we'd had a good time that evening we talked. The next day it felt like you turned on me."

Nodding his head in agreement, he said, "And you deserved better than that. Which is why I'm apologizing." He dropped a hand to her knee and squeezed it gently.

Kenzie gasped, his touch like an electrical current threatening to make her combust. She cleared her throat, desperate to shake away the sensations that were shooting up her spine. She gently pushed his hand away and shifted the subject. "What doors?"

He chuckled warmly, clasping his hands back together. "Excuse me?"

"What doors were you wanting to keep closed?" she asked, referring back to his earlier comment.

He hesitated before responding, seeming to drop briefly into thought. When he finally answered, the humor had left his tone. "My marriage, for one. That's a sore point for me, and you didn't seem to get the hint."

She nodded. "And I apologize for that. I wasn't pushing to make you uncomfortable. I just wanted to know if you were still emotionally invested in that relationship."

"Whether I am or not, the subject didn't have anything to do with your article," Zachary said with a slight shrug of his broad shoulders.

Kenzie met the intense look he was giving her. "Truth?"

"I expect nothing less."

"My reasons for wanting to know were strictly personal. I wanted to know if you were ready to move on or if pursuing you was a waste of my time."

The faintest smile lifted his full lips. His eyes skated along with hers. "Is that all?" he asked.

"What do you mean, is that all? Should there be more?"

"There could be. Because you like me, and we both know once your emotions get caught up in another person everything takes on new meaning."

She laughed. "I like you?"

He grinned and nodded. "Yeah. You really like me! And you spend a lot of time thinking about me."

The wealth of her laughter warmed Zachary's spirit as it resounded around the space, echoing off the water in the pool and dancing in sync with the twinkling lights that trimmed the trees bordering his property.

"And how do you know that I spend a lot of time thinking about you?"

"I know this, Kenzie, because I've spent a great deal of time thinking about you."

The few minutes they sat staring at each other felt like a lifetime, the moment surreal. The tension that had churned between them earlier began to slowly dissipate, giving rise to something else that was brewing thick and decadent between them.

"Truth?" Zachary questioned.

Kenzie smiled, her head bobbing against her shoulders. "Always, I hope."

He took a deep breath. "I'm scared," he said matter-of-factly.

A hint of surprise wafted over her expression. "You? Scared? I don't know if I believe that."

Zachary smiled again, nodding in response. "Well, I am! You throw a mean left hook when you get mad." He laughed heartily.

"Do you take anything seriously?"

"I take everything seriously. But I also know how to find the humor in every situation. You, on the other hand, don't know how to take a joke."

"That's not true."

He laughed again. "Time will tell."

Kenzie shook her head, frustration furrowing her brow. She hated that he seemed to know her so well when she was still feeling in the dark about so much. A soft sigh blew past her lips. "Tell me about you and Kai Tamura. He trained you, right?"

Zachary's eyes dropped to the ground as he seemed to drift into thought. A moment passed before he answered. "My relationship with Kai is a matter of public record. I trained with him. He was a great mentor. He left my employ many years ago. End of story," he finally answered, lifting his eyes back to hers.

"Do you know where he disappeared to?" she asked.

He hesitated a second time. "Your father left me too, Kenzie," he answered, his voice dropping to a soft whisper. "He left, and he didn't want to be found. I didn't like it, but I loved him enough to respect it."

Kenzie stared at him, the comment surprising her. For longer than she realized, she had imagined that Zachary would have had the answer to all her questions about her father, and in that moment it felt as if he was as lost as she was. Tears misted her gaze, her eyes batting them back. "I apologize for my comment earlier," she said, "about you not being worthy of Kai's friendship. It was a low blow, and you didn't deserve it."

Zachary nodded. "Something tells me that as we continue to get to know each other better, you and I are going to make each other mad a few times before we get it right."

She pondered his comment for a good few minutes, and then she laughed, releasing every ounce of tension that she'd been holding tightly onto. "I'm sure you're right," she said.

Zachary shifted his body closer to hers. "So, are we good?"

Kenzie was suddenly lost in the wave of heat that wafted off his skin, his temperature seeming to rise with a vengeance. She lifted her gaze to his, her eyes dancing an erotic tango with his. The ardor between them had risen to a new level, and she felt herself gasp ever so slightly. She bit down against her bottom lip to stall the quiver of desire that was suddenly all-consuming. She nodded. "I think we're very good."

Zachary nodded. His voice dropped to a low, seductive whisper. "Does that mean I can finally kiss you now?"

Kenzie smiled. "No," she said as she shook her head from side to side.

"No?" His eyes widened in surprise, a level of shock registering across his face.

She laughed, amusement dancing in her gaze. "What it means is that *I* can kiss *you*!"

Kenzie pressing her mouth to Zachary's was truly a dream come true. That first touch was satin gliding across silk, the touch so slight that it was the faintest flutter. Flesh brushed flesh ever so sweetly. Slow, simple pecks soon had them both open and gasping for breath. Then his tongue slid past her lips and the line of her teeth, probing and teasing, a heat-seeking missile on a mission of its own. In no time at all, the desire consuming the two was everything.

Kenzie wrapped her arms around his neck as she lifted herself up to straddle his legs. Zachary drew her close, wrapping his own arms around her waist and back as he pulled her pelvis tightly against him. She grabbed his head and buried her tongue down his throat. Their connection was suddenly intense, sweet shifting to wickedness with lightning speed.

Zachary slipped his hand into her thick curls, hugging her tightly. "I'm about to explode, I want you so badly," he whispered into her ear just seconds before plunging his tongue inside. He trailed his lips over her lobe, along her profile, around the curve of her chin, and down her neck. Seconds later their tongues were entwined once again, neither able to get enough of the tasting and teasing.

When Kenzie's mouth left his lips and began a slow trail down the length of his torso, Zachary was gasping for air, fighting to stall the wealth of sensations that had him near tears. She kissed and licked his neck, nuzzling that spot beneath his chin. Her hands were heated as they laid the path her mouth followed.

Since the first day she'd laid eyes on him, she had been enamored with his tattoos. He wore the ink like a badge of honor, each intricate design painstakingly chosen to tell a specific story. Both arms were sleeved, and the first outline of a full back piece had been started, the detail yet to be finished. He preferred black ink against his warm, brown skin, with hints of color here and there. His chest was still bare, free from the graphic storytelling. She traced every line with her fingertips and kissed and licked the patterns as if they were candy.

When she suddenly fumbled with the string tie that held up his athletic pants, Zachary took a deep breath and held it. When she eased her hands inside his waist band, he almost lost it, his control wavering from the excitement.

Kenzie focused her eyes on his face as she gestured for him to raise his bottom from the seat, allowing her to work his pants down to his ankles. She stole a peek downward and gasped before lifting her gaze back to his. Zachary wore no underwear. She imagined him suddenly feeling exposed and vulnerable as her fingertips lightly traced his flesh.

Zachary met the look she was giving him with one of his own. His gaze urged her on. His dick was hard, feeling like forged steel. It stood straight out with just the hint of a curve in the shaft. She gripped it between her fingers and thumb, pushing it gently back against his body until the tip hit his belly button. A slow grin filled her face as she stole another look toward his face, dropping to her knees between his widened legs. The sensation of her touch was sweeping, the heat too intense. If it could have gone on forever he would have been a very happy guy.

Kenzie traced patterns over his pecs and across his stomach, her mouth laying warm, wet kisses against his skin. She tipped her tongue into the well of his belly button, then teased it even lower toward the dark-brown tufts of pubic hair that met the lower edge of his abdominal wall. When her lips, warm and wet, blew a heated breath against his male member, his whole body quivered, the chill of a sensual current coursing deep into the pit of his stomach. His erection throbbed and pulsated and ached with the sweetest pain. And then she took him into her mouth.

Zachary shifted his buttocks to the very edge of the seat so that he hovered between sitting and standing. The angle let him watch his penis slide in and out of her mouth, fascinated by the way it bulged her cheeks. He was in awe of her oral skills, amazed that she could take as much of him down her throat as she did. She held him with one hand and played with his balls with the other. She sucked up and down his shaft, at the same time jerking the base and twisting to change up the pressures and frictions and suctions that had his head spinning. Kenzie brought him to the brink of orgasm multiple times, his dick going frantic, his heart racing. And then she'd pull him back just to ignite that fire in him one more time.

He didn't have to tell her when he was coming. His body told her, spilling out like a dirty secret kept hidden for far too long. His hips reared up from the chair as he drove his cock into her mouth. His hands gripped the back of her head, clutching the thick curls that tickled his inner thighs. His own head rolled from side to side as he suddenly fought the urge to scream from the intense pleasure of it all.

His body was out of control, his ass jerking up and down against the plastic surface beneath him. His orgasm was volcanic. For just a fleeting moment, he thought that he might die, the convulsions were so earth-shattering. She sucked him dry, and as he gulped air, he stroked her hair and whispered her name as if he were in prayer.

Zachary didn't know how long she stayed there, on her knees, her tongue flicking back and forth between his legs as she lapped at him, her touch light and easy. Time seemed to stand still as he reveled in the sensations she was still eliciting from his body. And then he hardened a second time, his male member engorged beyond his expectations. It surprised him, his body's recovery breaking all personal records. He was brick-hard and suddenly anxious to see where that would take him next.

Kenzie moved onto her feet, taking a step back. The smile on her face was taunting as she slowly brushed her thumb against her lips. The look was teasing, and as he reached for her, she took a step back, moving herself just out of his reach. She shook her index finger at him, and his eyes widened. He laughed warmly, the rich sound echoing through the late-night air.

She did a seductive striptease that had him salivating. She pulled her T-shirt over her head, dropping it easily to the concrete beneath her feet. When she stepped out of her shorts, standing in the sweetest pink lace lingerie set, his manhood surged, the muscle desperately twitching for attention. He stood up, done with being passive as she held control.

He wrapped his arms around her and lifted her into his embrace. His mouth captured hers in another tongue-entwined kiss. Kenzie moaned, the guttural tone rising from deep in her midsection. Heat wafted off her skin with a vengeance. Zachary's yearning was monumental, and all he wanted was to drop his body into hers and lose himself in the beauty of that connection.

Kenzie seemed to read his mind, her own desire as electrifying as his. It filled the air around them, an intoxicating current fueling a host of emotions. "Do you have protection?" she whispered.

His response was incoherent as he mur-

mured in her ear, his palm gently kneading her breast, his thumb and forefinger pulling at the protrusion of nipple. Kenzie kissed his mouth, licking his lips as he spun her around, carrying her in the direction of his bedroom. She gasped, loudly, when he suddenly snaked a hand between them, his fingers sliding past the line of her panties to tangle in her wet fold.

Zachary snatched the bedclothes and tossed them to the floor as he lowered her down to his bed. He was still fingering her unabashedly, his touch searing. Kenzie's body was moving of its own volition, her hips pressing upward, wanting him to touch her deeper, harder, faster. His fingers were slick, coated with her feminine moisture, and when he pushed himself from her to reach into his nightstand for a condom, he shoved his fingers into his mouth, savoring her taste.

Kenzie reached for the prophylactic, taking it from his hand. She tore the wrapper open and sheathed him quickly, pinching the end of the condom as she rolled it over his length. Wanting seeped from his eyes and hers, both drunk with their desire. The moment was exhilarating. Zachary hesitated, his eyes closed as he took a handful of deep breaths to stall the blood that surged so intensely. He dropped his head, his thick tongue teasing one nipple and then the other as he suckled her breasts, wrapping his lips around the lush tissue. It was almost too much as she cried out, her buttocks lifting off the bed to urge him on.

Zachary pushed her legs open, and as he dropped himself between them, he plunged himself into her. The moment was telling, the intensity of it so powerful that neither had the words to explain what they were feeling if their lives depended on it. Their loving was frantic and immeasurable, the wealth of it so abundant that it spilled out of every crack and crevice in the room.

There was a whole other level of excitement that danced hand in hand with their being together for the very first time. From that initial touch there was something wholeheartedly different from the years of casual encounters both had known. Breaking personal taboos as hands touched bare flesh, fingers caressed intimate places, the kissing, the sucking, the swallowing was greater than either could have anticipated. The room was a stereo of little moans and cries of pleasure.

Kenzie came first, her whole body beginning to buck as he stroked her relentlessly, driving himself in and out of her like a piston. Each time he rammed his cock back into her, a surge of pleasure radiated throughout her whole body. Zachary was large and abundant, and he filled her pelvis with the wealth of himself. He thrust himself into her hard and immediately retracted his body only to dive back in again. When she finally reached the peak and orgasmed, her whole body convulsed with pleasure. They were both shaking and trembling, and then his second orgasm spewed, sending them both over the edge of ecstasy together, both shuddering in sync with each other. Zachary fell against her, his weight pinning her against the mattress. Everything felt right as she cradled him against her, both panting heavily as they wallowed in the glowing aftermath of the experience.

Zachary tried to roll off of her, but she gripped him tightly and whispered, "Stay inside of me!" Her muscles pulsed around his organ, squeezing him gently. He pushed himself back against her, rolling enough to wrap himself around her body. He hugged her close, pressing a warm kiss to her forehead and her nose, meeting her lips as he sucked her bottom lip. His kisses were ravishing. Kenzie could barely breathe, all of the air knocked out of her lungs. She pulled a leg higher around him, teasing his backside, and they lingered in the easy caresses of each other's touch as they panted for air.

They lay together for some time before Kenzie finally pulled herself from him.

"Are you okay?" he asked as she moved onto her feet.

She nodded. "I'm better than okay," she whispered back as she headed toward the bathroom.

Zachary lay listening to the flush of the commode and then the running water. Minutes later she came back to the bedside, a warm washcloth in hand. He lay back, one arm resting over his head as she discarded the soiled condom and bathed him clean. Her touch was gentle and easy, and each pass of the washcloth felt like he was being babied in the most nurturing way.

When she was done, Kenzie fell back into his bed, and Zachary pulled the covers around them both. There, in that moment, everything felt right. They wrapped their arms around each other and rubbed noses like little kids. She giggled softly as she turned onto her other side, cradling her buttocks into his crotch. The curve of her back arched against his chest. He wrapped his arms around her waist, seeming to draw her even closer as they lay there pressed together.

Sleep came swiftly, pulling them both beneath a dark, quiet blanket of bliss. Their dreams were sweet that night, promises twinkling in the bright stars that peppered the dark sky outside his windows.

Chapter Seven

"I am not needy," Kenzie snapped. She sat on the edge of Zachary's soaking pool, dipping her toes into the warm water. "In fact, I am the least needy woman you will ever know."

Zachary lay reclined in the pool, his back pressed against the tiled wall. He shook his head. "I didn't say you were needy. I said . . ."

"I heard what you said. And I fully understood what you were implying," she said defensively. "Just because I sometimes allow my emotions to get the best of me doesn't mean I'm desperate for male attention. Yours or anyone else's."

Zachary rolled his eyes skyward. "Are you difficult by default or do you actually work at being such a pain?"

She kicked water in his direction. "It takes skills to do what I do," she said with a soft giggle.

She stared at him, her eyes dancing over his face. After their initial lovemaking they'd slept the night away, finally giving in to the exhaustion that had been teasing them both for days. It was a peaceful slumber, satisfying and rejuvenating. They had been so comfortable that neither had moved, waking up in the exact same position where they'd laid their heads the night before.

His eyes had opened first, the early rays of morning sun streaming past the open window blinds and shining over them. The morning air was unusually warm, and he knew that it was going to be an extremely hot day. He woke with an erection, his morning boner bringing a smile to his face. It took every ounce of his fortitude to keep his urgings at bay. As he'd rolled away from Kenzie, rising to relieve himself, she'd opened her own eyes, greeting him with the sweetest smile, and his fortitude was lost. They had started the day making love before breakfast and again after, and now he needed to get back to his responsibilities. Half the day was already gone without him leaving his home.

Zachary threw water back in her direction. "I need to get dressed," he said as he lifted himself from the water and reached for a towel. "I need to get a run in, and then

I need to go to my office for a few hours to get some work done."

She nodded. "I should go run with you."

He smiled. "You're always welcome. But don't expect me to hold back so you can keep up. I don't work that way."

"Why do you assume I wouldn't be able to keep up? I'll have you know I'm in excellent shape!"

He shrugged his broad shoulders. "I'm sure you are, but you're not in my kind of shape."

Light flashed in Kenzie's eyes, and a muscle at the edge of her brow twitched ever so slightly. It was like a switch turned on, igniting her competitive spirit. She followed behind him as he moved into the bedroom.

The expression on her face made Zachary laugh. "You better keep up," he said as he reached for his running shoes.

Kenzie grabbed her shoes and one of his T-shirts from a pile of clean laundry on the dresser top. "You better run fast," she said.

Zachary was dressed and ready a split second before she was. When she exited the house, he was in the front yard, bent at the waist as he reached for his toes. She stretched her own limbs, twisting first to one side and then the other. Zachary gave her a wink of his eye, and then he took off running, not bothering at all to count down or say go. Kenzie took off after him, the thought crossing her mind that maybe it hadn't been a good idea to think that she could keep up with him.

Zachary crossed the grounds at Revolution, running toward the lengthy driveway and out onto the main road. He ran purposefully, his lengthy strides at an even pace. Kenzie stayed close on his heels, determination motiving each of her own steps. They ran from Patong to Karon Beach. The route was one of the prettiest she had ever run. The spectacular views made the pain she was feeling worth it, and she was feeling pain. The round-trip trail offered some challenging hills, and the midday heat was just a few degrees from stifling.

Sweat poured from them both like water from a running faucet. Kenzie's lungs were feeling brittle and dried like crumpled paper. Her legs were concrete wrapped in rubber. She imagined that if she stopped, her whole body would be one gelatinous mess and she wouldn't be able to move a single step farther. She was just about to quit when Zachary suddenly darted in the direction of the beach, coming to an abrupt stop at the edge of the coastline where the warm blue water kissed the sand. They were both panting harshly.

She gasped for air. "Why . . . why you . . . why did you stop?" she finally managed to mutter.

He cut an eye in her direction. His hands clutched his hips, his broad chest heaving up and down, a drumline beating rhythmically beneath his skin. He laughed and then coughed, gasping for his own air. He shook his head, bemusement painting his expression. "You can keep running," he said. "You don't have to stop because I stopped!"

"I said I would keep up with you, not outrun you. I'll save that for another day!"

Zachary laughed heartily. He gestured toward the empty water bottle affixed to her waist. "I thought you might like to get something to drink," he said as he turned and pointed to a small shack at the end of the beach. "They make a great ginger water that will help energize you."

"Who said I needed to be energized?" she quipped as she followed him down the length of coastline.

Zachary tossed her a look over his shoulder, his expression smug.

The little restaurant was family-owned, and as they stepped to the counter, a young woman greeted Zachary by name. She was beautiful, with waist-length hair, a petite figure, and strong Thai facial features. Zachary introduced Kenzie to Preeda, as she looked Kenzie up and down, her narrowed gaze expressing her displeasure. Preeda turned her attention back to Zachary, her wide smile expressive, her eyes wishful. He greeted the young woman warmly, ordering two drinks in the native language.

Kenzie didn't miss the exchange between the two as Preeda passed him both drinks, allowing her fingers to glide seductively against his. He pulled several bills from his pocket, laying the Thai currency on the counter to pay for their drinks and leave a substantial tip. He passed one cup and straw to Kenzie and grabbed the other. With a warm palm pressed against the small of her back, he guided her to an empty picnic bench so the two could sit down. Preeda was still giving Kenzie the evil eye, watching them both intently.

"Something I should know?" Kenzie questioned, her gaze shifting toward Preeda and back.

Zachary shrugged. "If there's something you want to know, Kenzie, you just need to ask," he said. "I don't make a habit of volunteering unnecessary information."

"Did you sleep with her?"

He lifted his eyes to meet the look Kenzie was giving him. He wanted to laugh, but then he realized she was serious, a hint of jealousy wafting off her spirit like a ghostly mist. "No," he said with a head shake. "I've never had sex with her. I did train her brother for a few years, and I've given both her parents work when they needed it. But I have never even thought about Preeda in that way."

"Well, she's thought about you like that."

"I can't control what anyone thinks about me. If I could, it would eliminate a lot of drama in my life. And I definitely don't worry about anything I can't control. You should give it a try. It'll work wonders for you."

Kenzie pondered his comment for a moment, but she didn't bother to respond. She switched her attention to the plastic cup in her hand. She took a sip of her drink, surprised by the cooling effect of the ginger and citrus blend.

"So, let me ask *you* something," Zachary said. He set his cup down and clasped his hands together in his lap. "Why are you jealous?"

"Who said I was jealous?" She cut a quick

eye in his direction, then shifted her gaze toward the shoreline.

"No one needed to say it. I could see it on your face. That little girl actually had you seeing green."

Kenzie rolled her eyes skyward, the gesture exaggerated. "First, she is no little girl. She's a grown woman. And second, I was not jealous. Not one bit."

"Yes, you were. You were all caught up in your feelings."

Kenzie clenched her teeth, her jaw muscles tightening. Once again she hated to admit it, but Zachary was right. She had been in her feelings, her emotions drifting between jealousy and curiosity. The intensity of it had surprised her, and clearly, despite her best efforts, she hadn't been able to keep it off her face. She didn't bother to respond, feigning interest in her drink instead.

Zachary laughed. He shifted his body and extended his legs, then leaned his back against her chest, pulling her arms around his waist. Kenzie giggled as she let him settle his weight against her. She brushed her fingers across his abdomen. His skin was damp from perspiration, the T-shirt he wore saturated from sweat. He smelled like heat and manliness and the outdoors, his body odor musky and intensely sexual. She inhaled him, allowing his scent to fill her nostrils.

"You need a shower," she said, still trailing her palms and fingers back and forth across his chest and stomach.

He lifted an arm and sniffed his armpit. "I do," he said with a slight shrug.

He turned his head to nuzzle his nose between her breasts, pulling at her sports bra to expose the round tops of her breasts.

Kenzie's eyes widened, and she tossed a quick glance around to see if anyone was watching them. Preeda was still eyeing them intently. Kenzie swatted a hand at him. "What are you doing?"

"Learning your scent. There is something very sexy about a woman's natural body odor," he said.

She bit down against her bottom lip. "I need a shower too."

"After we make love again, we can both shower," he said.

She giggled as he nuzzled her again, his tongue lapping at the salty sweat on her skin. "You really should stop," she said, leaning to press her face into the top of his head. His dreadlocks were loose, falling past his shoulders in intricate waves. His hair was thick and soft, the twists feeling like cotton against her skin. The strands smelled of coconut oil and shea butter. "You've got me feeling all tingly, and we still have to run back."

He nipped at her skin, biting her lightly with his teeth. "I can't. Not yet," he said as he palmed her breast with a heavy hand.

Kenzie tossed a look over her shoulder. Preeda was gone, having disappeared back inside the small building. She looked over her other shoulder, her eyes skating the landscape. The beach was empty, nothing but water and sand and miles of sunshine around them. "Why can't you?" she whispered, pressing her palm over his hand and squeezing it gently.

Zachary nipped at her again. "Because you've got my dick hard."

They were insatiable. Zachary had waved down a tuk-tuk to take him and Kenzie back to Revolution, forgoing the return leg of their run. The driver of the mechanized, three-wheeled taxi had been excited to have the champion in his vehicle and had talked nonstop the whole trip. The entire time, the two had been in the back seat, sitting miles apart, fighting to keep their hands off of each other.

Zachary had tipped him generously when they'd been delivered to the front door of his home. Once inside, they'd left a trail of clothes from the front entrance through the living room and into the bedroom. Their loving had been intense and dirty, the physicality of the sexual act raw and hard. Everything about their coming together was animalistic, the two rutting like it was mating season. Kenzie had lost count of the number of times she'd orgasmed, each one more intense than the time before.

There was something seductive about the easy caresses and gentle nudges they shared. Their connection was intoxicating, and both felt an air of buoyancy that came with the newness of their relationship. The give-and-take between them was surprisingly easy, the two exchanging breaths with each deep inhalation and exhalation of air. They traveled in a parallel universe of their own making, and it was full of sheer bliss like they'd never known before.

As Zachary drifted off into the deepest sleep, he was in awe of his own stamina. Nothing in his past had prepared him for the fireworks between him and Kenzie. Just the thought of her would lengthen an erection in his pants and have him salivating at the prospect of tasting her. When he slid himself into her, it was as if he'd found world peace and the cure for cancer, and had righted everything wrong in the whole wide world. They came together over and over again, and it still wasn't enough. No woman before her had ever had him feeling so fulfilled and so ravenous at the same time.

It was dark out when they finally made it into the shower, slowly soaping each other and rinsing the suds from the other's body. When they finished bathing, they ate the leftovers from the night before, then Zachary excused himself to go check on the chores he'd ignored earlier.

Kenzie retreated to her own cottage for her laptop, sitting down to type out the finer points of her article. She'd been struggling with the words, unable to convey the message that had been spinning in her head for weeks. And then, just like that, it was as if the floodgates had opened, syntax spilling out with a vengeance. She wrote like a woman possessed, the words coming faster than she could get them onto paper. The feeling was incredible, a level of excitement rising that shoved her writer's block to the wayside and had her feeling like a contender for the next Pulitzer Prize. She still needed to visit Colorado and Alexander Barrett's athletic facility there, but she had more than enough data to write the story she was excited to tell. With the words hitting the paper like melted butter on hot toast, she fell into her zone and took up residence.

A few hours passed, and Kenzie had finished the first draft and a round of edits before she realized how late it was. She glanced at her wristwatch and then her cell phone, surprised by the time. After pressing the SAVE button on her keyboard she shut the computer down and tucked it back on the closet shelf.

She moved into the bathroom to freshen up, rinsing her hands and face with warm water. She stared at her reflection, marveling at the glow that seemed to shimmer in her eyes. It felt as if everything that had been weighing heavily on her spirit was gone. She felt something like joy, and the smile on her face refused to be moved. Zachary Barrett had her all in her feelings, and she couldn't begin to fathom that ever going away. She combed through her curls with her fingers and dressed her lips with her favorite gloss. After giving herself a spritz of perfume and one last look in the mirror, she went to search out Zachary, missing him something fierce.

"I think we should sweeten this game up a bit and play strip poker," Zachary said matter-of-factly. He peered over the top of the cards in his hand, lifting his eyebrows suggestively.

They were playing pitty pat, a card game that Kenzie had learned to play as a child; her mother's great aunt Janie had played it with her when she'd been a little girl. After a good hour of conversation, she'd been surprised when he had started dealing the deck of cards, asking her what she did or didn't know how to play. Apparently, he was skilled at gin rummy, poker, and a host of card games she'd never heard of before. She, on the other hand, was only proficient at pitty pat and go fish.

She laughed. "I told you, I don't know how to play poker."

"It would be my pleasure to teach you."

"I'm sure it would, and something tells me I'd be buck naked while you'd still be sitting around fully clothed."

Zachary laughed. "Maybe for the first few games. Until you got yourself acclimated to playing. Then I'm sure you'd give me a run for my money."

Kenzie said, "A run for your skivvies, you mean!" She laughed with him.

"Them too!"

"Pitty pat!" she said as she slammed her last card down on the discard pile. She jumped to her feet and did a little happy dance. Zachary rolled his eyes skyward. She'd beaten him in six straight games, and she enjoyed reveling in his defeat. "Do you want to play again?" she questioned.

He shook his head. "Nope! I'm done for the night. I'm going to take a swim, soak for a few minutes, then I'm going to take you to bed."

Kenzie laughed. "Just like that?"

He nodded. "Exactly like that," he said as he leaned in to give her a swift kiss. He stood as he swept his T-shirt up over his head and dropped it to the concrete beneath his feet. He moved in the direction of the pool, stepping out of his trunks along the way. His naked backside was a sight to behold, his buttocks full and firm like two oversized melons. Kenzie imagined he could have easily balanced a quarter on his hind parts with very little effort. As if he knew she was watching him intently, he jiggled one cheek and then the other, demonstrating the strength of his muscles. The gesture was a wave of sorts, beckoning her to follow after him.

Kenzie moved to the edge of the pool and watched as he slipped beneath the surface of the water, sinking his body low into the pool's depth until it covered his head.

Zachary held his breath for a few good minutes before he lifted himself up, shaking the dampness out of his eyes and hair. He gave her a bright smile, and then he swam laps from one end of the concrete tub to the other, back and forth until Kenzie was actually tired for him. When he finally came to a stop, leaning back against the wall to catch his breath, she realized that she'd been holding her own breath the entire time, air locked deep in her lungs. She blew a heavy sigh and then took a deep inhale of oxygen.

As Zachary lifted himself out of the water to sit on the pool's edge, she thought he was the most beautiful specimen of male prowess that she had ever seen. His warm complexion glistened under the water that trickled down his chest and against his skin. Everything about him screamed power, every hardened line, each sinewy muscle. He was absolutely divine!

Zachary found it exciting to watch her as she stood watching him. The expression on her face was intoxicating, an intense longing seeping out of her eyes. She was as mesmerized with him as he was with her. No woman had ever looked at him like that before. He found himself liking the reflection he saw in her eyes.

As if she were reading his mind, Kenzie

lowered her gaze coquettishly. The look she gave him sent a chill up his spine, and he shuddered as if he were cold. He shifted his body backward, crossing his legs in a lotus position. His dick was rock hard, standing straight up from his body, heavy and lengthy and swaying back and forth as if demanding attention. Their gazes locked as he wrapped his hand around his member and shook it at her, the gesture reminiscent of a magician waving his wand to effect a trick.

"Look at what you did," he said teasingly.

Kenzie laughed. "What I did?"

He nodded. "It's all your fault. Now what are you going to do about it?"

Kenzie bit down against her bottom lip. Her cheeks dimpled from the seductive smile she gave him, and her eyes half closed as she stared from his face to his hands and back. She moved slowly around the end of the pool to stand above him. As she did, she slowly eased the strap of her tank top from her shoulder, her fingers gently stroking her own flesh.

Zachary's face lit up like a kid who had just gotten his Christmas wish. He extended his legs, still stroking himself, slowly at first and then more forcefully, his hips pushing gently up and down against his palm. As he pleasured himself, his eyes watching her intently, Kenzie began to slowly remove her clothes. Her stripper game was on point as she gyrated seductively to the music playing in the background, removing each piece of clothing one by one. He watched her with an eager expression on his face, salivating ever so slightly.

Kenzie didn't speak. Soon she had stripped down to her panties and the high-top sneakers she wore. Then she began to taunt him. She pulled the crotch of her undergarment aside, giving him glimpses of her treasure box, only to quickly cover it up again. She pulled the fabric tight against herself and squatted down within inches of his face as she gyrated her hips. This aroused Zachary even more, and soon he was breathing heavily as he bucked his hips up and down in rhythm to his fingers and palm. He licked his lips. "Talk dirty to me," he commanded, his eyes beseeching.

Kenzie eased herself slowly out of those panties, and then she began to touch herself, talking dirty to him the entire time. "Do you like this pussy, baby? See how hot, and wet you've made me! Look how my fingers slide in and out!" She tossed her head back against her shoulders and purred. "And it feels so good!" she hissed, her voice a loud whisper. "I know you want to put that dick right up in here!"

Kenzie eased herself above him and straddled his head. Her crotch was mere inches from his face. She turned and leaned forward, supporting her weight by holding onto his thick thighs. "That's it, baby," she hissed as she eased her buttocks back and lowered her crotch to his face. "Rub that pussy good! Get me wet! You want me, don't you, baby?"

"Yeah! Oh, yeah," Zachary croaked, the words catching in his throat as he panted.

Kenzie dropped even lower over his face, covering his mouth until she felt his tongue lapping at her folds. He licked her from front to back. He drank the taste of her sex, the pungent aroma and flavor hardening him even more.

Kenzie moaned with joy and pleasure as he began to move her pussy around with his mouth, spreading the flow of her juices all over his face as his tongue dipped into each crevice. "Oh, God!" she exclaimed.

"Come for me," Zachary ordered in a low, throaty whisper. "I'm going to make you come!" He stopped stroking himself as he grabbed her butt, kneading the flesh with a heavy, heavy hand. He pulled her back against him and then pushed into her, his tongue plowing her like a piston in overdrive.

Kenzie bent her knees to lower her torso even more. She suddenly took him in her mouth, sucking him like he was an ice pop and it was noontime in the middle of the summer. They licked and sucked and lapped at each other in a twisted sixty-nine position until she felt her legs begin to quiver, her entire body beginning to spasm with pleasure.

Zachary suddenly pushed her forcefully, spinning her at the same time. He pulled her down against him, driving his dick deep inside of her. The intrusion into her secret spot was explosive, and Kenzie felt her body gush, the satin lining of her inner muscles squeezing and tightening around him. She pumped her body up and down, around and around, over and over again, until Zachary fell off the edge of ecstasy with her, screaming her name into the midnight air.

Their orgasms were earth-shattering, the two shaking and quivering intensely. Everything seemed bigger and brighter, smells more intense, touch more sensitive. Zachary pumped himself in and out of her until there was nothing left to push and pull, every ounce of himself drained. He fell back against the hard surface beneath him,

Kenzie falling against him as she clutched his arms and held on tightly. Her torso heaved up and down in sync with his as they gasped and panted for air, feeling as if there wasn't enough oxygen to share and needing to save the other with each breath.

Riding the last waves of their orgasms, neither noticed the slight scrapes against her knees and his back, skin red from the abrasive flooring they lay on. Neither paid any attention to the clouds that had darkened the late-night sky, the first sign of bad weather coming. And when the rains finally fell, they could have cared less, still lost in the beauty of being with each other.

Chapter Eight

Sarai hit the redial on her cell phone for the umpteenth time. When she didn't get an answer, she tossed the device aside in frustration.

"What's wrong?" Alexander asked. He lifted his eyes from his morning newspaper. "Who are you trying to call?"

"Your brother. Have you spoken with him? I've called Zachary a few times, left a ton of messages, and he hasn't called me back."

Alexander chuckled. "I spoke to him the other day. He's doing just fine."

"Are you sure? I got a message from Kenzie. She's canceled her trip here to Colorado. She's done all her interviews with the staff here by phone and video chat, and she's planning to submit her story in the next few days."

"Well, that's a good thing, right? She got everything she needed."

"I guess, but I wanted to make sure.

Which is why I want to speak with Zachary. To get his take on why she changed her plans."

"You worry too much. If I guessed, I'd venture to say that things are probably going very well with both my brother and Kenzie."

Sarai stared at her husband for a brief moment. Alexander Barrett was the most beautiful man she had ever laid eyes on. She'd been enamored with him since she'd been a little girl and her mother had received a Christmas photo card of him and his family, he and his twin brother looking like two bookends in little boy suits. Meeting him had been a dream come true. Becoming his wife had opened the doors to Eden, the two of them so in love that sometimes she was in total awe of how happy they were together.

He gave her a smile that melted her heart and had her legs quivering with anticipation. She loved his smile, the simple gesture warming her spirit.

Sarai laughed. "What do you know?" she questioned as she moved to his side and eased herself into Alexander's lap. She wrapped her arms around his neck and drew him close, meeting his lips with her own.

Alexander kissed her back, a deep, tongue-entwined connection that left them both panting when they finally pulled back. He took a deep breath before he spoke. "I know that my brother and that girl are doing just fine. They don't need either one of us in their business. And Zachary certainly doesn't need you running interference for him."

She hesitated for a brief moment, mulling over her man's comment. "So they're a thing now? Zachary and Kenzie?"

Alexander shrugged. "I don't know if they are or not. But I know that my brother likes her, and when he asked my opinion I told him to go for it. He has nothing to lose."

Sarai shook her head, and Alexander could almost see her mind working. His wife's relationship with his brother went back years, before he and she had met. He knew that other people often questioned the bond the two shared, wondering if that something between them was more than platonic, curious if their friendship came with any privileges. He himself had been skeptical of their relationship before he and Sarai had fallen in love and married. But he knew both their hearts. His brother had his back and would never betray him like that. His wife loved him as deeply as he loved her. He trusted them both, and he understood his wife's concerns. "Are you jealous?" he teased, his brow raised questioningly.

Sarai shook her head. "No, not at all. If he's happy, then I'm ecstatic!"

Alexander smiled. "He's very happy!"

She kissed him again. "You know he's going to mess it up, don't you? Somehow, some way he'll do something to push her away and blow it. He needs to call me so I can tell him what he needs to be doing."

Alexander laughed. "Let's hope not! Let's hope that he can get it right this time. But I'm sure the minute it goes left, you'll be the first person he calls looking for advice. Then he'll call me for a second opinion."

His wife nuzzled her nose beneath his chin. "You're right," she said. "I guess I won't worry." She trailed her tongue across his jawline. "Now, how much time do we have before we have to be at the gym?"

Alexander stole a glance down to his wristwatch. He stood, lifting her in his arms as he moved onto his feet, reclaiming her mouth with his own. His voice was a loud whisper, the tone inviting. "We'll make time," he said.

Zachary was humming. Zachary never

hummed. But many times that week he'd been caught uttering a rhythmic murmur under his breath, his staff and friends eyeing him curiously.

Gamon turned to stare at him as Zachary hummed from his desk to the file cabinet and back. He hummed as he sat back down to sign a stack of checks, and he hummed as he reviewed the week's employee schedule. Twice he exited the room, and when he returned he was still humming.

Gamon swallowed back a laugh, bemused by the other man's behavior. "You are very happy," he said, interrupting the chorus that had risen to a new pitch.

Zachary smiled sheepishly. "Sorry! I guess I got a little carried away."

"No need to apologize. If you are happy, then you are happy."

"I admit it. I'm in a really good mood!"

He and the older man exchanged a look.

"Is Miss Kenzie in a good mood, too?" Gamon asked, his expression smug.

Zachary shrugged, his wide smile spreading into a full grin that filled his face. He didn't bother to respond.

Gamon rolled his eyes toward the ceiling, his head waving from side to side. He crossed his arms over his chest. "You need to stay focused," he said, the slimmest hint of scolding in his tone.

Zachary scoffed. "How am I unfocused, Gamon?"

"You are missing classes. You are not spending time with your clients like you usually do. You haven't returned important phone calls, and you spend much time locked away in your home with Miss Kenzie. You are like a schoolgirl with a crush!" The man tossed up his hands in frustration.

Zachary laughed. "I am not that bad!"

"You are worse!" Gamon countered.

"Okay," Zachary said with a soft sigh. "I'll get focused and do better. I promise."

Gamon sucked his teeth, "Tch!" He waved a dismissive hand. "You will be just as bad as long as she is here. When is she leaving?"

Leaning back in his leather executive's chair, Zachary paused on the question. He met the other man's stare when he answered. "I don't want her to leave," he said softly. He lost himself in another split second of reflection, then said, "I like having her here."

Gamon eyed him intently before nodding his head. "We need the cottage she is staying in. She will move in with you so that we can have that space for new clients coming," the patriarch said, his comment feeling very much like an order.

"Fine," Zachary answered. "She can move into my spare bedroom."

The look the old man gave him made Zachary laugh and blush, his cheeks warming with color. "What?" he asked.

Gamon headed toward the office door. "We should call the monks," he said matter-of-factly.

"The monks? Why?"

"For the marriage blessing," Gamon said as he exited the room, closing the door after himself.

"The what . . . ?"

As the door closed, Zachary chuckled warmly, amused by his friend's attempt at a joke. Even though he knew Gamon well enough to know the man probably wasn't joking, he found him comical. Because Gamon knew marriage was the last thing on Zachary's mind. Having been there and done that, he couldn't imagine himself making such a commitment ever again with any woman.

Then he thought about Kenzie, and suddenly he wasn't so sure anymore. Kenzie had him wide open. Their sexual connection was off the charts. They were having a good time together, and with everything he discovered about her, he found himself excited to learn more.

Kenzie Monroe was an anomaly in his small world. She not only excited him, but she challenged him. She didn't fit into the box where he so casually placed all of his female relationships. She spilled past the boundaries he set between himself and the women he associated with. She soothed his soul, and he was fascinated with everything she said and did. And she frustrated the hell out of him; her sensitive nature, sometimes hyper behavior, and devil-may-care attitude gave him many reasons to pause and reconsider what he was getting himself into.

Zachary sat in deep thought for a good few minutes before turning his attention back to the paper work on his desk. He really did need to work harder on staying focused, but after an hour of being away from her he couldn't get the exquisite creature out of his head. Kenzie had that effect on him, and he didn't see that changing anytime soon.

Kenzie had found the perfect spot on the beach, under the most perfect tree. The weather couldn't have been better. The warm sun overhead sat in a bright-blue sky where marshmallow clouds floated lazily through the midday air. The water was crystalline, a shade of blue that was calm and soothing, sparkling like a collection of rich jewels beneath the light. It was as if the moon and the stars had aligned in perfect sync, the entire world rotating on its axis at just the right speed to insure the day was the best that she could have ever imagined. Kenzie felt relaxed and happy and like no one and nothing could push her off the pedestal she was sitting on top of. She imagined she was queen for the day and there wasn't a whim or wish that she would be denied.

Zachary had put her on that dais and had lifted her sky-high, making her feel like she was the end-all of everything he held near and dear. He spoiled her, teased her sensibilities, and had her feeling like an adolescent with her very first crush.

Kenzie found herself laughing out loud, the sound resonating through the warm air. She was happy, and she couldn't remember the last time she'd felt so incredible. With her article about the two brothers finished, Kenzie had no reason to still be in Phuket, but she wasn't ready to leave. She had pushed the SEND button on her writing days earlier, and her agent expected her to head back to New York, but Kenzie hadn't even given the possibility of leaving a thought. There was still so much she wanted to learn about Zachary and even more that she wanted to share with him.

Everything about her newfound friendship with the man moved her spirit. He had her questioning everything she thought she knew about herself and what she wanted for her life, and suddenly the thought of a man in the middle of that mix didn't feel so foreign to her.

She deeply inhaled the warm air, allowing it to fill her lungs and nourish her insides. Sitting there in reflection, Kenzie had to admit that she had never imagined herself wanting any man to be in her life for longer than a minute. And she blamed her parents for her disdain about marriage and relationships.

Kai Tamura and Tanya Monroe had met when he was touring the United States, trying to attain his own heavyweight title championship. The Madison Square Garden event had been one of many her mother had worked, taking tickets at the window, working the concessions stands, and whatever else helped pay her bills at the time. Running into Kai had been a fluke, fate interceding when neither had expected it. His English had been faltering, but he'd had the most brilliant smile. Their attraction had been instantaneous. At the time, Tanya couldn't fathom the cultural differences that would eventually tear them apart, only knowing that he made her heart flutter at the possibilities. Kenzie was born twelve months later. Her father had returned to Bangkok months earlier to prepare for the fight that would make him a household name. He had not been there to witness her birth. Her mother had often told her the story of their first meeting, Kai fawning all over his six-month-old baby girl. Kenzie often regretted that she had no memory of that moment.

Things between Kai and Tanya had gone downhill from there. His checks came like clockwork. But he was gone more than he was there, and there were other men who made her mother feel better about her situation. Kenzie had grown up never seeing either of her parents in a healthy, loving relationship with a partner. She'd always been angry about her father leaving, feeling abandoned as though she was unwanted goods. Her mother had tried often to assure her that the very adult issues between them had nothing at all to do with her, but Kenzie had never been able to wrap her mind around the truth of that.

When she'd been a little girl, her father had called often to check on them both. His professional fight career had him traveling more often than not. She'd often imagined him standing in telephone booths in Paris, Spain, Belgium, Morocco, and a whole host of other countries he would find himself in, always taking time to call and tell her he loved her. Then there'd be the fights between him and her mother about the money that was never enough as far as Tanya Monroe was concerned. For longer than Kenzie could remember, Tanya was always holding her hands out for more, for bigger, for better, bleeding her father dry of everything he had to give. Most especially his love.

An injury had eventually returned Kai back to Thailand to teach. Kenzie had been twelve and certain that her father would be back in her life to teach her about the boys to avoid and hold her hand at the father-daughter dances that her youth group sometimes hosted. But Kai Tamura had never come for her. Eventually his calls waned, their frequency starting to feel like leap years. The last time he'd called to wish her a happy birthday and tell her that he loved her, she'd been seventeen, surly and contentious, angry that her mother had yet another new boyfriend, some other man wanting to play daddy in their home. And she'd taken her anger out on her father, telling him to never call her again. Years later, when she'd finally reached out to make amends, Kai Tamura had vanished.

Not having her father in her life and watching her mother blow through one reject after another had kept Kenzie on the defensive when it came to her own relationships. She had never been willing to risk her heart. She learned early how to feed her natural desire for human connection, but giving her body had never come with any contingencies that involved her head or her heart. Lust didn't require commitment, only a condom.

And suddenly everything had changed. Kenzie was back in her father's country, following the desires of her own heart and a man who had her full attention. She wanted to get it right, to do it better than her parents had ever imagined, and she knew deep in her heart that flying back to New York wouldn't help that happen. She wanted Zachary, and her wanting him was about so much more than her body and how he made her feel with his touch. This time, whether she was ready to acknowledge it or not, her head and her heart were caught up in the fray.

■ ■ ■ ■

"Did you not think you should have checked with me first?" Kenzie stood with her hands on her hips as two staff members moved her personal possessions — a suitcase, her computer, her makeup bag, and a shopping bag of souvenirs — into Zachary's second bedroom. They were eyeing her out of the corners of their eyes, fearful that she might lash out at one or the other of them. "Maybe I don't want to be moved!" she screamed.

Zachary shrugged his broad shoulders as he took a sip from his bottle of beer. "What are you mad about? You haven't slept over there in weeks!"

Kenzie hissed. "That's not the point," she snapped as she cut her eyes toward the two men, who'd come to a standstill.

"Well, what's the point, Kenzie? Do you not want to be here? If you don't want to be here, I will personally help you pack your bags and check you out. I'll even arrange for a ride to the airport!"

"So now you want me to leave?"

Zachary rolled his eyes skyward. He pointed the two men toward the door, closing it after them. He turned to give her a look, then walked past her, not bothering to respond to her comment.

"Aargh!" Kenzie screamed, fury washing over her expression.

Zachary tossed her a look over his shoulder. A wry smirk painted his expression. "Keep it up, and see if it I don't put you over my knee."

"You wouldn't dare!" she gushed as she stomped after him.

He suddenly turned toward her, and she came to an abrupt stop, taking a quick step back. "Why are you having a fit?" he asked. "I moved you into my home. I didn't excise your kidney."

"You didn't *ask* me," she said, crossing her arms over her chest. "You just assumed and did it without my consent. That's not cool."

Zachary took a deep breath, blowing it out slowly past his full lips. "I apologize if I upset you, but there are going to be times that I'm going to make a decision that's in the best interest of our family that you're not going to agree with. I'm the head of our home, and you're just going to have to get over it because I'm not going to ask you to vote or weigh in. There's no democracy here!"

Kenzie bristled, her eyes widening. "That's whole-heartedly arrogant and sexist! And I guess you want me barefoot and pregnant, too?"

"*Naked,* barefoot, pregnant, and on your knees works well for me."

The look Kenzie gave him made Zachary laugh out loud. He turned back toward the outside and stepped out onto the patio, still chuckling heartily.

She was suddenly struck by the absurdity of their conversation. *Our family. Our home.* Since making the announcement, Zachary had been talking about the two of them as if they were already an old married couple. And she'd responded in kind; their bickering was reminiscent of a duo who'd been together longer than dirt and sand. She was suddenly just as amused by their exchange as he was. She giggled softly, her head waving from side to side.

"You are so crass," she said as she joined him outside. "On my knees? Really?"

He shrugged his shoulders a second time. "A man can dream, can't he? You do that thing with your tongue so well," he grinned.

She tossed up her hands. "You really are impossible!"

He met her gaze as he wiggled an index finger and gestured for her to come to him. She moved slowly, still wanting to linger in her anger for a moment longer.

"What?"

He tapped his lap, then opened his arms, holding them out wide.

With her own eye roll, she eased herself against him, settling down comfortably as he wrapped his arms around her waist. He kissed her forehead and then her cheek before letting his lips connect with hers.

It had taken very little to send her over the edge. They had already cleared out her cottage when she'd come back from the beach, finding all of her belongings being carted off. He'd been excited to share his plans for the two of them — her coming to stay in his space since she'd already taken up residence in his bed every night. But Kenzie hadn't taken the news lightly, going from one to a hundred in a split second. For a brief moment, he'd second-guessed his decision, but the shimmer of energy in her eyes had told him they were definitely on the right track. Kenzie wasn't going to be a passive partner. She would be fully engaged, and she would keep him on his toes. She was everything he needed in a woman multiplied by ten.

One of his hands slid between her legs, and she pressed her knees tightly together to trap his fingers. The other traced her full buttocks, his fingers teasing. Heat radiated through them both, and he gasped for air as they broke the connection.

"You said *our family* like we're a couple or something," Kenzie muttered.

"We *are* a couple," he replied, lightly licking her lips.

"I don't remember you asking me if that's what I wanted with you," she whispered loudly.

He chuckled softly. "You really need to learn how to just go with the flow. You're going to give yourself a heart attack the way you go off about absolutely nothing." He kissed her again.

She inhaled a deep breath when he finally let her lips go. "It might be nothing to you, but it's something to me. You need to keep that in mind when you catch yourself taking charge." She nuzzled her cheek against his. "I'm not interested in being with a tyrant."

"And I don't plan to be with a brat."

"I'm not a brat."

"You have brat-like tendencies."

"I do not!"

"Yes, you do. You're spoiled, and you're bitter, and you have a tendency to be hostile toward men."

"And you are self-absorbed, egotistical and . . . well . . . you just piss me off sometimes!" Kenzie snapped, instantly dreading that they were going tit for tat.

Zachary shrugged. "Sounds like we're perfect for each other."

"Sounds like it."

He tightened the hold he had around her waist. Neither said anything for a good few minutes, settling into the silence. In the distance the sun was beginning to set, disappearing past the line of trees that bordered the property. Instinctively, both knew things between them had changed, the dynamics of their relationship having morphed into something neither had expected. The wealth of it was overwhelming and intense and wholeheartedly comfortable.

Zachary cupped his palm beneath her chin and twisted her face to his. He kissed her lips again, his mouth gently brushing hers. When he pulled back, he closed his eyes for a quick minute and took a deep breath. Blowing it out slowly, he opened his eyes and stared into hers. "I'm falling in love with you, Kenzie," he whispered. Their gazes were locked tight, the bond suddenly formidable.

Kenzie felt her body begin to shake. She wasn't sure how to respond, not sure she had the words for all the emotion she was feeling, so she didn't say anything at all.

"It's okay," he said, reading her mind. "It

scares the hell out of me, too."

They sat together for a good long while, trading easy caresses and saying nothing. The sun had completely disappeared, and the automatic nightlights had switched on. It was a moment Kenzie knew she'd never forget as she reflected on everything he'd said, most especially his last comment. Because she was scared, and if she were honest with herself, and with him, she wasn't *falling* in love with Zachary Barrett. She was already there. Zachary owned every square inch of her heart.

Chapter Nine

Zachary's secrets were suddenly haunting him. And they were haunting him because he suddenly felt obligated to share everything with a woman who had gotten under his skin. Kenzie was like a deep itch he couldn't scratch, everything about her crawling deep beneath his skin. She had him out of sorts, and he was feeling beside himself with regret and concern because he knew something he needed to share with her and didn't have a clue when or if he'd ever be able to tell her.

He had never had a relationship where he kept things from his partner. His ex-wife had played those tricks, and after the fiasco that had been his first marriage, he had sworn to never purposely deceive any woman he claimed to care about. He would never lie to the woman he loved, and he was determined to get that same respect back.

What he was feeling for Kenzie was more

than casual concern. He saw her occupying every aspect of his life. He trusted her and looked forward to the moments they would inevitably share and the opportunities that would propel them into their future together. And wanting theirs to be a love of a lifetime had his past haunting him.

Sarai could hear the frustration in his tone when he finally answered her call. "Hey, what's up?" Zachary said.

"That's what I'm trying to figure out. How are you doing? It's been a minute since we last spoke."

"It hasn't been that long!"

"It's been a good few weeks. You haven't returned any of my calls. If my father hadn't kept me updated, I wouldn't know what was going on."

"That's why I knew I didn't need to call you. Gamon wasn't going to let you miss out on anything. I'm sure he's kept you all in my business."

"Your business, yes, but he hasn't answered any of the questions I wanted to know. Like what's up with you and Kenzie? How are things going?"

"They're good."

"What did you think about her article?" Sarai asked.

Zachary's gaze shifted to the advance copy

of the sports magazine that rested on his desk. He and his brother graced the cover, his image front and center, while his brother was at his side, his profile visible. The two held onto his fight belt, the photo taken right after his last title win. The bruise on his cheek had been airbrushed away, and both men actually looked *GQ* ready. It was a good photo.

He'd read the article a few times. Kenzie had done them both well, even when she had pointed out that everything wasn't always roses and apple pie with him. She'd called him out on his bad behavior, but she'd been right, so he couldn't even begin to be mad about it. All in all, it was one of the better articles ever written about him.

"Kenzie did a good job. I'm not mad about it."

"Alexander liked it too." Sarai took a deep breath. "So are you and Kenzie a thing now?"

"We're friends."

There was an awkward pause, and Zachary could almost see the exasperation on his friend's face.

"You really like her!" Sarai suddenly exclaimed, unable to contain the excitement in her voice.

Zachary shook his head as he grinned into

the receiver. "There you go!"

"There I go? I'm just looking for information. She's still in Phuket, so something must be going on. Her article comes out next week, so she doesn't have any reason to be there. At least none that anyone is sharing with me."

"We're getting to know each other, so she decided to stay for a little longer."

"So you moved her into your house?"

"I thought you didn't know anything?" Zachary laughed heartily.

"I know enough to know there's more going on than what you're actually saying."

"I think I might be in love with her!" Zachary gushed, suddenly spilling information like a hydrant gone awry.

When he finished updating her, Kenzie was laughing with him. "Why does this sound really serious?" she asked.

"Because I think it is, Sarai! I really want to keep her! Is that crazy?"

Sarai laughed. "She's not a pet, Zachary. You just don't get to keep her like she's some kind of toy!"

"You know what I mean."

"I do. You don't want to lose her. She's become important to you."

"That too," he said casually.

There was a moment of pause before

either spoke, Sarai continuing the conversation. "My father says she's Kai Tamura's daughter."

The laughter in Zachary's tone suddenly fizzled. "Yeah."

"Does she know?"

He shook his head as if she could see him. "No. Kenzie doesn't know anything, and you know I can't tell her."

"Well, you have to tell her," Sarai said matter-of-factly. "She deserves to know."

"I promised him, Sarai."

"Zachary, you can't commit to Kenzie without telling her the truth. A relationship based on lies isn't a relationship."

"And how is that conversation going to go? Oh, by the way, I know where your father is, and he doesn't want to see you?"

"How about telling Kenzie that her father is dying and he didn't want her to know?"

"Don't say it like that, Sarai." There was a wealth of melancholy in his voice, his whole demeanor suddenly weighed down with sadness.

Understanding swept between them. It wasn't the first time they'd had a conversation like this, but it was the first time Zachary understood why his friend had always advocated for him to do what was right, not necessarily what his mentor had begged from him.

Sarai's compassion was abundant. "You know it's the truth, Zachary. It's a burden you've carried for far too long. Tell her, but be prepared for the fallout."

"What fallout?"

"Kenzie is going to be upset. And she's probably going to be very angry with you. Don't be surprised if she reacts badly."

Zachary cussed, spitting a long line of expletives past his full lips.

"She really has rubbed off on you," Sarai said with a giggle, remembering how casually the other woman would curse.

He blew a loud sigh. "If it were your father and I didn't tell you, how would you feel?" he questioned.

"I would never forgive you," Sarai said. "It would destroy everything between us. And that's why you need to tell her. Don't let it ruin what you two have if being with her means that much to you."

He sighed a second time, pausing to reflect on her comment.

Sarai was shaking her head on the other end. "Do you want me to pass your brother the phone now or do you want to call him later to get his opinion?"

Zachary grunted softly. "I'll call him later."

"Whatever, but I'm sure he's going to

agree with me. Alexander is going to tell you the exact same thing!"

"Yeah, yeah, yeah, whatever."

"I'm still not sure if she's good enough for you, Zachary!"

He laughed. "Trust me. She's as perfect for me as you were for my twin!"

Zachary and Sarai continued to talk for a good hour or more before finally ending their conversation. After he'd disconnected the call, he realized just how much he had missed bantering back and forth with his friend. She was happy, and he could hear it in her voice. She genuinely wanted the best for him, wishing him and Kenzie well. He also knew she was right about needing to be open and honest with the woman who kept him on edge. But the thought of telling Kenzie the truth stirred up feelings he wasn't able to confront yet, feelings that kept him up at night.

He didn't bother to call his brother. Alexander had texted a quick message, reiterating what Sarai had said. Zachary knew he needed to tell Kenzie the truth, and he needed to do it sooner than later. But he couldn't fathom where to begin.

His time with Kai had seemed like a lifetime ago. He'd been young and determined to make his mark in a business and culture he knew nothing about. It had been his ex-wife's suggestion that they just pack up their lives and move to Thailand. Lacking maturity and being naïve, he'd trusted that the ex-Mrs. Barrett had his best interest at heart. Once he'd arrived, he realized he was in way over his head.

Finding Kai had been a twist of fate. Alexander had tried a number of boxing gyms before finding his way to Tamura's. The grand champion had been larger than life, mean as spit, and an amazing instructor. The two had taken an instant dislike to each other.

It had taken months of fights and sparring with better-known Thai fighters before the day Kai had stood ringside, seeing something in him that Zachary himself hadn't known was there. Days later, Kai had called him to the office of his training facility and had personally taken Zachary under his wing. Zachary had been ecstatic. Then real fear set in. Zachary's natural talent and his love of the sport had meshed nicely with all that Kai had brought to the table. But building a bond between them had come after much hard work.

Kai Tamura had been a legend for a reason. The man's talents far exceeded anything Zachary had ever known. Kai had sometimes pushed him well past his limits and had never once allowed him to quit. The two men had eventually become more family than friends, with Kai a surrogate father of sorts. Zachary respected Kai with every fiber of his being, and there had been nothing that he wouldn't have done for him. Even promising to take his friend's secrets to the grave.

Zachary had held his first title belt and was preparing for his second title fight when Kai had been diagnosed with a rare form of early-onset Alzheimer's disease. He'd been dealing with Kai's descent into dementia ever since.

Statistically, Kai was among the one percent of people with Alzheimer's who get the early-onset form of the illness. The series of changes in his brain had begun decades before the symptoms of his disease had been noticed by those closest to him. When it had become clear that something wasn't right, the official diagnosis had been devastating to them both.

As his memory problems had begun to seriously affect his daily life, Kai had put a plan into place to control the last days of his life. All of his needs had been accounted for, and then he'd dropped the bomb, the kind that Zachary had prayed would never explode while on his watch. Discovering that Kai had a child had been a surprise. Learning that Kai and his offspring were estranged had been difficult. Promising to never let Kai's daughter be affected or burdened by her father's illness had been Zachary's last act of selflessness. He'd sworn on everything he cherished that he would honor the oath he had pledged to his friend. And now that bomb had imploded, everything suddenly going *boom!*

"We're going away for a few days," Kenzie said. She tossed a pile of T-shirts into her carry-on bag.

"Away where?" her friend Stephanie asked.

"Zachary didn't say, and I didn't ask."

"So when are you planning to come back home?"

Kenzie paused as she took in the question. She'd been asking herself the same thing but hadn't made any plans to return to the United States. She liked being in Thailand. And she loved the time she was spending with Zachary. She didn't want it to end, and as long as he was happy with her being there, she saw no reason to leave.

"You are planning on coming back home, aren't you, Kenzie?"

"I'm sure I'll be back to get my things at some point."

"You have lost your mind. You don't know anything about his man."

"That's not true. I know a lot about him. I did just write a whole six-page article about him, and we've been spending all of our spare time together. I think I know him very well."

Kenzie imagined Stephanie rolling her eyes skyward before she responded. "I swear, Kenzie. This is taking impulsive to a whole other level. You're going to drive me crazy."

"I'm really not that bad."

"Yes, you really are."

"Zachary is just a great guy, Stephanie, and . . . well . . . I . . ."

Her friend interjected. "Don't you dare say it!"

"What?"

"Do not use that four-letter word I think you're going to use."

Kenzie laughed. "But it's how I feel. I love him."

"How many times do I have to tell you about that foul mouth of yours?"

"Love, love, love, love, love," Kenzie quipped. "I love him."

Stephanie laughed. "Someone bring me

some damn soap and water, so I can wash this heifer's mouth out!"

Kenzie laughed with her friend. "Girl, Zachary and I are good together. Hell, we're *great* together, and he's so good to me!"

"Your article makes him sound like he might be a little bit of a narcissist."

"He's actually a lot narcissistic. But I like that about him."

"You're killing me! And I'm happy for you, but you really do need to come home. Let that nonsense go!"

"Thank you. I appreciate all that love and support. You know I do," Kenzie responded, a hint of teasing in her tone.

"I still want to know where he's dragging you off to. Just in case you don't come back or something."

Kenzie laughed. "I wish I could tell you, but it's a surprise."

"You don't like surprises, remember?"

"I love Zachary's surprises!"

Kenzie sat out on the patio, her luggage packed and ready. After disconnecting the call with Stephanie, she'd finished throwing a few things into her carry-on bag and had even packed a suitcase for Zachary. He was off somewhere handling his business, fulfilling the last of his training obligations before they'd be able to leave. He had told her to be ready when he got back, and she was, her excitement brimming like a bubbling pot on the stove.

Kenzie was overwhelmed by the wealth of emotion that had claimed her soul. It was almost as if she'd been claimed by a body snatcher from some sci-fi drama. No man had ever had her feeling so out of sorts. But what she was feeling for Zachary was voluminous. It filled the air around her, swelling full and thick like the mist after a monsoon of rain. An outsider looking in would have thought she had tossed Christmas, New Year's, and her birthday into one big balloon, and Zachary had popped that bubble, showering her with confetti of enthusiasm and energy. He was steering the cloud she was floating on, and Kenzie was gladly following after him. Clearly, she suddenly thought, she had lost her damn mind.

She reached for her computer and turned it on. A lengthy list of email messages was awaiting her attention. One by one she went through them, appreciating that over half required absolutely nothing from her. She couldn't focus and had no interest in anything that might require her to be fully engaged. Kenzie was beside herself with giddiness; it was unlike anything she'd ever experienced before. As she sat reflecting on all the things she attributed to her emotional overload, she was suddenly grateful that she had never been in love before. Going through this time and time again would have driven her crazy. She couldn't begin to imagine how women who went from relationship to relationship managed to do it.

Zachary coming through the door pulled her from her thoughts. Her smile was canyon-wide as she jumped excitedly from her seat. "Hey, baby!"

Zachary kissed her mouth, his lips lingering sweetly. "Hey, are you ready?"

Kenzie nodded. "So, are you going to tell me where we're off to?"

He hesitated as his eyes locked with hers. "I just wanted you all to myself for a few days," he said, his voice dropping to a loud whisper. He wrapped his arms around her and hugged her tightly.

Kenzie sensed that something was on his mind, his spirit floating in a sea of turmoil. A wave of anxiety pierced her midsection, and concern washed over her expression. "What's wrong? You seem out of sorts."

Zachary shrugged. He kissed her forehead, the tip of her nose, and her cheeks. "Just a lot of stuff on my mind, baby. That's why I need to get away for a few days. So let's get out of here. Let's go have some fun!"

The drive was quiet as they meandered through downtown Phuket and out of the city. Neither spoke as Zachary headed north, driving along one of the most scenic coastal routes in Asia. The landscape was a panorama of limestone hills densely covered with jungle and thickly planted greenery along limestone boulders. It was breathtakingly beautiful, a feast for the eyes.

Taking it in, Kenzie had no need for words. She was comfortable, and being in Zachary's presence felt all kinds of right. She was glad to be there, and he knew it without her having to say so.

There was so much to see as they took in the sights. They passed Thai people working massive rice fields, large Buddha statues in the most obscure places, amazing displays of flora, and children skipping in rows of dust. Kenzie found herself drafting a travel article in her head. By the time they made it to the Sarasin Bridge that connected the island to mainland Thailand, she had written a pitch in her mind, excited about passing it by her agent.

Around the base of the bridge, there were fish trawlers and anglers bobbing in the deep blue water, hoping to catch dinner. In the distance, there were views of the tropical forests, lush vegetation, and stands of mangroves. Wherever they stopped, everyone recognized Zachary, and people were excited to shake hands with their champion. He spoke to each of them in their native tongue. Continuing on, they stopped at the infamous Phang Nga Bay where the James Bond movie *The Man with the Golden Gun* had been filmed, then stopped at a beautifully secluded beach to take a quick swim. They reached their destination in under five hours, just in time to see the sun beginning to set in the distance.

Kenzie wasn't expecting the hustle and bustle of Krabi Town. The area had a quirky feel with the sheer volume of buildings that were packed into the compact area. Everything about the downtown area belied what she'd come to know and love about Thailand, with its white sand beaches and blue waters. The town was congested with cars and crowded with natives and tourists.

Kenzie didn't know what to expect when Zachary left the downtown area and turned onto a private road. She sat forward in her seat as she spied the beachfront villa at the end of the roadway. The meticulously landscaped property was extraordinary with its tropical fruit trees and lush vegetation.

"This is beautiful," Kenzie exclaimed as she cut an eye in Zachary's direction.

He winked an eye at her. "I think so." He pulled the car into a parking space and shut down the engine.

Before either could comment, the front door of the villa flung open and a man rushed outside to greet them. He was robust and gregarious, reminding Kenzie of the Pillsbury Doughboy, with a balding head and a thick, blue-black mustache and matching goatee. It was his lengthy lashes, blue eyeshadow, meticulous makeup, and silk kimono that threw her off guard.

He rushed to shake Zachary's hand, clearly excited to see him again as he pumped the man's arm up and down.

"Zachary, welcome! Welcome! I was just about to worry. We were expecting you hours ago," he said, his accent clearly European and extremely feminine.

"We took our time. Kenzie wanted to enjoy the sights," Zachary answered as he gestured in her direction. She had moved to his side, and he wrapped an arm around her shoulders. "Kenzie, meet my friend Franklin Smith. Franklin and I have been friends since forever. Franklin, this is Kenzie Monroe. The woman I was telling you about."

Kenzie cut a quick eye in his direction, surprised to hear that he'd been talking about her. She smiled as she greeted his friend. "Hello!"

"It's a pleasure to meet you, Kenzie," Franklin said as he grabbed her hand. "But call me Barbie. Or Doll! All of my good friends do, and I answer to both. This one is the exception!" He winked an eye at Zachary, his smirk causing her to laugh out loud. "Zachary didn't lie about you being so beautiful! You are absolutely exquisite!"

"Thank you," she said, her smile widening. "It's a pleasure to meet you, too, Barbie!"

"Come inside!" he said as he pulled her along, Zachary following on their heels. "You must be famished by now. We have plenty of food and drink ready for you."

She laughed. "Thank you. Something to drink would be very nice."

The home's interior was as stunning as the outside. Kenzie was instantly taken by the cathedral ceilings and the floor-to-ceiling windows, which allowed impressive panoramic views of the outside.

"Zachary, the beer is cold, just like you like it. Kenzie, what can I get you to drink?" Barbie questioned as he moved to the bar. "I can make any pretty drink your heart desires. I'll even dress it with one of those pretty umbrellas, if you want. Just name it! Your wish is my command!"

Kenzie was still grinning from ear to ear. "Actually, a beer would be perfect. I don't do a lot of *pretty* drinks."

Barbie clasped his hand to his chest. "A woman after my own heart!" he exclaimed as he grabbed a bottle for each of them. He passed one to Kenzie and one to Zachary, then gestured for them to take a seat.

"Kenzie, Zachary tells me you're a journalist. What made you want to write a story on this scoundrel?"

"He and his brother are somewhat of an anomaly in the sporting world — beautiful black athletes making names for themselves in business. They had a story that needed to be told, and I wanted to tell it."

"Yes!" Barbie exclaimed. "I hope you spilled the tea on a few of his secrets! This one can be very guarded when he wants to be."

Zachary rolled his eyes skyward as he took a sip of his drink.

Kenzie laughed. "I think I probably should have met and talked to you before I turned in my article," she said.

Barbie nodded as he fanned a hand in her

direction. "Darling, the stories I could tell you!"

"He has no stories," Zachary interjected, shaking his head at his friend. "Nothing!"

Kenzie and Barbie both laughed. "We'll talk later," he said as he tapped her knee.

"So what do you do, Barbie?" Kenzie questioned.

Barbie suddenly jumped to his feet and practically ran from the room.

Kenzie's eyes widened. "Was it something I said?" she whispered, leaning toward Zachary.

Zachary laughed, amused by her confusion. Before he could explain, Barbie suddenly rushed back into the room. He had donned a Marilyn Monroe wig and stiletto heels that were easily five or more inches high. He swept the skirt of his kimono aside to expose one extremely hairy bare leg. "*Cabaret,* darling! I own the premiere cabaret club in the area featuring the prettiest *kathoey* to be found! It's called Club She, and it's chic, divine, and absolutely spectacular!" He took a deep bow, his arm gesturing in front of him.

Kenzie nodded, chuckling warmly. The *kathoey,* or lady boys, were popular in Thailand. They were transgendered women or gay men with feminine qualities who were seen as a third gender in Thai culture. "Zachary will have to take me to a show before we leave," she said.

Barbie dropped back down into his seat. "If you're looking for an interview, I'm available. Just ask me anything!" he gushed. He quickly changed the subject. "How long will you be staying this time? I want everyone to meet your beautiful woman, so we should throw you both a party at the club to announce your engagement!"

The couple cut their eyes at each other. Zachary laughed. Kenzie stammered. "We're not . . . it's not . . ."

Barbie looked confused. "What?" he said as he looked from one to the other.

"We're not engaged," Kenzie quipped.

Barbie fanned another dismissive hand. "Oh, please, this one always said the day he brought any woman here would be the day he burned his little black book. Only the woman he intended to marry would ever gain entry to his private circle. And you are the only woman he has ever brought here. You, *darling,* are something special!"

Barbie jumped again, steeling a quick glance down to his wristwatch. He reached for her hand and pulled her to her feet. "Let me give you a tour and get you settled in before I have to go to work."

Barbie's enthusiasm was infectious. As he pulled her from room to room, he excitedly told her about how he and Zachary had become acquainted, a casual encounter that turned into a lifelong friendship.

"He was so green, that one! Like a cute little puppy. He and a mutual friend had come to my club to drink, and one of my dancers had taken a serious liking to him. He was a big, hulking stud, and these girls love their *farang dam.*"

Kenzie smiled at his use of the term for black foreigners.

"It was his first time being up close and personal with a lady boy, so you can imagine his surprise when he discovered she was actually a he!" Barbie laughed. "Most foreigners know what to expect, and the few who don't and get surprised are sometimes mean and abusive to the girls. But not Zachary. He was the perfect gentlemen, and he let her down gently. It broke that beauty queen's heart!

"But he had some choice words for me! Oh, the names he called me that night! And then he laughed and apologized, and we had this wonderful conversation and have been the best of friends ever since. He comes to stay every month now."

"Every month?" Kenzie looked surprised.

"Yes! He comes to stay every time he visits . . ."

Zachary suddenly interrupted their conversation. "Can I have my woman back, please? Or do you plan to talk her ear off?"

Barbie giggled. "So afraid he's going to miss out, that one," he muttered as he winked an eye at her. "You and I will talk more later," he said. He leaned in to kiss Kenzie's cheek.

He swept his robe around him as he moved past Zachary, brushing a single, manicured nail over the man's chest. "Be good to her," he commanded. "I like her! She's absolutely adorable!"

As Barbie moved down the length of hallway, Zachary shook his head, bemusement painting his expression. "So, now you've met my old buddy."

"He's a riot! And such fun! I really like him."

Zachary smiled. "I'm glad. He's been a good friend, and I really want you two to like each other. So, what do you think of the house?"

"The house is gorgeous!" she exclaimed.

And it was. All of the rooms had unparalleled views from the oversized windows. There were ocean views on one side and mountain views on the other. In the backyard there was a private infinity pool. The deck surrounding the pool had steps leading down to landscaped gardens bordering a private beach. The entire property had been designed for privacy, intimacy, and comfort.

There were four individual, air-conditioned suites situated around a central, open-air living and dining space and a television and media room. The fully equipped island kitchen was a chef's dream come true, and the adjoining dining area was a convivial communal space boasting its own views over the water. Their luggage had been taken to a master suite with direct access to the swimming pool from the terrace. There was a circular Jacuzzi tub in the marbled bathroom, along with an oversized dressing room. All of the bedrooms came with plush, king-size beds and were lavishly decorated from floor to ceiling.

Kenzie had been surprised when Barbie told her there was a private chef, an on-call masseuse, and a driver at their beck and call. "I don't think I've ever stayed any place as pretty as this," she added.

Zachary nodded. "Well, that's good, because I own it. It's ours."

"You own this?" Kenzie questioned, her expression incredulous. "I thought Barbie . . ."

"Barbie manages the property for me. He actually lives in the guest house on the other side of the property. I rent the house out to guests when I'm not here, and Barbie makes sure the tourists don't burn it down during their stays."

"Wow!" she exclaimed. "I'm surprised."

"Why?"

"I don't know. The property in Phuket seems more like you. This is extraordinary, but I would never have imagined you to have invested in such a luxury home."

He smiled. "Well, I guess you're going to discover a lot about me this weekend that you don't know."

Kenzie pressed herself against him, lifting herself up on her toes to kiss his lips. She whispered. "I find that very exciting," she said as she kissed him again.

Barbie called out from the other end of the hallway. "I'll be at the club if you need me! Have a wonderful night, and I will see you both in the morning!"

"Good-bye, Franklin!" Zachary called back, tossing the other man a look over his shoulder.

Kenzie chuckled. "Why don't you call him Barbie, like everyone else?"

Zachary rolled his eyes. "What the hell

would I look like calling another man Barbie Doll? Even if he is wearing a dress!"

"Zachary!" she exclaimed, her eyes wide with surprise.

He grinned. "Hey, Franklin is my friend — one of my best friends — and he knows I'd do anything for him. But calling him Barbie is not one of them. He's good with that, and so am I."

Chapter Ten

Dinner had been amazing. The chef, an elderly Thai woman who spoke no English, had prepared a meal of fresh fish, curry stir-fry, sticky noodles, and a platter of Thai pastries and treats that left them both salivating for more. After dinner they changed into their swimsuits and went into the pool for a late-night swim.

As Zachary swam laps, Kenzie bobbed beneath the warm water, floating easily as she allowed her body to relax. She jumped ever so slightly, surprised by his touch, when Zachary swam beneath her, lifting himself against her body.

"You feel good," he whispered into her ear, his hands gently trailing over her torso. He licked the line of her earlobe, then nibbled her neck as he pulled her closer to him, spinning her around in his arms.

"You feel better," she said as she wrapped her legs around his waist, feeling the wealth of his erection growing abundantly beneath her bottom. Her body reacted of its own volition, her pelvis grinding against him.

They traded easy caresses as they held tightly to each other. Zachary traced his finger along the line of her bikini top. He gazed at the fleshy mound squeezed into the cup of the black bra top. Her breasts swelled over the lace edge of the patterned cup, jiggling in time with her sensuous gyrations against his manhood. He leaned, shifting her slightly as he licked the curve of her mounds. His tongue was hot and wet, and Kenzie gasped at the sensations his touch ignited.

Emboldened, he dove in for more, exploring the exquisite flesh and probing into her bra cups with his mouth. Kenzie felt her insides becoming heated. He cupped one full breast as he slid her top aside, pushing the straps from one shoulder and then the other. He groped her as the two bobbed in the water, the water's buoyancy keeping them afloat. Kenzie's entire body was heated, her bottom soaked from more than pool water, her sweet spot tingling.

He suddenly gave her nipple a hard squeeze, biting it between his full lips like he was sucking on the sweetest candy. Kenzie let out an involuntary yelp of pleasure that echoed in the late-night air. It was music to Zachary's ears as he lapped at the circle of her areola. The soft flesh was tight and ridged, and he was rewarded with a candy-hard nipple at its center. He licked and gnawed like he'd been given a prize.

When he sneaked a finger past the line of her bikini bottom he found her juices flowing in vast quantity, her slick moisture coating his fingers. His mouth moved back to her ear, his tongue probing as he traced her crotch with his hand. Pulling her bottoms aside he entered her easily, her body opening to welcome him inside. He was thick and full and filled her perfectly.

Theirs was the gentlest give-and-take as he stroked her with the wealth of himself. He loved her slowly and easily as she rode the vastness of his thick member. His cock danced to its own beat, the silk of her body strumming the tune. They moved in perfect sync until they both found themselves at the edge of ecstasy, and then they fell together, the beauty of it like the sweetest dream.

Making love to Zachary had become Kenzie's favorite thing in the world to do. Every time was like the first time, the sweetness of his touch almost unimaginable. They made love in the pool, on one of the deck chairs, in the shower, and finally on the bed before falling into a deep sleep curled tightly against each other. The new box of condoms he'd opened had disappeared quickly.

Hours later she woke to him snoring softly, his face pressed into a pillow, one arm looped around her waist. She eased herself from his side, moving into the bathroom to pee. After flushing the commode, she washed her hands and face and moved back to the bed. Zachary had rolled onto his back, his eyes wide open, one arm pulled over his head.

"Hey, I didn't mean to wake you," she said softly as she slid her body back beneath the sheets. She eased herself against him, throwing one leg over his.

"I missed you," he said as he wrapped his arms around her. He kissed the top of her head and nuzzled his nose into her hair.

She smiled, melting into the heat from his body. "You like it here, don't you?"

He gave her a light squeeze. "Why do you say that?

"I think this is the most relaxed I've seen you since we met. At Revolution you always seem to be waiting for something to happen. Even when things are going smoothly, you're ready to jump."

Zachary nodded. "I do like it here. This place means a lot to me. One day I plan to retire here. I have even imagined myself raising my kids in this house."

"You want kids?"

"Please don't tell me that you don't want kids."

She laughed. "I've never really thought about it. I never thought about being in a serious relationship or getting married, so kids definitely never crossed my mind."

There was a moment of pause as he reflected on her comment. When he finally spoke, his voice was a gentle whisper. He was suddenly vulnerable as he told her something he had never imagined himself saying to any woman since his wife broke his heart. "I do want kids. And I want to have my kids with you, Kenzie. I can't imagine anyone else being the mother of my children." He lifted himself up on his elbow, staring down into her face. Her eyes skated back and forth with his as she fell headfirst into the look he was giving her. He drew a finger along the line of her cheek.

Kenzie pressed a kiss into the palm of his hand. Her touch was tender and endearing. She nodded her head, suddenly realizing that Zachary was her future. She wanted what he wanted without him ever having to ask.

"I love you, Zachary," she whispered. "I love you very much! And I'd be honored to be your baby mama!"

He laughed heartily, and then he leaned to press his mouth to hers.

They spent the rest of the night perfecting their baby making, intent on insuring they got it right for when they were ready to make that actually happen.

When Kenzie woke the next morning, Zachary was nowhere to be found, his side of the bed empty. She found herself disappointed not to find him there when she'd reached for him, sleep still lingering in her closed eyes. She sat upright, stretching the length of her limbs as she stared out to the pool outside the glass doors.

Rising, Kenzie walked naked across the bamboo floors to slide open the glass doors and move outside. The air was already warm, and the temperature was rising. The sky was a deep shade of blue with the barest wisps of clouds floating about. The sun sat majestically, shining down brightly, and birds chirped as if they hadn't a care in the world. Kenzie took a deep inhale of air, filling her lungs, her body warming nicely.

Moving back inside to the bathroom, she noted the dull ache between her legs, the sweetest reminder of her and Zachary being together. Making love to him sat on the same list as eating and breathing, and she couldn't begin to imagine what a day would be like where they weren't near enough to touch each other when the moment moved them. Her body tingled at the memories of what they'd shared that previous night, and a quiver of heat shot up the length of her spine.

Minutes later, she was showered and dressed, having tossed on a floral-print sundress but no shoes. She'd tamed the mane of curls atop her head into two braids down her back, and she didn't bother with eyeliner or lip gloss.

Moving to the center of the house, she called out Zachary's name. Barbie answered in his stead, greeting her from the designer kitchen. "Good morning, beautiful lady!"

"Good morning, Barbie. How are you?"

"Fabulous, darling, and don't you look simply spectacular!"

"Thank you! Did you have a good show last night?"

"We have a good show every night!" He flounced toward the refrigerator, a bright smile filling his pale face. He was wearing a satin muumuu in a brilliant shade of red and matching high-heeled slides adorned with feathers. Everything about him made Kenzie smile.

"What would you like for breakfast, darling? I can fix whatever your heart desires," Barbie asked. He eyed her with a lifted brow, his eyes wide.

Kenzie reached for a ripe mango that rested atop a bowl of fresh fruit. "Actually, this and a cup of coffee are really all I need right now."

Barbie gave her a nod. "One cup of my special coffee coming right up!" he exclaimed as he moved to the pot percolating on the stovetop. "I brew it with a hint of kava root in it."

"Kava root? What's that?"

"It's an organic plant. It's used for medicinal purposes."

"You don't smoke it, do you?" she asked teasingly.

Barbie laughed. "I don't! I can't speak for anyone else."

"And it's safe?" she asked.

Barbie shrugged. "It all depends on who you ask on which day. Some people say it might not be good for your liver, but no one's one hundred percent sure. I get checked regularly and have had no problems."

"Does it have any side effects?"

"It'll make you horny as hell!" Barbie said with a hearty laugh.

Kenzie watched as he poured the dark brew into an oversized mug. "Barbie, do you know where Zachary has disappeared to this morning?" she asked. She took a seat on a stool at the oversized counter.

Barbie hesitated as he set her mug in front of her, sliding a carafe of cream and a bowl of sugar cubes toward her. Kenzie sensed he was trying to determine what to say without saying the wrong thing. He gave her one of his brightest smiles before he spoke, and she sensed that whatever he was about to say was going to have only an inkling of truth to it.

"Zachary went for a quick run . . . I think." Barbie turned from her as he finished his statement, moving back to the stove and coffeepot.

Her gaze was narrowed as she eyed him. She nodded her head slowly. "I'm surprised he didn't wake me. We usually run together."

"Do you?" Barbie fiddled with the knobs on the stove, seeming desperate to avoid her scrutiny. He continued, "I'm sure you were sleeping so soundly that he didn't want to disturb you." He changed the subject, doing an about-face to stare in her direction. "So tell me, Kenzie, do you dance, darling?"

She laughed, amused by his question. "I guess that depends on what kind of dancing you're talking about," she said, letting him off the hook with a slight giggle. She flavored her coffee with two cubes of sugar and a spattering of cream, then took her first sip, savoring the rich flavor.

Barbie laughed with her. "Dancing is good for the soul, no matter what type of dancing you do."

He moved swiftly from the kitchen to the living room and turned on the sound system. The room filled with the sound of Latin music with a distinctive Caribbean flair. It was rich and seductive and incited shoulder shimmies, hip gyrations, body isolations, hand styling, and some serious leg work. It was so Barbie-like that Kenzie instinctively knew that whenever she heard that type of music again she would always associate it with the chubby man who was suddenly doing a side-to-side shuffle in her direction. She laughed, the exuberance racing across her face.

Barbie gestured with both hands. "Come

dance with me!" he exclaimed, his own enthusiasm like a beacon of light spotlighting everything in his view.

He reached her side and pulled her to her feet, both hands tugging her along with him. Kenzie laughed at the absurdity, but she began to shuffle her feet from side to side, and before she knew it, she was doing some kind of salsa-mambo thing that had her grinning like a Cheshire cat.

When Zachary finally found his way back home, they were perfecting their Rockettes kick, one leg and then the other, toes pointed skyward as they kicked up and out. He paused for a quick minute in the doorway, eyeing the two of them, clearly amused.

Kenzie laughed at the expression on his face as she gestured toward him with both hands, calling him to her.

He shook his head as he eased himself inside. "You two started the party a little early, didn't you?"

Barbie waved a dismissive hand as Kenzie danced her way to Zachary's side, pressing her body against his. She lifted her lips to be kissed. Zachary wrapped his arms around her waist and drew her close as his mouth danced against hers. It took nothing at all before they were doing a seductive bachata against each other, their two bodies connecting in the sweetest places. One of his palms was pressed against the small of her back, and her hand clasped the other. His body was so close to hers that there was barely breathing space between them.

"I missed you," she whispered.

He grinned. "I missed you too."

"Where did you disappear to so early?"

Zachary cut an eye toward Barbie, who was grinning at the two of them. He gave them a nod of his head and skipped his way down the hallway toward the rear of the house. Kenzie looked from one to the other as Zachary shrugged his shoulders.

"I just had an errand I needed to run." He kissed her cheek before letting her go. "That coffee smells good."

He had changed the subject as deftly as his flamboyant friend had. Kenzie instinctively knew something was amiss and that the two men were trying to keep it from her. She and Zachary exchanged a look before he cut his eyes to the floor.

She shook her head. "It tastes good. Let me pour you a cup," she said as she pulled herself from him and moved into the kitchen. Barbie had already laid out an empty cup, and she filled it, the early-morning octane still steaming hot. After she topped off her own cup, they sat down at the marble counter.

"So, what's on our agenda today?" Kenzie asked. She took a sip of her drink and then another.

Zachary blew a cooling breath across his own cup. "We need to do something different. I thought we'd go do some rock climbing."

There was an awkward pause, Kenzie's brow furrowed as she stared at him. "Rock climbing? Really?"

Zachary laughed. "I promise. You'll enjoy it."

Her smile teased the edges of her eyes and the soft bend of her mouth. "Rock climbing?"

"It's one of my favorite things in the world to do."

"I think we could make lounging by that beautiful pool and you doing that thing you do to my inner thigh one of your favorite things to do too."

He chuckled, his head bobbing. "That's an idea, too. I could do that thing and you could suck on my big toe."

Kenzie laughed. "I am *not* sucking on your big toe. Your feet are not going anywhere near my mouth!"

Zachary held up his sandaled foot. "What's wrong with my feet? I have really pretty feet."

"You have hammer toes!"

"Like hell I do! There is nothing hammer-like about my toes."

Kenzie laughed. "Okay, if you say so."

"See how you do me! I'd suck on your toes," he said as he reached for her leg. He brushed the dust from the bottom of her foot as he pulled it into his lap.

Kenzie smiled as she eased her toes into his crotch, taunting his manhood beneath his shorts. "Are you *sure* you want to go rock climbing, because I can think of a few things we could do that you'd enjoy much more?"

He gently stroked the bottom of her foot, kneading and massaging the sole and toes. "I plan to do that too. We might even do it at the top of the mountain. You never know about me!"

She laughed again, the wealth of it coming from deep in her midsection. "I guess we're going rock climbing then. I need to go change my clothes."

He nodded. "You should do that. I love the dress," he said as he slid his hand up the inside of her leg, his fingers teasing the edge of her G-string, "but it's really not practical."

She squirmed slightly. "So maybe we can

do that *thing* before *and* after rock climbing."

This time he laughed. "We should probably conserve our energy and save that *thing* for later."

Kenzie feigned a pout. "You are so not fun right now."

"Actually, I'm a really good time." He slapped her thigh, stinging her flesh ever so slightly. "Let's get moving so I can show you how much fun I can be!"

"Ouch!" Kenzie exclaimed as she rubbed her skin. "That hurt."

"It did not."

"It stung . . . a lot!"

His eyes closed slightly as he eyed her.

"Okay, so maybe it was just a little," she concluded.

Zachary took the last sip from his coffee cup. He stole a quick glance at his wristwatch. "I'll clean up the dishes while you get ready," he said as he stood back up onto his feet.

Kenzie rose with him. "Okay. I'll go get ready," she said.

As she turned, Zachary tapped her on her ass, the gesture causing her to jump. He laughed, and she giggled as she moved down the length of hallway and back to the master bedroom.

Zachary moved from the counter to the sink, depositing the dirty dishes into the stainless-steel container. He'd washed and rinsed the last saucer when Barbie suddenly moved into the room behind him. The two men exchanged a look, and Zachary watched as his old buddy stole a quick look down the hall to make sure that Kenzie's bedroom door was still closed.

Barbie leaned against the counter and crossed his hands together in front of himself. "How was he today?" he asked, Zachary understanding the he Barbie was referring to.

Zachary shrugged his shoulders. He held out his hand, the palm down as he waved it from side to side. "He didn't know who I was."

"Some days he's really, really good. Some days not so much. I was hoping this was one of his good days."

Sadness settled in Zachary's stare. He didn't bother to respond, thinking about the last couple of hours he'd spent visiting his friend Kai.

Barbie continued the conversation. "When do you plan to take her to visit?"

Zachary's shoulder jutted skyward for the umpteenth time. "I'm not so sure this is a good idea. I still have doubts about telling her."

"Normally I would agree with you, but now that I've met her and had some time to talk to her, I think you have to bring them together. Besides, I've said it before: Kai was not in his right mind when he forced all of us to make that damn promise!"

"Yeah . . . still . . . it was so much easier when none of us *knew* his daughter. I'll be honest with you. I never really thought she'd come looking for him."

"Well, I did. He always spoke so fondly of his baby girl that I just knew there'd be a day when she would come calling. It was inevitable. What surprises me is that you have fallen head over heels in love with her!"

Zachary shot his friend a look.

Barbie laughed. "No need to confirm or deny. I see it all over your face every time she comes into the room. Kai would have paid her off and put her on a plane back to where she came from with the way you're acting. It's a good thing you don't have a fight coming up because she would have you all off your game!"

Zachary laughed. "I'll admit she's been a bit of a distraction."

"What does Mr. Montri think?"

"Gamon thinks I need to make this reunion happen and then get back to work."

"I'm more of a romantic. Make it happen, and then you and she should have whatever happy ending your little hearts desire!"

"Well, I don't know if we can get happy out of this situation. It's a total cluster fuck, and unfortunately my girl is going to be hurt. And it's my fault. I should have told her weeks ago."

"Told her what?" Kenzie suddenly interrupted the conversation, moving into the room. "What are you two talking about?"

The two men both looked stunned and nervous, each eyeing the other as if they'd been caught with their pants down. Both spun around to face her.

"Don't you look beautiful!" Barbie exclaimed excitedly. He clapped his hands together, his head nodding his approval.

Kenzie had changed into a pair of black stretch leggings, a black printed, long-sleeved T-shirt, and her running shoes. A black cotton sweater was tied around her waist, and she'd twisted her two braids into a bun at the nape of her neck.

She shook her head. "Don't change the subject. You two were whispering about me, so one of you spill it. What does Zachary need to tell me?" Her eyes darted back and forth between the two.

Zachary chuckled. "That is just like a woman. Nosey!"

She cut her eyes at him. "Don't try it. You're trying to avoid the conversation. First, you sneak out and this one covers for you, and now you're trying to turn things around on me like I'm crazy or something. But I know what I heard, and I know how squirrely the two of you have been acting this morning."

Zachary shook his head. "We'll talk about it later. We need to go."

"I don't want . . ."

"Cut me some slack, please!" Zachary exclaimed, tossing up his hands in frustration. "I swear it was no big deal. Franklin was telling me how perfect we are for each other, and I needed to point out some of my flaws. It wasn't that serious!"

"At least you addressed your flaws first," she said matter-of-factly.

Barbie laughed. "I really like her!" he said as he wrapped his arms around Kenzie and gave her a tight squeeze. "She is definitely a keeper!"

"You don't get off that easy either," she said, squeezing the man back. "I know you're covering for him. And I know you two are up to something. Don't think I won't figure out what it is and why!"

Both men chuckled.

"You got us," Zachary said smugly. He rolled his eyes. "Franklin, we will see you later."

"You're bringing Kenzie to my show tonight, I hope?"

"We wouldn't miss it," his friend answered.

"Fabulous!"

Chapter Eleven

It turned into a fight, and neither Zachary or Kenzie had wanted that. But by the time he pulled his jeep into the parking area at Dan Pier in Phang Nga Bay, both had said some things that they'd instantly regretted.

Zachary shut down the car's engine. They both stared out to the long-tail boat that rested just off-shore, awaiting them. He blew a loud sigh, air rushing past his full lips. "Kenzie, I don't understand why you're making an issue out of me not being there when you woke up. It's not a big deal!"

She tossed up her hands, ire washing over her expression. "It's not about you not being there when I woke up!" she hissed. "I could care less if you're there when I wake up! I don't like that you are keeping me in the dark about something that's bothering you, Zachary. I don't like it at all. You're keeping secrets. Add that to you sneaking around, Barbie covering for you, and it all feels wrong! *That's* what I'm saying!"

"I don't know what you want me to do," he finally muttered.

"I *want* you to be honest with me. I just *want* you to tell me what's going on! Is that so damn hard? Don't you trust me?"

Zachary blew another sigh, his head shaking. "Fine. Tonight we'll sit down and talk, and I'll tell you whatever you want to know."

"Tell me now."

"I said we'll talk later," he snapped. He pushed the car door open. "Let's go, Kenzie. Let's try to have a good time, please!"

"Aargh!" Kenzie screamed, frustration furrowing her brow. "I swear you are this far from me pushing you off this damn rock you want to climb!"

Light suddenly flickered in his eyes. "If you push me, I won't be able to tell you all my secrets," he said, a smug smirk piercing the look he gave her.

He exited the car, grabbed his gym bag and slammed the door. Kenzie sat in her seat, watching as he moved toward the entrance of the pier. Zachary turned, tossing her a look over his shoulder. She hoped the look she gave him back showed her displeasure, and then she snatched her gaze away to stare down into her lap. She was suddenly kicking herself for ruining what should have been a good time between them. It had not been her intent to pick a fight with him, but she'd had questions, and when it became obvious that he wasn't going to give her answers, it had all just rubbed her the wrong way.

She looked up and he was gone, having disappeared down the length of the pier, and it dawned on her that Zachary might actually leave her sitting there until he returned. Zachary didn't coddle her mood swings, and he would have found it quite amusing to go climb rocks by himself while she sat pouting in the car. She had no intention of giving him that satisfaction, she thought.

Jumping from the vehicle, she grabbed her own bag and hurried after him, practically tripping her way to the boat, where he and two other men sat waiting. She stopped abruptly as the trio turned to stare at her. Zachary smiled, meeting her gaze briefly before turning his attention out to the oceanic waters. A thin Thai man extended his hand to help her into the boat. When she was settled, he untied the launch, and they set sail.

Minutes later, Zachary shifted forward in his seat, inching his body closer to hers. "You still mad?" he asked, lifting his eyes to her eyes.

For a good few minutes, they sat staring at each other, Kenzie not bothering to respond.

Zachary shook his head "Are you always this stubborn?"

"Mad and stubborn. I must be making quite an impression on you," she finally answered.

"Oh, you've made an impression alright." He smiled and lifted his eyebrows.

His mouth was lifted in the sweetest bend, and Kenzie suddenly wanted to be kissed. She licked her own lips, her tongue slowly rolling from one side to the other. Zachary grinned, and he inched even closer, a large palm dropping against her knee. Kenzie lifted her gaze skyward, feigning disinterest. Zachary laughed.

Taking a deep breath, Kenzie eased her body against his, falling into the warmth of his body heat as she slid into his side. She leaned her head onto his shoulder as he reached his hand out to hold hers. The rest of their conversation was silent, everything that needed to be said exchanged in the gentle touches, his fingers tap dancing inside her palm, her fingers entangling with his. As she stared out to the blue waters that carried them to their destination Zachary pressed a damp kiss to her forehead.

The trip took thirty minutes. Kenzie had a ton of questions that she asked in Thai, their guide excited to converse in his native language with the exquisite woman. The captain of the long, lightweight canoe hull eased his watercraft through the still waters with the help of a second-hand engine and a propeller mounted directly on the drive-shaft. There was a makeshift canopy to shield them from the sun if they were so inclined, but she and Zachary both were enjoying the ride beneath the mid-morning sun.

They landed at Ko Panyi, a fishing village in Phang Nga province. Nicknamed the "Sea Gypsy Island," it was a floating land-mark on stilts built within the protection of the bay. Forty limestone islands surrounded them, rising some thirteen hundred feet above the calm, blue-green waters that filled the bay. The entire area was rich with history, and Kenzie enjoyed the stories their hosts shared.

Her introduction to rock climbing began with basic climbing techniques and safety training. An old pro, Zachary interjected as the moment moved him, but there was no ignoring that he was anxious to get started. For Kenzie, learning how to climb and rappel on the limestone cliffs was not without its challenges. But his enthusiasm and her own competitive spirit had her excited to do what she was witnessing him do.

They started with top rope climbing, a climbing style that was typical of indoor climbing walls. A sturdy rope ran from the foot of their climbing route through one or more carabiners connected to an anchor system at the top of the route and back down to the climber's harness. A climbing team stood at the bottom of the climb to help her up and down. After she got the hang of holding on and pulling herself up, she was ready and excited to test the training further, moving from a straight up-and-down route to ones that were more difficult.

They took a quick lunch break of fresh fish and grilled vegetables over rice noodles. It wasn't until the first bite that Kenzie realized she was hungry, that cup of coffee and sliced mango long gone. After the short break, they moved her to the rock formation that Zachary was besting.

Kenzie was in awe. What they had her doing was safer, less demanding physically, and psychologically easier. Zachary was a true sport climber, and he clipped preplaced bolts in the rock as he ascended. He took risks, testing his abilities beyond her comfort zone, and he was having the best time doing so. She couldn't wait until she was there, following in his footsteps, pushing past her own limits by his side.

After his final climb, she threw her arms around his neck and kissed him. With one arm holding his equipment and the other looped around her waist, he kissed her back.

"That was so much fun!" she exclaimed. "When can we do it again?"

"I told you it would be a good time," Zachary laughed. "We can come back again soon."

She hugged her arms around his neck, leaning up to whisper into his ear. "I'm sorry," she said softly. "I don't like when we fight."

Zachary nuzzled his nose in her hair. "Neither do I. So stop."

She laughed. "I'll own it. I know I start things, but you don't help matters."

"I probably don't, but I'm not going to let you push my buttons and not do or say anything. If you want to fight, I will give you a fight back."

"But you don't fight fair. You spar and then throw one big punch that always takes me out, and sometimes you do it by *not* doing or saying something, which totally infuriates me!"

"Fighting is my career, remember? Letting my opponent get the best of me isn't what I do. I will always give as good as I get. So if you throw a punch at me, I'm throwing one right back."

"Well, stop, because I will. I hate when we're ugly at each other."

Zachary grabbed her hand and squeezed it. "Let's go home, baby!"

Their late-afternoon nap had absolutely nothing at all to do with getting any sleep and everything to do with makeup sex. They had stripped out of their clothes, pouring themselves into a hot shower and then their bed before either could remember what it was they were fighting about in the first place.

It was bliss! Kenzie sat straddled above him, her body plunging up and down against him. He filled her, the length of his erection bottoming out with each downward stroke. She controlled the momentum, her gyrations slow and easy one minute, then hard and fast the next. He clutched the cheeks of her ass to guide her and then palmed her breasts, twirling her hardened nipples between his fingers. Their loving was heated and intense as she teased him, pulling him to the edge of ecstasy and pushing him back.

When it became too much for either to bear, the intensity of their connection painfully sweet, Zachary lifted his torso from the bed and wrapped his arms around her. In one swift move he rolled them both, her body lying flat beneath his as he plunged himself into her. He orgasmed, screaming her name, and she came at the same time, her whole body convulsing with pure pleasure. Muscles quivered, nerve endings burst with sheer joy, and then he captured her mouth beneath his own, kissing her until the last twinge of heat and fire ceased to simmer.

That nap lasted a whole forty-five minutes before they had to get ready for their night out with Barbie at his cabaret show. Pulling themselves from each other, they showered a second time. An hour later they were dressed, standing in front of the full-length mirror to take in their reflections. Zachary wore a silk suit in a beautiful shade of gray, with a white dress shirt, no necktie, and Gucci red suede smoking slippers. His dreads were freshly twisted into two French braids down his back.

Kenzie was totally in love with the dress that Barbie had surprised her with. It was strapless, form-fitting, and stopped just a smidge above her knees. It was a chevron print in white and silver, the bodice shimmering with silver sequins. It complemented her warm complexion and flattered her curves. With her thick curls flowing free and full, she was stunning.

Zachary extended his elbow, and she slipped her hand through to hold on. She lifted her face to his and smiled sweetly.

"Damn!" Zachary said. "We look good, girl!"

As they moved into the other room, Barbie echoed the sentiment. "Fabulous! Aren't you two just the prettiest!" their friend exclaimed. He clapped his hands together excitedly.

"Thank you, Barbie! I think so, too," Kenzie said. She pressed one palm to his chest as Zachary pulled her close, the two posing for Barbie's camera. After a series of snapshots and selfies, they were all out the door, headed to Barbie's favorite place in the whole wide world.

Club She was a hidden gem nestled in one of the area's historic neighborhoods. Go-go bars lined both sides of the street. Hawkers with megaphones and girls barely dressed stood outside trying to lure tourists and residents inside. The entrance to Club She was staid, lacking the bright neon lights of the establishments next door and across the street from it. Everything about the exterior belied what was hidden behind the entrance.

The club was all Barbie, from the hand-painted floors to the lush, velvet fabrics that dressed the windows. The interior was theatrical, dramatic, and totally unexpected. Kenzie stared about in awe as she took it all in. Just past the entrance was a hand-carved, walled courtyard with pools of goldfish splashing about. It was like entering a whole other realm with walls of murals, original art, crystal chandeliers, and sumptuous silks.

As they moved farther inside, the stage sat room center, elevated a few feet off the floor, and there was an extended carved-wood bar along the back wall. The entire space was upscale and sexy, the clientele pretty, and obviously wealthy. Barbie moved off in one direction, and one of his staff escorted the couple to a VIP table that was front and center, in the middle of all the action.

Having the local champion in the room had everyone beside themselves with excitement. For the first few minutes, Zachary signed autographs, shook hands, and took pictures. When he'd had enough, he signaled their waitress to bring a bottle of champagne and gestured for the club's bouncer to wave off any lingering fans. By the time they'd poured their second flute of drink, he and Kenzie were grateful to have a moment alone.

The music playing was seductive and dirty, an intoxicating mix of jazz and blues. Everything about the rich sounds encouraged slow, cheek-to-cheek dancing and much pelvic grinding; to Kenzie, it felt like a blue-light basement party from years gone by.

"This is pretty cool," Kenzie whispered as she leaned against Zachary. He sat with his arm draped casually over her shoulder, his fingers playing with her hair.

He nodded. "This place is special. Barbie has put a lot of his heart into this space. He loves it, and the clients love him."

She nodded. "The women are beautiful," she said, her eyes skating around the room.

Zachary laughed. "Most of them aren't women," he said casually, his eyebrows raised.

Kenzie shot him a look. "Really?"

"If I'm correct I think Keiko, the girl behind the bar, is the only one who was actually born female."

Eyes wide, Kenzie glanced around a

second time. "Damn!" she exclaimed. "Then the men are beautiful!"

"They'd be offended if you said that out loud. They're transsexual, and they consider themselves women. Franklin gives me a lecture every time I come here."

"Do you visit often?"

Zachary laughed, his head shaking from side to side. "No. I wouldn't like that kind of surprise because they are beautiful." He leaned to kiss her cheek. "But not one of them is as beautiful as you are!"

"Good answer!" Kenzie said with a giggle. "Very good answer!"

He smiled. "I try hard."

"Is Franklin transsexual? I've been saying he and him. I haven't offended him, have I?"

Zachary shook his head. "No. He's a gay male who makes his living dressing in drag and singing show tunes. And if you had offended him, he would have set you straight. Trust me!" He smiled.

"You seem very comfortable with the culture and all of this," she said gesturing with her hands. "That surprises me, with you being so macho!"

Zachary shrugged. "It is what it is. I don't have any reason not to be respectful or accepting. Franklin has proven himself to be a great friend. How he lives his life doesn't have anything to do with how I choose to live mine. He deserves to be happy as much as anyone else does, maybe even more so because there are people who are judgmental about who and how he is. How all of these women choose to live their lives is their personal choice. I can't judge. I don't have a heaven or hell to put them in."

The room lights suddenly flickered, and the sound system was lowered until it felt like background music. A single spotlight was focused on the stage, and the velvet curtains rose slowly. Stepping into the light, Barbie was a sight to behold. He'd changed into a ruby-red dress and matching stilettos. The dress was split thigh high, exposing fishnet stockings and a white garter belt. His wig was big and bold, a black afro that seemed miles wide. His makeup was flawless, his lips crimson, black eyelashes forest thick, and his eyeshadow a complementary shade of gold.

His voice was loud and booming as he spoke into the microphone. "Good evening, darlings! Welcome to Club She! I'm Barbie Doll, but call me Barbie or Doll . . . just call me!" He laughed heartily. "I'm your hostess with the most-est, and I'm here to insure you have a fabulous time!" He glided from one side of the stage to the other, his wide hips leading the way.

The music suddenly boomed, and a cavalcade of dancers joined Barbie on the dance floor. He was suddenly doing an impressive Beyoncé karaoke, claiming that he and his brigade ruled the world. They followed that number with what Barbie called his diva hit list. There was some old school Tina Turner, Diana Ross's "Love Hangover," Celine Dion's "All By Myself," and Shakira's "Hips Don't Lie." The mix was big and bold, but nowhere near as big as Barbie's stage presence. He commanded attention, grabbed it by the throat, shook the life out of, and held on with everything in him.

Kenzie understood completely why the space was suddenly standing room only, eager patrons pushing to get inside. When Barbie's show was done, his team of dancers took center stage, lithe young bodies twerking and shaking with everything in them. The men in the crowd went crazy, and the tips flowed like water. Even the few females in the crowd showed their appreciation, sending money raining down like it was storming. Everything about the entire night was one good time.

"I want to be just like Barbie when I grow up!" Kenzie exclaimed.

Zachary laughed. "Do you sing? Dance?"

"I can hold a note, and my two-step is always on point."

"I'll put in a good word for you then. I'm sure Franklin will love to have you!"

"I heard my government name. Who's talking about me?" Barbie suddenly exclaimed, moving to join them at the table." He hugged one and then the other.

"I was saying how spectacular you were!" Kenzie exclaimed, imitating her new friend's flamboyant gestures. "You stole the show!"

Barbie giggled. "I was good, wasn't I?" he responded, his bright smile filling his face. He pulled his fingers through his thick goatee. "It's such a chore being so beautiful!"

Kenzie laughed as the three fell into an easy conversation with each other. Barbie kept her laughing with stories about Zachary and their friendship; then it dawned on her that the two had known each other since the beginning of Zachary's career.

"Barbie, did you know my father, Kai Tamura?" She looked curiously from Barbie to Zachary and back. The two men exchanged a look, and it suddenly felt as if someone had dumped ice water over the table.

Barbie sat back in his seat, folding his

hands together in his lap. "I did know your father. He was a dear friend, and of course, his championship status made him quite the local hero. People would flock in to sit with him when he would come to visit."

Kenzie sat forward in his seat, her expression hopeful. "You don't seem surprised to hear that he had a daughter."

Barbie's gaze shifted toward Zachary.

"I told him, Kenzie. I wanted him to be ready in case you decided to interrogate him," Zachary said. He reached for his glass and took a sip, then gestured for another bottle.

"So you warned him off, is what you're saying?"

Barbie laughed. "Not at all. Zachary thought you might have questions, and he thought I should know about your connection to my old friend."

"So you and my father were friends?"

"We were. We were very good friends. He introduced me to this scoundrel!" Barbie gave Zachary a wink of his eye.

"I haven't had any luck finding him. Do you know where he is? Have you heard from him?"

Barbie took a deep breath. "Kai was notorious for disappearing when he didn't want to be found."

A wave of sadness washed over Kenzie's expression, fueled by disappointment and one glass of champagne too many. Tears suddenly burned hot behind her eyelids.

"Don't," Zachary said, reaching his hand out to caress her shoulder. "Don't cry. Please!"

She shook her head, her posture stiffening. "I wasn't going to cry," she muttered, avoiding his eyes. She stood abruptly. "I need to go to the restroom," she said as she shuffled off in that direction, her high heels clicking against the floors.

Zachary blew out a heavy sigh, suddenly feeling like the weight of Kenzie's small world rested on his broad shoulders. Barbie had shifted forward in his seat, crossing his thick arms over his chest. He eyed the younger man intently.

"I know," Zachary quipped, seeming to read the other man's mind.

"It's for the best, Zachary. She needs to know the truth. We've all been complicit in keeping the truth from her, and she deserves better from us."

"You aren't telling me anything I haven't told myself a half dozen times. I just know . . . well . . . ," he hesitated.

"What?" Barbie asked.

"She's going to hate me, and it may mean

the end of our relationship. I don't want to lose her, Franklin. I love her."

"And she loves you. She's going to be hurt, but you two will work through it. I have faith!" Barbie blessed him with an endearing smile that actually made Zachary feel better.

"I have faith, too, my friend. I will do whatever I have to do not to lose her. I'm not above begging and groveling if I have to," he said with a soft chuckle.

They both spied Kenzie as she stood on the other side of the room. One of the dancers had grabbed her by the hand, trying to entice her to join in one of their burlesque numbers. She was laughing, joy having returned to her eyes as the other women cajoled her into joining in. Watching her attempting the choreography they were trying to teach her made both men laugh. Seeing her happy again made Zachary's heart sing. But knowing that he was just hours away from breaking her heart had his nerves on edge, his stomach doing major backflips.

Zachary tossed back the last of the bourbon he'd ordered and stood up. Barbie gave him a thumbs-up and waved him away as he headed across the room to reclaim his woman. He stepped between the throng of partiers, moving his body against Kenzie's.

Her smile widened as she wrapped her arms around his neck and drew him to her. A slow, seductive love song was playing in the background. They moved instinctively together, their bodies moving as if they were a singular unit. And in that moment they were, the love between them in perfect sync. It was so immense that it filled the room. They were beautiful together, and all eyes were on them as they danced the rest of the night away.

CHAPTER TWELVE

Kenzie had fallen asleep minutes after dropping into the bed, and she'd been resting well ever since. Zachary had tossed and turned, unable to get comfortable, not even when he wrapped his body around hers, cradling her in his arms. He'd been watching her for over an hour, memorizing the slow and steady inhale of her breath and the gentle exhalation that blew like a whisper past her lips.

Everything about Kenzie warmed his spirit. She moved him to new heights, and there wasn't anything he wouldn't have done for her. And now he had to burst her happy bubble and pick up the pieces when it all went left. He was single-handedly going to cause her a wealth of hurt, and there was absolutely nothing he could do to keep her from it.

He shook his head, pulling his legs over the arm rail of the chair he sat in. They needed to talk, and it was a conversation he didn't look forward to. But he'd promised her, and himself, that he was going to be honest with her, sharing every dirty secret he'd ever had in his lifetime. The truth about her father was going to devastate Kenzie, because it had devastated him, and it continued to do so with each day the disease progressed.

Zachary was a holy mess each time he came to Krabi Town, and he came regularly. He'd been coming ever since his best friend and mentor had been diagnosed. He'd been coming since Kai had purchased the property down the road and had hired a team of medical professionals to help him navigate the inevitability of his disease. Kai had a loyal and devoted team of nurses and doctors and other health-care professionals monitoring him daily. There was the live-in nurse, the visiting nurses, and physical therapists, all engaged to make his days as comfortable as possible.

Zachary had purchased this home to be close to his friend, but not so close that either felt they were intruding on the other's privacy. With both lots substantial in size, there was significant space and an acre or two of lush tropical gardens between them. When Kai had no longer been able to handle his day-to-day responsibilities, Zachary had stepped in to take over, fulfilling the promises that his friend had asked of him. Promising to never let Kai's daughter see him as he deteriorated had been the biggest mistake Zachary had ever made, and now he was going to have to pay the price for having done so.

He blew another sigh. As he did, Kenzie rolled onto her back, both arms thrown over her head. She snored softly, and he found the lull of it comforting. In that moment, he knew that he would watch her until the sun rose, a new day welcoming them together. He would watch her, and then he would tell her Kai Tamura's story, praying that when it was all said and done, there'd be more nights that he could just sit and watch her.

The morning sunshine had just begun to stream through the windows when Kenzie opened her eyes. Zachary was sitting in the recliner when she sat upright, rubbing at her eyes with both fists. He was amused at how she had reached for him in the bed, her face skewing in frustration when he wasn't there.

"Good morning," he said, his tone soft.

"Good morning." She stretched her arms over her head as she yawned. "Why are you over there?" she asked.

He smiled. "I was watching you. Did you know that you talk in your sleep?"

"Do I really?"

He nodded. "Yes. You were fussing at someone!" he laughed.

Kenzie laughed with him. She tapped her palm against the mattress. "Come snuggle me," she said as she tossed back the covers.

Zachary stood, then crawled into the bed beside her. He pulled her into his arms, wrapping himself around her. Her body was soft and warm, her bare skin teasing his. Neither spoke; no words were needed as they settled into each other. He drifted off into his thoughts, and she drifted off into her own.

Outside it had begun to rain, the cloud cover spoiling the earlier hint of sunshine. Zachary had left the glass doors open to let the fresh air blow through the mesh screens. The gentle drip of rain hitting the ground resounded through the air.

"What's wrong? Kenzie suddenly asked.

Zachary had tensed, and a tear had rolled over his chiseled cheeks. There was no missing that something wasn't right, and his show of emotion caused her to tense with worry. He hugged her tightly and kissed her cheek as she swiped away his tear with the pad of her thumb.

"Did something happen, Zachary?"

"I was just thinking that I didn't want to lose you, Kenzie. Ever! It would kill me."

"I don't want to lose you either. I like what we have together, and I'm excited to see where we go from here. I'm not planning on going anywhere."

Zachary nodded. "I have a friend," he started. "He's ill. Terminally ill, and knowing that he doesn't have much time left breaks my heart."

"Baby, I'm so sorry!" Kenzie exclaimed. She shifted so that she was holding him in her arms, their positions reversed. She pulled his head to her chest. "Do I know this friend?"

He shook his head, spilling another little white lie. "You've never spent any time together," he said, the only truth he could get out in the moment.

She nodded. "What's wrong with him?"

"He was diagnosed with early-onset Alzheimer's. It's been aggressive and has affected him at an alarming rate. Just a few months ago, he still remembered who I was, and now I'm a stranger to him."

"I've never known anyone with Alzheimer's, but I know it's particularly difficult for the caregivers and family."

"We all saw the signs early. There were a lot of memory problems. Small things at first, and then they began to affect his daily life. He had trouble making plans and sticking to them. He couldn't concentrate on detailed tasks, and where he'd always been meticulous with numbers, he suddenly couldn't keep track of his bills or balance his checkbook!" Zachary took a deep breath before continuing.

"He used to come to the gym every day, and then he started having trouble making the drive. Everyone made jokes about it at first, but I knew something was wrong. He couldn't judge distance anymore or tell colors apart, and reading became problematic. Things we take for granted were suddenly big challenges.

"Now he has trouble with his vocabulary. I can't tell you the last time we actually had a full conversation that made any sense."

"I am so sorry," Kenzie said a second time. "I can only imagine how hard this is on you."

Zachary nodded. "I need to go see him this morning, and I'm not ready."

"Well, you know I'll go with you. You don't have to go alone."

Zachary sat upright. "I want you to go, Kenzie. In fact, it's important that you do, but I don't want you to be frightened. He can be aggressive, especially if he's not remembering who people are."

"I'm sure I'll be fine."

He took another deep breath. "There's something else you need to know about my friend, baby."

His tone suddenly scared her. A wave of anxiety pierced her midsection. "What is it?"

"My friend . . . ," Zachary hesitated briefly, then he just spat it out. "Kenzie, my friend is your father. He's Kai Tamura."

Explaining everything that had gotten them to that point seemed to go on forever. Kenzie had questions, and she didn't want to wait for answers. Tears streamed down her face, her emotions wafting from sadness to frustration to anger and back again.

Zachary sighed heavily. "Get dressed, baby. We can grab some breakfast, and then I'll take you over to see him."

Kenzie snapped. "Don't call me baby! And I can't eat. I need to see my father."

Zachary nodded. "That's fine. Just get dressed, and I'll take you there."

Kenzie didn't bother to shower. She rinsed her mouth, swiped a soapy washcloth over her face, pulled her hair into a high topknot, and threw on a pair of shorts and a T-shirt.

In the kitchen, Barbie eyed them both anxiously.

"Did you know, too?" she asked, speaking sharply.

Barbie nodded. "He swore us to secrecy and made us promise not to betray his trust. We did what he wanted us to do."

"Did either of you ever think about me? Or how this might affect my life?"

"To be honest," Barbie said, "I didn't know he had a daughter until after he became sick and made us swear."

Kenzie turned to stare at Zachary, her stare questioning.

He answered. "I knew, but from what he told me, your mother didn't want to have anything to do with him, and once you were old enough to decide for yourself you weren't interested either. He never expected you two to reconcile, so neither did I."

"I never had a chance," she suddenly shouted. "You took my chance away!"

The two men cut their eyes at each other. Neither bothered to respond. Both knew she was angry and hurt, and she needed someone to blame. Zachary was the most convenient option.

She stomped toward the door, her arms

crossed tightly over her chest. "Please, take me to see my father."

Kenzie couldn't believe that Kai Tamura literally lived next door to Zachary, their backyards bordering each other. The walk took no time at all before they were standing at her father's front door.

The woman who answered the door greeted them both in English. She was middle-aged, blonde, and blue-eyed. She wore a simple shift dress and flats. She greeted them warmly and both by name.

"Mr. Barrett, Miss Monroe, good morning."

"Good morning, Angelika," Zachary responded. "How is he this morning?"

"It looks like it might be a good day. He's in good spirits. We haven't had any outbursts. I was just about to feed him his morning meal."

The woman named Angelika gave Kenzie a smile, but she didn't say anything to her, just gesturing for them both to follow behind her.

The home was immaculate. It had a warmth to it that instantly relaxed Kenzie. There were photos on the walls and cases lined with books, and in that space she got the first sense of who her father was. She was suddenly even sadder than she was just minutes before.

Kai Tamura was sitting at the table in the kitchen when they stepped into the room. He looked up from a plate of scrambled eggs, bacon, and toast that he was eating with a spoon, his fist wrapped around the utensil like he was three years old. He eyed them both suspiciously, pulling his spoon close to his chest.

The former champion was a reduced semblance of the man Kenzie remembered. Her father had always been large and magnanimous in her eyes. But sitting there he was frail and vulnerable, completely childlike. It wasn't the reunion she had often imagined, and sitting there, he wasn't the man she had wanted him to be.

"Mr. Tamura, you have company!" Angelika exclaimed, her singsong voice ringing warmly. "Mr. Barrett is here, and he brought your daughter."

Kai looked from one to the other, but he didn't respond. He shoveled another spoonful of food into his mouth.

Zachary spoke in Thai. "Hey, big guy, how are you this morning?"

Kai nodded his head, but he didn't answer. His gaze shifted back to his plate.

Kenzie pushed her way past Zachary.

"Daddy? It's me, Kenzie."

Kai bristled visibly, eyeing her with reservation. Kenzie took a step closer, and his eyes widened.

His caregiver suddenly stepped between them. "He doesn't like to be touched," she said softly. "You need to take things very slow until he gets comfortable with you."

"He's my father!"

"I know. But he doesn't."

Kenzie's tears began to fall again. She bit down against her bottom lip and took a step back. Zachary stepped behind her, his hands gently caressing her arms. Kenzie leaned back against him, allowing herself to use his chest for support. The weight of the moment was suddenly too much for her to bear alone.

Zachary leaned to whisper in her ear. "It's okay. I've got you."

Her head bobbed almost frantically, and although she didn't say so, she was grateful that he was there. He reached for her hand and pulled her along beside him as they took seats at the table.

"Would you like something to eat?" Angelika asked.

They both shook their heads.

"No, thank you," Kenzie muttered.

Kai suddenly startled her, his voice loud

as he cried out. "Who are you? I don't know you! Go away! Go away! Go away!" he screamed as he threw the spoon at Zachary's head.

She grabbed Zachary's arm, but he didn't flinch. "My name is Zachary. Zachary Barrett. We used to train together. You and I were best friends!"

"No, no, no, no, no!" Kai hit his forehead with a clenched fist.

Angelika knelt down in front of Kai. She grabbed his arm, stalling the slams he was inflicting upon himself. "Shhh! Stop, Mr. Tamura. It's okay."

"Make them go! Make them go! I don't know them," he muttered in Thai.

Angelika nodded. "Why don't we go sit in the sunroom? You can watch the television," she said as she gently pulled him to his feet and guided him into another room.

Zachary blew a breath. He cut his eye at Kenzie. "Come on," he said. "I want you to see something." He rose from his seat and extended a hand in her direction.

Kenzie slid her palm against his. She didn't have any words, so she just expressed her appreciation in her eyes, her gaze locking briefly with his. Zachary kissed her lips, the gesture brief and gentle.

They moved in the opposite direction,

toward the master bedroom at the rear of the home. Zachary opened the closed door and gestured for her to go inside. Kenzie clutched the front of her T-shirt as she spun in a slow circle around the room. The entire space was a tribute to Kai's life and career. There were photos of moments in time that he had shared with people who'd been important to him. His trophies and belts were neatly displayed, and a stamp collection rested on a table.

One wall had been dedicated to the time he'd spent training Zachary. There were photos of the two together and framed articles about their partnership. And every one of Zachary's championship belts and trophies was lined up neatly in a glass case against the opposite wall.

Kenzie stood taking it all in. She moved from one side of the room to the other, taking note of each and every item. She came to an abrupt halt at the nightstand by the bed. She tossed Zachary a quick look before she reached for a photograph that rested there. The image was old, a black-and-white photograph of Kai and her mother holding her between them. Her father held her in his arms, and they were both smiling as if it was the happiest time in their lives. Her father had been a giant then, and his smile was the prettiest thing she'd ever seen.

There was one more photo that rested on the table, a collage of Kenzie's school pictures: kindergarten, first grade, third grade, middle school. Only her twelfth-grade graduation photo was missing. Kenzie's hand quivered as she stood staring at the images. And then she really cried.

There was no stopping Kenzie's tears. She was bereft, her loss unfathomable. She could only begin to imagine how it could have been had her mother been a more forgiving woman and her father had fought harder for the two of them. And then she wondered what might have been had she not been so angry at the world, allowing her teenage angst to hammer the wedge between the two of them. But there was no going back, and their future together was slipping away with the darkness that had intruded into her father's life. So she cried; there was nothing else that she could think to do.

"He's not always like this," Zachary said, breaking the silence that had risen between them. "There are times when he's very lucid and he remembers. It doesn't happen often, but it happens."

She wrapped her arms around her torso and hugged herself tightly. "Why do you keep some of your trophies and belts here?"

she asked, pointing at the wall dedicated to his career. "The ones you lied about being in storage," she said tersely.

"I have them because of your father. It's my way of sharing those victories with him since he can't be with me. If he hadn't gotten sick, he would still be with me ringside when I fight. He'd still be training me."

She nodded. "You two were very close."

Zachary nodded. "There's nothing I wouldn't do for him. And what I did do I did because I love him. Because he asked me to and I couldn't tell him no."

Then their conversation lapsed into silence, both understanding there was nothing else that could be said. He hadn't told her about her father. It was what it was. Although she wanted to be thankful since Zachary could have continued to keep the truth from her, she was angry, unable to find anything to be grateful about.

"Do you want to go back to the house?" he asked. "We can always come back later."

She shook her head. "No. I'm staying. I'm not leaving my father."

Zachary stared at her briefly, then nodded. He turned back to the door, and she followed.

In the sunroom, Kai was watching a really bad Thai soap opera. He was completely engaged, shushing them as they entered the room.

"Shhh! He's not her boyfriend!" he said excitedly as he pointed to the screen. He suddenly turned his attention toward Zachary; his gaze narrowed as he stared at the man. "You say you're a fighter?" he suddenly asked as he leaned forward in his seat.

Zachary sat down on the ottoman beside the man. "Yes, sir."

"You don't look like a fighter. You're too skinny. We need to get you bulked up."

"Yes, sir."

"And you need to keep your hands up! You can't win if you keep getting hit!" Kai laughed, and Zachary smiled, his eyes misting slightly.

"Mr. Tamura, I want you to meet someone," Zachary said. He gestured for Kenzie to move to his side.

Kenzie sat down beside him. "Hello!"

Kai tilted his head in greeting. "Women are a distraction. And they are trouble. You do not need trouble. You are going to be the champion one day. You don't need trouble, and this one looks like trouble." He winked an eye at Kenzie, which made her smile.

Zachary grinned. "She's okay. I promise. This is Kenzie. She's Tanya Monroe's daughter. This is your baby girl."

Kai looked at her and him and back again. "Who is Tanya?" he asked, confusion washing over his expression. "I don't know any Tanya."

There was a moment of pause, and then he sat forward. "Are you my nurse? I need my medicine. Can you get my medicine?"

Zachary reached out to squeeze her hand. She pulled away from him abruptly, not looking in his direction.

"I'm not a nurse," she said softly. "I'm your daughter."

Kai twitched as he tried to focus, trying desperately to remember. You could almost see his mind working, fighting to put the pieces into place. He suddenly looked up with blank eyes. "I need my medicine," he said.

Kenzie took a deep breath. "I'll go see if I can find it for you," she said, and then she stood up, practically racing from the room.

Kenzie refused to leave her father's home. She returned to Zachary's place just long enough to claim her bags, and then she took up residence in the only spare bedroom in Tamura's home. Every day, she woke when her father woke and rested when he rested. The rest of the time, she tried to talk him into remembering who she was. Into remembering anything about his life when it had included her or her mother. She talked nonstop, and Kai sometimes listened and most times didn't.

There were occasional moments of lucidity when he gave her brief hints of his past: his fight career, his training days, the women he'd loved, the places he'd seen. He'd talk, and she would become someone he'd known back when, but never once did he call her by name or give her any inkling that he knew who she was.

Zachary had come and gone from the gym in Phuket a few times. He always returned to check on her, on them, always hoping that Kenzie would be ready to kiss her father good-bye and leave. And every time, she told him no and little else, not having much to say to him. Barbie kept tabs on her, tried often to convince her to return to Phuket, and to Zachary, but she would not be moved.

"Jason Williams was my first boyfriend. He's a minister now, but there was nothing Christian-like about him back then!" Kenzie laughed. "He was also my first kiss, but it was the absolute worst. The boy was like a Hoover vacuum on steroids!" Kenzie grimaced.

Kai sat in his recliner with his eyes closed.

He heard her, but he didn't. If he understood, he didn't show it. Mostly he slept, waking to memories of other people and things that she had never been a part of or sometimes waking to darkness, an empty world where no one existed but himself and the muddled memories he could never quite piece back together.

Kenzie wiped her eyes with the back of her hand. Her father was snoring, and although she'd spent an hour regaling him with stories about her cheerleading days, he had barely been able to look her in the eye. He had dozed on and off, and now that he was on again, she tossed a throw blanket over his thin frame and headed outside.

They had drained the water from the pool in her father's yard and had covered the concrete hole. Apparently the patriarch had been prone to wandering, and they feared him falling in and drowning. Kenzie wanted to swim, so she took the short walk next door and threw herself into the warm blanket of water that filled Zachary's pool. She came every day, needing the time to herself to regroup.

She missed Zachary. She missed him when he was gone. When he came, she wanted them to be good with each other again, but she couldn't move herself past the anger. Because she was still angry. Angry as hell that she had her father back but that he was lost to her. She was angry with Kai for having failed her, and she was angry that Zachary had gotten caught up in the fray. Hell, she was angry that it was Thursday and she'd gained five pounds and that she hadn't written anything at all since the day she learned her father was living in the house right next door to the man she was in love with.

She was furious that she couldn't write — no words fluttered in her heart. That made her angrier than any of the other stuff. Because she needed the words to make sense of it all. She needed to write, wanted to write, believing that somewhere in the midst of her father's hell was a story she needed to tell.

She swam until she was too tired to do anything else, lap after lap until she was taxed and ready for it to be over. When she couldn't swim any longer, she lifted herself from the pool. She smiled when she spied the clean towel resting on the chaise lounge; Barbie had snuck in and out like a ninja. Wrapping it around herself, she dried the moisture from her skin. She stood beneath the warm afternoon sun for a good long while, allowing the day's heat and the sun's bright rays to dry her.

For a brief moment, she contemplated going back to her father's, but knowing he wouldn't miss her changed her mind. Kenzie sauntered past the sliding glass doors into the master bedroom where she and Zachary had slept. She walked out of her swimsuit and into a hot shower. After she'd shampooed and conditioned her hair, she stood beneath the spray of water until it started to run cold. Her fingers and toes were wrinkled, and she was slightly waterlogged, but she was slowly but surely beginning to feel like her old self.

She wrapped a towel around her wet hair and moved back into the bedroom. Dropping down onto the bed, she contemplated her next moves, trying to decide if she should stay or go. Every day she asked herself the same questions, and every day had no answers. She thought about calling Stephanie, but she knew her bestie wouldn't have any answers for her either. She was alone, and she imagined that in some ways it must be how her father often felt.

She lifted her legs onto the bed and crawled beneath the clean white sheets, pulling them up and over her torso. Then she let her mind go blank, too tired to be scared and angry and frustrated and lonely one minute longer.

Kenzie jumped, startled out of her sleep by the sound of Zachary snoring softly beside her. His body was curled close to hers, heat wafting from his skin. *He felt good,* she thought, suddenly remembering everything she was missing. She snuggled closer to him, moving her buttocks into his crotch and her back against his chest. As she nuzzled herself against him, Zachary wrapped his arms around her and pulled her even closer against him. He pressed his face into the back of her neck and kissed her behind her ear.

"Are you okay?" he whispered softly.

She shook her head as she whispered back. "I'm not sure," she said. "Everything feels so strange. I don't know what I'm supposed to be doing anymore."

Zachary kissed her again. "How can I help?"

Kenzie turned, rolling herself over until she was facing him. "Tell me you still love me. Even though I've been a complete and total jerk to you, I'm praying like hell that you still love me. Even if it's just a little bit."

Zachary laughed. "You know damn well that I love you more than just a little bit.

You know that I love you even if you are a complete and total jerk."

"I still need to hear it. Especially since I will probably never hear my father say it."

Zachary pressed his palm to the side of her face. "Kenzie, I'm sorry about that. I really am. I never imagined that keeping Kai's secret would ever cause you this kind of pain. I didn't agree at first, but as his disease progressed I understood why he wanted to spare you. He didn't want you to see him like this. He didn't want you to be in the room with him and have you feel what it's like for him not to know you. He understood it better than I ever did." He took a breath and held it for a split second before he continued.

"I know how much your father loves you. And I will remind you of that every day. Kai can't say it himself, and I have no problems saying it for him. But know that when I tell you *I* love you that it has nothing at all to do with your father and everything to do with the hold you have on my heart. You've become my air, and I need to breathe you if I'm going to survive. So don't you ever forget that." He brushed away the tear that had fallen from beneath her eye.

"Thank you," she whispered. She gently

kissed that spot beneath his chin, allowing her lips to linger there briefly. “Thank you.”

CHAPTER THIRTEEN

Zachary stood at the sliding glass doors staring out and watching the torrential rain that was gushing from the sky. It had been raining for hours, with no sign of relief. Kenzie eased herself into his side, wrapping her arms tightly around his midsection. He felt good, and his being there made her extremely happy.

"Are you okay?" he asked as he draped his arm around her shoulders and hugged her close. He gently kissed the tip of her nose and then her cheek.

She nodded. "I have a lot going on in my head."

"Do you want to talk about it?" he questioned.

She shrugged her shoulders as she pulled herself from him, moving to one of the wicker chairs that rested in the corner.

Zachary dropped down into the other,

pulling it up close to hers. "Talk to me, baby."

"What's going to happen? After . . . well . . . when my father . . ." She hesitated, seeming to search for the words to say what was in her heart.

He nodded and took a deep breath, filling his lungs with warm air. His eyes shifted back to the downpour still happening outside. "It'll be hard for a while, I'm sure, and then we'll push forward and go on with our lives. It would be what Kai would want for us."

"What's going to happen with *us*, Zachary? I know we joke about being a couple and . . ."

He smirked. "Who was joking?"

She smiled, the lift to her mouth ever so slight. "You know what I mean."

He nodded. "I hope that you'll stay her with me in Phuket. That's what I want. And we can get married when you're ready and have lots of beautiful babies."

"You make it sound so easy."

"You want to make it complicated, and it doesn't have to be."

"You want me to leave my life in the States behind. My friends, my family, everything I know."

"I want you to claim everything that you

can have here in Thailand with me. Our friends, our family."

"What if . . . ?"

He stalled her question, holding up his hand as his head waved from side to side. "There is no what if. What if a frog fell from the sky and bumped his ass? Whatever we have to do to make this work I am willing to do. Are you?"

She met his stare, the intensity of his gaze all-encompassing. She nodded. "Yes. Yes, I am."

"That's all that's important. We can figure out the logistics later. Baby, you just have to trust that it will all work out."

Kenzie leaned forward in her seat, reaching to kiss his mouth. Her lips lingered with his for a good minute, as she fell into the warmth of his touch. When she sat back in her seat, Zachary was grinning, looking like he'd just won the biggest prize at the state fair.

They continued talking. About everything. Her feelings. His feelings. Her dreams. His future ambitions. And they talked about the goals they wanted for each other and what they aspired to as a couple. It reminded them of that first time when they'd spent hours in conversation, learning about each other. They regained a sense of balance with each other, and by mid-afternoon it was as if they had never been out of sync.

Kenzie had not spent the entire day with her father. Instead, she and Zachary had walked over together, sitting down to share lunch with the man. Kai's gaze had skated back and forth between them. Despite a growing level of comfort having them around, he still didn't have a clue who either was; both were still a mystery to him. And then there came a moment of clarity.

"You won that last fight. Are you training for the next one? You know there will be a next one!" The comment came out of nowhere, and it surprised them both.

Zachary grabbed his napkin and swallowed the bit of the turkey sandwich he'd been eating. He tossed Kenzie a quick look before turning his full attention back to the man. "No, sir. I haven't been training. I don't know if I'm ready to sign the next fight yet."

The old man shrugged his narrow shoulders, wincing slightly as if he might be in pain.

"Are you okay?" Kenzie asked, concern ringing in her tone.

Kai nodded. He fanned a hand in her direction. "Who is she?" he asked, looking back toward Zachary.

"That's Kenzie, your daughter."

Kai stared at her. Then he nodded. He looked back at Zachary. "You're running out of time. You're not that young anymore. Either do it or get out while you're on top. You're good, and you can always turn to training other fighters, like I did. What does Montri think?"

"Gamon thinks I should take one more fight. Maybe even two."

"Listen to him. He's a good man. He'll give you good advice. You can trust him."

Zachary nodded. "Yes, sir."

There was a moment of pause, and then he turned to stare at Kenzie a second time. "I need my medicine."

Holding hands, Zachary and Kenzie walked the length of roadway for what felt like the thousandth time. The two had been walking up and down the road between the two houses, back and forth as if they had nowhere else to go. Although Kenzie was still disappointed that her father saw her as a stranger, the ache of it was no longer as catastrophic as it had previously been. The more she learned about his condition, the more she understood, and understanding bred a level of acceptance that made it all just a little bit easier to handle.

The sky had gone a dull gray, and you could smell the rain in the air. Suddenly there was a loud clap of thunder, and the sky opened, like the parting of the seas, dumping a torrent of water over their heads. Neither bothered to run for cover, and in no time at all both were drenched, soaked through to the skin.

Kenzie felt Zachary staring, an amused grin pulling at his mouth. Her nipples had gone erect from the chill of being wet. His eyes were fixed on her breasts, and when she looked down she realized that she was fully exposed, her full bustline pressing against her soaked white T-shirt. She hadn't bothered with a bra, and the outline of her breasts and nipples were detailed and clearly in view. If it had been a wet T-shirt contest she would have clearly claimed the championship. Kenzie felt herself blush slightly as one of the neighbors stood in his yard and stared. She crossed her arms over her chest, and Zachary laughed.

Zachary tapped her backside, and she rolled her eyes. The neighbor eyed them both with a narrowed gaze, clearly not amused. Zachary pressed a large hand against the small of her back as he guided her back toward the house.

His lips captured hers before they could

get inside and get the door closed behind them. He kissed her with an intensity that had them both reeling. Soaked, they didn't waste the energy to find towels, leaving a trail of wet clothes from the entrance into the bedroom. They were both heated, their damp skin sizzling from the other's touch. Their loving was intoxicating, both drunk with wanting. Kenzie welcomed him back into her heart and her core, reveling in how much she had missed the nearness of him.

Weeks later, her father's condition began to decline. Kai had not had a good day. His breathing had been labored, and he had difficulty eating and swallowing. He had needed assistance walking, and fearing that he had pneumonia, Angelika had insisted he be moved to the hospital for a chest X-ray. Kai had been too weak to object, allowing himself to be taken without a word of complaint. The experience had worked all of their nerves, and even when the doctors had released him, warning them that they would see more bad days than they would good, no one had been able to relax. Kenzie had taken it the hardest, frustrated that she couldn't do more for her beloved father.

That night, she couldn't sleep and unable

to even rest well. Slipping out of the bed, she slid open the sliding doors and stepped outside. The sky was dark, just the sliver of a quarter moon sitting high in the sky. She needed to move, and she hoped a late-night swim might help to settle her down. Kenzie jumped into the pool naked. The water was warm, and the shimmer of moonlight and the stillness of the night eased the tension from her spirit.

Standing in the doorway, Zachary watched her. She was exquisitely beautiful, and with the hint of light that illuminated her, she looked angelic. He had tried for most of the day to remember the mantras her father had given him, hoping that the directives would help her move past the sadness that seemed to be consuming her. But he had nothing in him, and the little that he did have didn't seem to be helping her.

He watched her, wanting to slide into the water with her, but he stopped himself. He understood that Kenzie needed the time alone to work through the discord that had become all-consuming. And he needed some time to regain a semblance of control, suddenly thinking about himself. His heart was as broken as hers, but there was nowhere and no one for him to turn to. He needed to be a pillar of strength for her, even when he felt himself failing and in need of his own support. Easing his way back inside, he let her swim, crawled back into bed, and tried to go back to sleep.

"Stop!" Zachary commanded, ire rising in his tone. "You really need to stop." He shook his index finger in Kenzie's direction. She'd been bitching and moaning about her circumstances for ten minutes longer than he could take, and he'd had enough. It had become a bad habit that she resorted to on a regular basis. They no longer had any sense of time, their days melting one into the other, and it was all beginning to weigh heavily on their spirits.

"Why are you yelling at me?" she snapped.

"Kenzie, I'm not yelling. But you need to get over yourself."

"Get over myself?"

"Yes. That's exactly what I said."

"My father is dying!" she shouted, her voice rising an octave.

"I know that. And I've been dealing with it far longer than you have. I know how you're feeling, but Kai would not want this for you. He would want you to focus on living your life, not falling into despair over his."

"Falling into despair? Really?"

He took a deep breath. "You've thrown yourself a major pity party, and you need to get over yourself. You act like you're the only one hurting! This is affecting me too, damn it!"

Kenzie jumped to her feet. Something like rage seeped from her eyes. "You need to go to hell!" she exclaimed as she stomped out to the yard and across the grass to the property next door.

Angelika greeted her at the door. The two women had become a team of sorts, as Kenzie had tried to help support the health-care professional Zachary had hand-selected to care for her father. The woman didn't talk much, but she was a consummate professional, and Kenzie liked her. She always seemed to know when Kenzie needed a kind word and when she just needed to be left alone.

She nodded her head in greeting and stepped aside as Kenzie swept past her, tears brimming in her eyes. Kenzie moved to her father's room, pausing at the door for a brief moment. She wiped her hand across her face before reaching for the doorknob and moving inside. Kai lay in the newly purchased hospital bed, his torso slightly lifted. He appeared to be resting comfortably, his eyes closed. She eased inside and moved quietly to the rocking chair that sat by his bedside. The radio on the nightstand was playing traditional Thai music, and as she started to rock back and forth, she realized he wasn't sleeping.

He stared, his gaze clouded but meeting hers. He stared at her, his head bobbing easily in time to the beat of a hand drum. Kenzie listened closely, realizing that he was humming, the tune familiar to him. He hummed, and she found the soft lull of it comforting. She closed her own eyes and fell into the moment, knowing that Zachary was right and hating to admit it. Feeling sorry for herself had suddenly become second nature, but it was not at all indicative of her true personality.

The quiet and the music were suddenly interrupted by her father's voice. "You look like your mother."

Kenzie's head snapped up suddenly, shock widening her eyes. She took a deep breath before she spoke, fighting to stall her excitement. "Do I?"

"Tanya was the most beautiful woman in the world, and you look just like her. But you are even more beautiful because you look like me too!"

Kenzie smiled. "Thank you," she said, her voice a loud whisper.

Kai smiled. "I missed your graduation. I am very sorry."

"It was my fault. I was mad, and I acted badly."

The man chuckled softly. "Just like your mother! You have her spirit too!"

"I've missed you, Daddy!" Kenzie exclaimed, struggling not to cry.

He laughed again. "I missed you, too, my angel."

Kenzie shifted the chair and inclined her body forward until she was directly by his side. She leaned her head against his arm, grabbing his hand. He held hers tightly, giving her fingers a little squeeze.

"I love you, my angel," he said. "And, Kenzie, I promise I won't miss your next graduation."

Kenzie reached up to kiss her father's cheek. "I love you, too, Daddy," she said, her voice barely a whisper.

Kai went back to humming along with the radio. He hummed, and Kenzie relaxed by his side, continuing to listen to the soft respite of his voice. Hours later, he jumped out of a deep sleep, startling Kenzie from her own slumber. His eyes locked with hers and held her gaze, the two eyeing each other.

Kai fanned a hand at her. "I need my

medicine. Are you my nurse?"

Two weeks later Kai Tamura died in his sleep. He asked for his medicine, closed his eyes, and slipped peacefully away. That first time that he had called her name and professed his love had been his last. Her father had not remembered her once after that moment.

Zachary insured that he was given a traditional Buddhist funeral. His friend had insisted on the formality of ceremony, and nothing would have kept him from honoring the man's one last wish.

The bathing rite took place on the evening of the first day. The service was reserved for those who had known him personally. Barbie had stood with the couple, holding them up as they'd laid Kai's body out on a table and covered it with a cloth. His head and one hand were all that was exposed. Everyone present took turns pouring scented water over his hand. The opportunity was given to ask for forgiveness for past transgressions. His ankles and wrists were bound with white string, his hands held together in a gesture of prayer. A coin was placed in his mouth, and then the body was laid to rest in a coffin. The casket was surrounded by flowers, and a portrait that Kenzie had selected was prominently displayed.

The monks had been invited to chant daily for the loss of her father. The sequence of sutras, or scriptures, was intended to guide Kai on his spiritual journey and to protect and comfort those he'd left behind. It was believed that the sacred utterances would lift followers from the ordinary to a higher level of consciousness. The chanting lasted for seven days until the day of the cremation. It was quite the social event and not a completely sad affair. Between the chanting, mourners would listen to traditional Thai music, a melodious mix of strings and percussion instruments. Despite wanting to crawl into a hole and pull in the dirt, Kenzie was the perfect host. She was generous with the snacks and drinks, even insuring there was enough food for a full meal if someone was so inclined. The time passed quickly.

After the week of chanting, her father's body was ready for cremation. There was more chanting and the ordaining of a novice monk to merit her father's dead body in the afterlife. It was a full ordination, in which the novice's hair and eyebrows were shaved. More chanting, and the monks were fed one more time.

As the coffin was moved to the crematorium, Kenzie clutched Zachary's arm as if her life depended on it. Her nails bore into his skin, but he seemed unbothered, lost in the depths of his own mourning. They led the processional, carrying her father's portrait as the coffin was pulled along behind them by the monks. Those who'd known and loved Kai Tamura followed the procession to the Thai temple, walking three times around the holy structure. The casket was left at the crematorium doors.

Barbie gave Kai's eulogy, recounting the most significant moments in the man's life just before a team of dancers performed the fong, a traditional Thai dance characterized by its slowness and distinct storytelling poses. There was more praying from the monks, and then it was over. Flowers made from wood shavings were placed under the casket. As Kenzie tapped the coffin with her flower, she said a short prayer of forgiveness, as she'd been instructed, releasing her father and herself from the heartbreak that had kept them apart for so many years. She put their wrongdoings in the past, then placed her flower with the rest, as if she herself were lighting the funeral fire.

When the final tributes had been made, most of the mourners went home, having paid their respects. Kenzie and Zachary were the last of his family, and they stayed until the coffin was pushed into the cremation chamber.

The following day, the couple returned to collect Kai's ashes. The monks were present for the ceremony, and there was another presentation of food and robes to honor them. Kai's urn was then taken to the prayer hall, where there was more chanting.

Kenzie had chosen to scatter her father's ashes over the water. There were those Thai people who believed that floating the ashes of their loved ones in a river or in the open sea would not only help wash away their sins but also help them go more smoothly up to heaven. Kenzie wanted to make sure her father was nestled somewhere in the clouds, having found a sense of peace wherever it was that he rested. And then it was all over, and the young couple was left to pick up the pieces and move on.

Chapter Fourteen

"We should go run or something," Kenzie said, her hands on her hips as she stood over Zachary.

He lay supine on the sofa, his arm tossed over his head, his eyes closed. It had been his position of choice for a day longer than necessary, and Kenzie was ready for them both to get past it and move on.

"I'm really not in the mood," he said, not even bothering to look in her direction.

"You haven't been in the mood for anything lately," she said softly. She moved to sit beside him, her hands clasped together in her lap as she nudged him aside with her hip.

He shifted his body from hers, sinking back into the cushions. With a deep sigh, he finally opened his eyes to meet the look she was giving him. He smiled slightly. "Yeah, sorry. I don't know what's wrong with me. I'm just a little . . . ," he paused and shrugged.

"Depressed?"

"No. Hell, no! I'm just tired. I'm not depressed."

She stared at him for a moment, saying nothing.

"What?" There was a hint of annoyance in his tone as he snatched his gaze from hers, visibly unnerved.

"I think you should go talk to someone. We've been through a lot with my father, and it might help . . ."

"Why are you coming at me with this?" he suddenly snapped, a hint of hostility in his tone. "I don't feel like running! What's the big deal? Yesterday you didn't feel like writing or working, but I didn't give you a hard time."

"Like hell you didn't," Kenzie snapped back. "You lectured me for thirty minutes!"

"Well, I should," he said as he drew his knees to his chest and swung his legs past her. He sat upright. "You need to get back to work. I haven't stopped."

Kenzie's jaw locked as she bit back her retort. She and Zachary had been bickering off and on since the funeral. Each spat started over absolutely nothing and escalated too quickly to be good for either of them. She took a deep breath and held it, struggling to contain her own rising emotions.

She stood up. "I'm going to go for a run. When are we going back to Phuket?"

He shrugged his shoulders. "I thought you wanted to stay a little longer."

"No. I think we should head back."

He nodded. "Whatever," he said dismissively. "I have some things I need to take care of, and then we can head back." He stood up.

Before Kenzie could respond, Zachary's cell phone chimed, vibrating against the glass-topped coffee table. He shot her one last look before he pulled the device into his hand. "It's my brother," he said as he headed toward the bedroom, putting the phone to his ear.

Kenzie watched as he disappeared, closing the door behind himself. She blew a low hiss of air past her lips, a blanket of sadness settling around her shoulders.

Barbie suddenly moved to her side from where he'd been standing in the kitchen, listening. He wrapped his arms around her and hugged her tightly. "He'll be okay. It's going to take some time," their friend said, his head bobbing with conviction.

"Yeah, but he's not okay now," she said softly. "Neither of us is, and I just want things to go back to normal."

Barbie squeezed her hand. "You just have to stay strong for the both of you," he said.

Kenzie gave him a slight smile. She took another deep breath, and then she headed for the front door.

"So tell me the truth," Alexander said. "How are you really doing?"

Tired of the small talk, he put his twin on the spot, demanding an honest answer. There was a lengthy pause as Zachary pondered his question. When he didn't respond, Alexander persisted. "What's going on, Z? I know this hasn't been easy for you."

"It's all good," he finally responded. "I've been trying to hang on for Kenzie. She's had a hard time, and things have been tense between us. But it'll get better, right?"

"You are both mourning. That's going to take some time. You're trying to hold Kenzie up, but who's holding you up?"

Zachary didn't bother to respond, going radio silent a second time. He was grateful that his twin couldn't see the anxiety that furrowed his brow or the tears that suddenly misted his gaze. He tried to change the subject. "I've been trying to get Kenzie to get back to work. She's not writing, and I'm sure that's not a good thing."

Alexander changed it back. "And are you working? Have you gone back to your regular routine?"

"I'm trying. I . . . well . . . I have a lot on my plate."

"You need to take some time for yourself, Zachary. You can't help Kenzie if you're falling apart yourself."

"I've got this, A," Zachary said, trying to convince himself more than his brother.

"And I'm not so sure about that. I'm worried about you, bro. I can come if you need me. You know I'll be there."

Zachary nodded into his receiver. "I know, and I swear, if I need you, I'll call."

The house was quiet. Angelika had already moved her belongings out, and nothing was left but Kai's things. Although Zachary and Barbie had coordinated the packing of his possessions and had everything transferred to Phuket, Kenzie had insisted on taking a moment to gather a few things herself. She'd already packed the bedside photos and a shoebox full of letters that her father had written to her but never mailed.

When Zachary moved into the room, she was standing in front of his trophy wall, admiring the many belts and awards and photographs of his career wins and accomplishments. For a brief moment, he stood watching her from the doorway. There was an air of melancholy that lingered like a dark shadow behind her. Despite her efforts to shake it away, it had found sanctuary in her spirit and was holding on for dear life. He would have done anything to shoo the darkness from her, but he had no answers, and he had his own issues to contend with.

His eyes shifted from her to the wall and back, wondering what she was thinking. He would have asked, but things had been tense between them; the two had been unable to find any sense of balance with each other. He knew he was at fault for most of the disagreements that seemed to be plaguing them, but he couldn't seem to shake the demons that had latched onto his own back. He wasn't in the mood for another argument or even the start of one, so silence was suddenly better than gold.

He was about to turn and leave when Kenzie suddenly floated her stare in his direction. Their gazes connected and held, the two eyeing each other intently. There was an abundance of love in both their eyes but also something else that neither could identify or define. Something cool and distant and too scary to put into words.

Finding it easier to push the emotion aside, they both chose to ignore it.

Kenzie was the first to speak, breaking the silence. "We'll need to find someplace to put these. Maybe we should display them in the office."

Zachary shrugged. "I don't know if I want them. They can go into storage."

"No!" Kenzie exclaimed. "You worked so hard for these. You should show them off. Share them with your family and friends!"

He moved to her side, lifting his eyes to stare where she had stared. "I'll figure it out later," he said, his shoulders pushing up toward the ceiling.

Kenzie shook her head. "Why can't we figure it out now? Why do you keep dismissing all of my suggestions? It's starting to get on my nerves, Zachary."

"Don't start."

"I'm not starting. I just want to know . . ."

He snapped. "Give me a break. Please! I am not in the mood. Are you ready to go?"

They stood toe to toe, adding bricks to the wall they'd been slowly building between them. When she didn't answer, he turned abruptly and headed back toward the door. He called over his shoulder. "If you're riding back with me, I'm pulling out as soon as I make sure Franklin has everything he needs. Be in the car."

As he rounded the corner and disappeared, Kenzie muttered under her breath, "Whatever."

It was a month later when Kenzie laughed, and Zachary realized that it had been forever since he'd last heard the sound. Since her father's passing, the two had settled into two different lanes, gliding past each other like two lost ships.

Everyone had expected that Kai's death would have hit Kenzie hard, but it was Zachary who seemed to be suffering the most. He stared out to the property; the gym facility was ripe with activity. Leaving Krabi Town and returning to Revolution had been easy, as neither wanted to stay a day longer than necessary. Now that they were back, Kenzie was laughing, and he couldn't begin to imagine what she could find so funny.

He moved back into his bungalow and the bedroom where she sat, lotus-style. She was on the telephone, lost in conversation, a smile actually filling her face. He stood in the doorway, watching her, until the conversation was done and she had disconnected the call.

She eyed him curiously. "I thought you

had a class?" she asked, lifting her eyes to his.

"I canceled. I wasn't in the mood."

She eyed him for a moment before nodding her head slightly.

Zachary shrugged. "Who were you talking to?" he asked.

"Stephanie. She has a job for me, a feature on the new owner of the New York Knicks."

"That's good."

She nodded again. "But I need to go back to the States. I think I'm going to try to leave at the end of the week."

"Leaving? When were you going to tell me?"

"I just did, Zachary."

"Don't you think we should have talked about it before you told her yes?"

Kenzie bristled slightly. "I'm not sure where you're going with this, but you're the one who's been telling me I need to get back to work."

"I said you need to get back to *writing.* Not that you needed to leave."

"My writing sometimes makes it necessary for me to leave, Zachary."

He shook his head. "Whatever . . ."

"What does that mean?"

"It means go. Do whatever you want. I don't care."

She blew a loud sigh. "I really don't want to fight. We keep going back and forth, and it doesn't make any sense to me."

"I'm not fighting."

"You're trying to pick one."

Zachary shook his head from side to side. "I've just signed to fight Antonio Barrera. I thought you should know. I need to start training, so it's probably better that you're gone anyway."

Shock washed over Kenzie's expression. She shook her head. "I thought we agreed that you weren't going to think about taking on a fight until next year? No major life decisions for at least six months, remember?" She briefly thought back to one of the few conversations they had had since her father had passed.

"They pitched a deal I couldn't turn down."

"And when is this supposed to happen?"

"We have a good few months. The UFC still needs to approve the deal, and then there's some logistical stuff that needs to happen. It'll definitely be after the holidays and probably sometime in the early New Year."

"And Gamon is okay with this?"

"Gamon works for me. I don't work for him," he said snidely. He tossed her a look, then cut his eyes in the opposite direction, refusing to look directly at her.

Kenzie's fists clutched her hips. Concern painted her expression. "Do you really think this is a good idea, Zachary? Are you ready to take on an opponent so soon? Because I don't think your head is in the right place for a fight right now. I really don't."

"Don't you, Kenzie? Let me worry about me."

She bristled, her eyes narrowing into thin slits. "What's going on with you, Zachary? What's going on with us?"

He shrugged as he turned, moving out the door. "Clearly, not a damn thing! You're leaving, remember?"

Zachary stormed back into the front room. He wanted to run. He *needed* to run, to forget, in the dust and dirt roads, the rise of frustration that was suddenly consuming him. He slid his feet into a pair of running shoes and slammed out the front door. And then he ran.

The trek took him off the property and through the streets of Phuket. He paced himself, determined to run until he dropped, no end goal planned at all. He rounded a narrow passage that dropped him at the bridge that connected the island to the mainland. From there he followed the route to Haad Sai Kaew Beach, an endless stretch of sand and sun. Miles of solitary beachfront property lay before him, the area completely deserted. Above his head, the sun lingered behind a wave of cumulus clouds, just the right amount of bright light peeking through. The water that kissed the sand's edge was an extraordinary shade of blue, but in that moment Zachary couldn't appreciate the beauty of it.

He ran until he was kicking up sand and the spray of ocean water was hitting him in the face. His calves had begun to burn, and there was a hint of ache in his knees. He had broken out into a sweat and was panting heavily, his chest tightening. His lungs were beginning to burn, and breathing was starting to be a challenge. When he reached an incline that began the path back to the gym, he suddenly came to an abrupt stop, his hands falling against the slight rise of his hips. Tears streamed down his face.

Zachary sobbed. He cried like a baby, his chest heaving up and down. His heart ached, the pain almost unbearable. He hadn't felt as lost, or alone, since the time he and his twin brother had been estranged and his marriage had fallen into dissolution. He sobbed, tears clouding his view as he dropped down against the loose sand and wrapped his arms around his knees. His hulking body heaved up and down as he wept, and then he wailed, oblivious to the curious stares from the few people who were walking along the beach.

CHAPTER FIFTEEN

When Zachary hadn't come back, Kenzie went looking for Gamon. His training manager and friend was in the office trying to catch up on paperwork that the star athlete had left unhandled. Frustration furrowed his brow, and when he looked up to see Kenzie standing there staring at him, it was clear that he was not in the mood. But neither was she.

"He is not here, Ms. Kenzie. I have not seen him today," Gamon said, mumbling with a thick Thai accent.

"I know. We had a fight, and he took off on a run. We probably won't see him for the rest of the day."

Gamon sat back in his seat. He folded his hands together in his lap. "Why did you two argue?" he asked.

Kenzie dropped down into the empty seat in front of the desk. "I'm going back to New York on Thursday. I just booked my flight. I have a new assignment."

Gamon nodded. "So he is not happy about you leaving."

"No," she said, her head shaking. "He's not happy about anything lately."

"Your father dying is weighing heavily on his spirit. He doesn't know how to deal with the loss."

Kenzie blew a loud sigh. "It's been hard for both of us."

Gamon nodded his agreement. "Grief will sometimes take your life to a crossroads. We all handle that differently. He may need a little help finding his way."

"So how do I do that, Gamon? He told me to get back to work and move on, and now he's having issues because I'm doing that."

"You need to just give him time. He is getting back to work. He will need to train, and when he is focused on that, things will get better."

"A title fight is too soon, and with Antonio Barrera? He's not ready for that, Gamon. His head's not in that kind of game."

"That is true. But he will be ready," the man said matter-of-factly. "I'll make sure of that."

Kenzie nodded. "Zachary trusts you. And so did my father. I don't know if I'm convinced, but I'm willing to trust you too. So what do I do until then?"

"Give him some space. Go handle your business. It will all work out the way fate intends for it to."

"Just like that?"

"Exactly like that."

Stephanie Guy met her best friend at the airport. Kenzie's flight had landed an hour past its originally scheduled arrival time due to the weather conditions in New York. An untimely nor'easter had blown through days earlier, and LaGuardia Airport had just reopened to air traffic. Primped and pretty, the four-foot, eight-inch spitfire in stiletto heels had bulldozed her way through a crowd to stand front and center with a handmade sign that read WELCOME HOME.

Kenzie laughed as she hugged her bestie. "Really, Steph? You're wearing high heels in this weather?"

"How many times have I told you that you never break formation? I have an image to uphold."

"That's going to be hard to do if you slip on some ice and bust your ass!" Kenzie laughed, her friend laughing with her.

"It's a risk I have to take. How was your trip?"

"Long! I flew from Phuket to Bangkok to Tokyo to Los Angeles to Chicago and then from Chicago to here. I've been on a plane for an eternity!"

"At least you flew first class. You did fly first class, right?"

Kenzie laughed. "Yes, and I will expense it, thank you very much! But you didn't have to come get me. I could have gotten a taxi."

"That would have cost one of us an unnecessary fortune! It didn't make any sense. Besides, I've been dying to find out what happened with you and the boyfriend."

Kenzie rolled her eyes. "Well, I appreciate you coming."

"Appreciate it when you make me forget that we're sitting in a boatload of traffic for an hour when the ride should only take thirty minutes. That snow has the roads completely jacked up!"

Kenzie nodded. "Let's grab my luggage and get on the way then."

Minutes later the two sat in bumper-to-bumper traffic on the Grand Central Parkway West, headed in the direction of the Triborough Bridge. They should have been mere minutes from the East 233rd Street exit, but it didn't look like they were going to be there anytime soon.

"So what happened?" Stephanie asked again. "It looks like you brought all your stuff back. I was sure you were going to tell me to sell your apartment and that you were headed back to Thailand for good."

"I did, too. But after my father died we just disconnected. It's been hard for us to find our way back to each other. I left because we needed some time apart. Right now, I don't know what's going to happen with us."

"Did you try? Because I know you, Kenzie. Did the pretty boxer fail some expectation of yours and suddenly become disposable? Because that would not be cool!"

Kenzie sighed, turning to stare out the window at the familiar landscape. She shook her head. "No. It wasn't like that. I think we're just afraid. Both of us." She cut an eye at her friend.

"Afraid of what?"

"Of losing each other. Walking away felt like it would just hurt less in the long run. So we walked away."

"Did you two at least talk about it?"

"We haven't talked much about anything since Kai's funeral."

"Do you love him, Kenzie?" Stephanie shifted in her seat to stare at her.

Kenzie nodded. Tears suddenly misted her

eyes. She didn't need to say anything; her eyes said it all.

Stephanie reached out and squeezed her hand. "Maybe you'll still get your happy ending."

"I don't believe in that fairy-tale crap, remember?"

"Well, I do. Maybe it'll be one of those *Pretty Woman* endings where he comes for you and climbs the fire escape as he professes his love, with the limousine waiting to whisk you both off to Neverland!"

Kenzie laughed. "Did you already fall down and bump your head?"

"I'm just not as jaded as you are."

"I'm not jaded. Not anymore."

"So why didn't you call me before you got on a plane? You always call me for advice about everything else."

"Because you would have talked me out of leaving, and I needed to put some space between me and him."

"And now you're regretting that decision, I'm sure."

"Why do you always have to be right!" Kenzie exclaimed. "I can't stand you!"

Stephanie shook her head as she finally steered the car off the exit and turned left. Ten minutes later they were pulling into the parking area of Kenzie's apartment building. "I stopped by earlier to turn the heat up. I watered your plants too."

"I didn't have any plants."

"You do now. I replaced that dead thing that's been sitting on your shelf since you moved in."

"I had a dead thing?" Kenzie laughed. "How's my cat, by the way?"

"You don't have a cat!" Stephanie eyed her with a raised brow and a bright smile.

"Yes, I do. Mr. Whiskers or something, I think."

"Girl, that's my cat. You babysat for him once. He was traumatized when I got him back, and I swore I'd never do that to him again. And his name is Chubby."

"Whatever."

The two women entered the immaculate one-bedroom apartment in the desirable Woodlawn section of the Bronx. When Kenzie had purchased the unit, it had been a dream come true. During the day, the modest space, a corner unit, was sun-drenched and boasted beautiful hardwood floors, custom crown moldings and trims, and ample closet space. The kitchen had been newly renovated, with stainless-steel appliances, and there'd been new fixtures in the bathroom. The apartment wasn't very large, but it had been enough room for

Kenzie, her computer, and the dreams that had followed her. The fact that the building was in commuter heaven, just blocks from Metro North, the express buses, and only a half hour from Manhattan was the icing on some very sweet cake.

But as Kenzie stepped inside, reacquainting herself with her surroundings, nothing about it felt like home. She turned to look at Stephanie, beginning to shake as she struggled not to cry. "So do you think Zachary really might come for me?"

Stephanie hugged her. "I sure as hell hope so, otherwise you're going to be miserable to deal with until you figure out you need to take the first step and just go back!"

Kenzie shook her head. "You mean even more miserable than usual?"

Stephanie chuckled. "Exactly!"

Kenzie shrugged. "Oh, well! Do we have anything to drink in this joint?"

"No, but if you want, we can walk up to Charlie's Bar and Kitchen."

Kenzie grabbed her coat and slipped it back on. "Last one there buys the chicken tacos!"

For the second time in his lifetime Zachary came home to find a woman he loved gone. This time his furniture was intact, but the emptiness was still as deep. Kenzie had flown out a week earlier. He imagined she was settled and content, but since neither had bothered to call the other, he didn't know. He knew she arrived safe and sound because she'd sent Gamon a message. She knew he was still being an ass because Gamon had responded that nothing with him had changed.

Gamon had taken her to the airport. Zachary had kissed her cheek good-bye, professing that he couldn't make time to take her himself. The moment had been awkward for them both, and now it was just lonely. He was suddenly kicking himself, his frustration deep. Truth be told, he hadn't wanted her to leave, but he didn't want her to see him beg.

Once Kenzie was gone, Zachary retreated into the fight ring, beating up on one sparring partner after another. He was robotic, moving by rote, refusing to allow an ounce of emotion get in his way. His routines were consistent — sleep, fight, run, fight, eat, fight, run, sleep — over and over again until he could do it with his eyes closed. Weeks later, when Sarai called to check on him, he was a semblance of his former self, completely lost in his heartbreak.

"You let her go?" Sarai admonished him

over the telephone line.

"She had an assignment. What was I supposed to do?"

"Fight for her. If you wanted her to stay, you should have told her. Kenzie loves you. She would never have left if she'd known that you had needed her."

"Do I?"

"Do you what?"

"Do I need her?"

"Don't we all need someone? Something in our lives that helps us make sense of the nonsense?"

Zachary shook his head. "Sarai, I don't know how it went so far left so quickly."

"You stopped communicating with her. You were hurting and trying to be so macho you didn't let her see that. You wouldn't allow yourself to be vulnerable with her."

"She needed me to be strong. To hold her up. I couldn't afford to be vulnerable."

"She needed you to be honest. We have all told you that time and time again. You hide behind your bravado when all you have to do is be truthful. Then you just got stupid and mean."

There was a moment of silence that filled the space between them. Sarai broke through the quiet.

"What do you want to do, Zachary?"

"I don't know, Sarai. I don't know what I want."

"Well, you better figure it out. If you care about Kenzie, don't let her get away!"

He changed the subject. "Did your father talk to you about the fight in Vegas?"

She blew a soft sigh. "He did. I've already started putting things into place. Alexander found a gym. I've coordinated your promotional schedule with the UFC, and you just need to let me know when you want to travel."

"I need Alexander's help again. I'm screwing up here, and the training's not what it should be. My form's bad, and all I'm doing is hammering away at these guys. I'm trying to decide if I should come back to Boulder before going to Vegas."

Sarai shook her head. "You need to fix what you've broken. Until you do, you're never going to be able to focus on this fight the way you need to, Zachary. You need Kenzie by your side. You know you do!"

A pregnant pause bloomed full and large between them. Sarai held her breath, quietly wishing a prayer that he would see the light and come to his senses. She could hear in his voice that he was ready for things to change. He was tired of being tired, ready to turn it back around and make it right.

She also knew he was embarrassed and his ego was waging war with his common sense. But she trusted he would come around and do right. He broke the silence by asking about his brother and his parents and catching up on the family news. The conversation was casual at best as he purposely avoided any serious discussion that wasn't about his business or his title fight. Then out of the blue, Zachary broke stance, the subject changing so swiftly that it almost threw Sarai off guard.

He whispered. "I want Kenzie back. I'm scared that I might lose her for good, and that breaks my heart."

"Then go get her!"

"I've been horrible to her. I don't know if she would even want me back."

"You need to call her."

"I would, but I'm mad."

Sarai laughed. "You're mad. Why are you mad?"

"Because Kenzie hasn't called me. Not once. She's spoken to your father twice, but she hasn't called me one time!"

"I swear! You are such a baby!"

"Whose side are you on?"

"Well, I'm definitely not going to support that kind of stupidity. She hasn't called me, so I'm not going to call her!" Sarai said mockingly.

Zachary hesitated, and then he laughed. He laughed until tears rained over his cheeks, and he had to fight to catch his breath.

"Are you okay?" Sarai questioned when he finally settled down, lightly gasping for air.

"Yeah." He coughed, clearing his throat before he continued. "I've just been so sad, Sarai! It hurt so much when Kai died. I didn't think I could hurt that much. And I was trying to hide it and be strong for Kenzie. When she suggested that I might be depressed and should talk to someone, I really withdrew. I didn't want to admit it."

"And now?"

"And now I think I'm ready. I think I am," he said hesitantly.

"Well, Kenzie was right, and she was hurting too. Now you need to go get her and beg her to come back to you. And I mean on your hands and knees begging!"

"Is that what you would want my brother to do?"

"He had better!" she said with a slight giggle. "Every woman wants to know that the man she loves will fight for her if it ever came down to it."

Alexander, who'd been listening in on the

line the whole time, finally interjected, adding to all the advice his brother was getting. "You better go get your woman!"

Zachary had been stuck in Chicago's O'Hare International Airport for half the day. He was frustrated and anxious to get to New York, but because of the inclement weather, it didn't look like anyone would be flying out anytime soon. The first five-hour leg of his travels, from Phuket to Beijing, had probably been the best part of his trip thus far. Beijing to Chicago had been fourteen hours of hell, with one baby crying nonstop and two frustrated old women complaining about everything, even the air they were breathing. And now he was snowed in. His only saving grace was that his brother had flown in from Boulder to meet him. Alexander eyed him with a bemused expression.

"You really need to relax. The departure board just changed, and they said we'll be boarding in the next hour." Alexander smiled.

"What if she doesn't want me back?"

Zachary's twin shook his head. "You really need to relax. Why haven't you called her anyway?"

"Because I didn't want her to tell me not

to come. I need to lay eyes on her and beg!"

"And you're begging for . . . ?"

"A second chance to get it right."

Alexander nodded. "I can appreciate that. I know I've had to beg Sarai a time or two."

Zachary finally dropped into the seat beside his brother. "Does it ever get easier?"

"When you get out of your way and you keep the lines of communication open, it gets easy as hell."

Zachary sat in reflection for a moment, pondering his brother's comment. He sighed heavily.

Alexander leaned forward in his seat. "I was really sorry to hear about Kai. I know how close you two were."

Zachary nodded. "Keeping his secrets took a lot out of me, A. The fact that Kenzie was hurt by what I did is what really tore me up."

"You can't look back, Z. You just need to look ahead to the future."

Zachary sighed again. "I guess, but that seems easier said than done. I can't imagine a future without Kenzie."

"And that's what you need to tell her."

The two sat quietly together for a good few minutes. Zachary suddenly sat forward in his seat. He looked his brother in the eye. "I need a favor after I get my girl back."

"What's that?"

"Antonio Barrera. He's gunning for me, and I really don't want to get my ass kicked! Not by a teeny bopper!"

Alexander laughed. "That *teeny bopper* has an impressive fight record. You know the bookies are betting against you, right?"

"Sons of bitches say I'm getting old!"

"You are!" Alexander grinned.

Zachary smiled back. "It's a damn good thing I have you on my side then. As soon as I get my girl back, I'm headed to the gym, and I want you to train me."

"Didn't I train you for that last fight?"

"That's why I want you to do it again. I won that fight, remember?"

Alexander laughed. "I guess I will. If I don't, my wife will kill me, and then I'll have to beg my way back into her good graces. Things are good with us right now, so I'd like to keep them that way."

The brothers bumped fists.

Zachary leaned back in his seat. "After this, I'm officially retiring. Then I'm going back to Thailand to make babies."

Alexander chuckled. "How many are you planning on making?"

Zachary winked his eye. "One set of twins. That's all. After that I just plan to practice a lot."

■ ■ ■ ■

He hadn't made any effort to call her, and Kenzie was past the point of being royally pissed. She couldn't begin to understand how Zachary could just dismiss her so easily. She stomped the hardwood floors for the umpteenth time, throwing her cell phone back against the bed. She pulled a hand through her hair, the tangled mess beginning to become a problem she had no desire to deal with.

Although she knew she needed to attempt to pull her Denman brush through the thick waves before her meeting at Madison Square Garden to interview some of the New York Knicks team and their owner, she could only think of Zachary, wondering where he was and why he wasn't trying to fix their broken relationship.

For a brief moment, she thought about calling Gamon and the main number at Revolution, but she didn't want to be embarrassed if Zachary rejected her. She didn't want to blow a gasket and have whoever answered remember who she was in case she did ever go back. Frustrated, she stomped in the opposite direction.

"Aargh!" she screamed, grateful that the

walls were thick and the likelihood of one of her neighbors hearing her was slim and nil.

The knock at the door surprised her. She knew Stephanie was already knee-deep in work at her office, so she wasn't expecting anyone to just drop in. As she moved toward the entrance, she prayed that it wasn't the old woman from the apartment at the other end of the hall. She talked too much, and Kenzie didn't want to be bothered.

She snatched the entrance open, not thinking to look through the peephole. The Barrett twins stood outside her home, both men looking contrite.

Zachary waved. "Hey, can we come in?"

Her eyes widened. "What are you doing here?"

He pushed past her, his brother stepping inside too as Kenzie looked from one to the other. Alexander leaned to kiss her cheek. "Hi, Kenzie."

"Alexander, hey!" Confusion washed over her expression.

"I hope we're not interrupting," Alexander said as the couple stood in the center of the room, staring at each other.

She shook her head. "Why didn't you call me?" she asked, her gaze connecting with Zachary's. Attitude seeped from her stare.

He reached into his jacket pocket for his cell phone, passing the device to her. "It's dead. I lost the power cord, and I haven't been able to charge it."

Kenzie shot Alexander a look. "And what's your excuse?"

The man's eyes widened. "Did you try to call me?" He looked down to the phone in his hand.

"No. But you could have lent your brother your phone to call me since his has been dead *since I left Thailand,*" she said sarcastically. "I was worried to death about him."

Alexander laughed. "He didn't ask, so I didn't volunteer. Sorry."

Her gaze rolled skyward in annoyance. She stepped against Zachary, her arms moving around his neck as she pressed her mouth to his. She kissed him, her mouth reclaiming his lips, her tongue darting past the line of his teeth as he pressed himself against her. His arms circled her waist and held her close.

She suddenly stepped out of his grasp. "I am so damn mad at you right now!"

Zachary nodded. "I deserve that."

Alexander laughed again. "I'm going to head to the hotel and get settled in. Give you two some privacy. The meter on that taxi is still running downstairs." He shook his brother's hand and kissed Kenzie one last time. "Go easy on him," he whispered in her ear as she walked him to the door. "He really feels bad!"

She nodded. "Is he doing okay?" she asked, whispering back.

Alexander nodded. "He's better. He'll be great once you two fix whatever it is that's broken between you."

Kenzie smiled. "Thank you," she mouthed as she closed the entrance after him.

She turned back to face Zachary. He'd moved into the living room, eyeing the things that decorated her space and spoke to who she was. There were framed articles that she had written on the walls. Her journalism awards. Pictures of friends and family who were near and dear to her. He drummed his fingers against a desktop that held an old typewriter. And there were books, title after title of stories that had captured her interest.

She took a deep breath. "How have you been?"

He turned around to face her. He shook his head. "I'm not good without you, Kenzie. Nothing feels right anymore."

Kenzie nodded, understanding completely. "I was afraid that you'd broken up with me."

He chuckled. "I was thinking the same thing about you. You left me!"

"You didn't try to stop me!"

"I thought about it. I really did. I just couldn't get it out. Or right. Or have it make sense so that you didn't think I was crazy."

She shook her head, her arms crossing over her chest. "That is such a load of . . ."

"I'm here to get you back, though," he said, cutting her off. "I love you, Kenzie. That has never changed."

She gestured for him to take a seat on her sofa. When they were settled side by side, she continued their conversation. "What went wrong with us, Zachary? After my father died you pulled away from me, and I really thought that our going through the same heartache would have pulled us closer together. None of it made sense to me."

He nodded. "I was struggling, baby. I was trying so hard to be strong for you, but I didn't feel worthy, and then I didn't have the strength to keep up that façade. It all just seemed to fall apart after that."

"I know we joke and make light of things, but I think we hit a serious impasse. I can't be in a relationship with a man who goes on the attack when we hit a bump. And I felt like you were attacking me, Zachary."

He nodded as he leaned forward, dropping his elbows to his thighs and his head into his hands. "I can only apologize again for my bad behavior. I know I was wrong on multiple levels. I let my feelings get in the way of what was right. I pushed you away, and . . ." Zachary suddenly choked, his words catching in his throat. Tears misted his eyes as he sat back, his fists clenched tightly together. He took a deep breath. "I pushed you away because I was scared that if you saw how weak I was, you would leave me."

Kenzie dropped a warm palm against his tightened fist, pulling his arm to her chest. She pressed his palm to her heart as her fingers lightly trailed over his wrist. "And I left you because I was scared too. I was scared that what I thought we had was ending. That it had all been a beautiful dream and we were suddenly falling into this horrific nightmare. And I didn't want to be that woman who put her whole heart into a man to have him just trash it. I didn't want you to see how much that was hurting me."

He sighed. "I didn't tell you enough that I love you. I didn't say it every day, or multiple times a day, because I assumed you knew it and trusted it. Because I do, Kenzie! I love you with every ounce of breath I have in my body!"

"Don't assume. You know we both have trust issues!"

He smiled. "I promise I'll do better."

"You're going to have to do *much* better. If you're going to be in a relationship with me, you need to work on that stank attitude of yours! That shit's just not cool!"

"If you promise to work on that foul mouth of yours! I swear you cuss too damn much!" he laughed.

Thirty minutes later the two had talked until they'd both heard everything they felt they needed to hear. The emotions had run high a time or two, but both trusted that what they were feeling for each other was what would sustain them in the years to come. It felt good. It felt right. And both believed wholeheartedly that the other was their future, fate sealing the deal between them.

"So what now? Where do we go from here?" Kenzie asked.

Zachary stared at her, his eyes skipping across her face. He suddenly dropped to one knee in front of her, reaching for her hand. "Marry me."

Kenzie's eyes widened in pure shock. "Zachary!"

"Marry me. Be my wife. I'm committed to fighting some damn good fights with you because I love you more than anything else in the world."

Zachary reached into his coat pocket and pulled out a black velvet box. Kenzie's eyes widened even more, her stunned expression moving him to smile. He slowly lifted the lid on the box, exposing the sweetest engagement ring. There sat a princess-cut diamond set in a 14K gold band. He extended it in her direction.

"Your father asked me to hold onto this for you. He had bought it for your mother, and since that didn't work out, he tucked it away to save for you. He said that he had planned to give it to the man you fell in love with, and he entrusted me to do just that. I don't think he imagined that I would have been that man. But here it is. Now, if you don't like it, we can always get you any ring you want, baby, but I couldn't come here empty-handed, and I think Kai would have definitely approved. So marry me, Kenzie!" he said as he slipped the ring onto her finger.

Tears of sheer joy rained down Kenzie's cheeks. She dropped to her knees beside him, her arms sliding around his neck. She pressed her mouth to his and kissed him passionately. "Yes!" she exclaimed. "Yes, yes, yes, yes, yes!" she screamed excitedly.

Zachary reclaimed her mouth, kissing her possessively. It was a tongue-entwined connection that reminded them of everything they had shared and the wealth of love that had grown from their experiences together.

"We need to plan," he said as he sat back on the couch, pulling her into his lap. "We have so many decisions to make!"

She nodded. "We do, but we're going to have to do it later," she said as she stole a glance toward the clock on the wall. "I have an interview, and I need to get ready." She tugged at her hair.

He nodded. "Is this your Knicks thing?"

"Yeah! I'm meeting with the owner one last time and a few of the players at Madison Square Garden."

"Let me help," he said. He reached for the hairbrush that she'd rested on the coffee table.

She smiled as she turned around in her seat to give him access to her whole head. With the skills of a professional, Zachary parted her hair into four sections and slowly brushed the tangles from the strands. Before braiding each section away, he scratched and oiled her scalp. His touch was gentle and comforting, and Kenzie knew that there would be many times more when she would want him to play stylist, and she looked forward to him doing so.

When he was done, he kissed the back of her neck, pressing his lips gently against her skin. "Are you going to wear it down?" he asked.

She shook her head. "It's too cold. I'm going to wrap it in a turban, I think."

"It is freezing, and it's March. I'm really hoping you don't want to stay here in New York."

She laughed. "You would stay?"

"Baby, I'd do whatever you want. If you want this to be base camp for us, then it will be. What I'm not going to do is lose you."

She smiled. "I really like how you think, but I love living in Phuket. I'll take the rainy season over these New York winters any day of the year!"

"Boy, am I glad you said that," he said teasingly.

Kenzie rose from the seat and moved into the bedroom. He followed behind her, dropping down onto her bed as she stripped out of her clothes and moved into the shower.

"Hey, can I borrow your phone?" he called out.

She poked her head out of the bathroom. "Of course. Who are you calling?"

"My brother. I need to tell him I got my

girl back!"

When Kenzie stepped out of the shower, wrapping her bathrobe around her body, she could hear Zachary snoring. He'd fallen into a deep sleep, his body stretched across the length of her bed. She reached a hand out to touch him, wanting to be sure that he really was there and she hadn't been dreaming.

As she pulled on a pair of black slacks and a black turtleneck sweater she was tempted to call and cancel the interview, but she knew the sooner she finished, the sooner she would be able to head back home with Zachary. She wanted to go home.

She dropped down onto the bed by his side, suddenly marveling at the fact that she was going to be Zachary Barrett's wife. They intended to form a lifetime union, and that was no small step. Even in the dynamics of the apology and the reclaiming of what was most important to them both, the fire in their personalities had them bumping heads. But it was that fire that made their being together possible in the first place. They challenged each other. They pushed each other. They motivated one another, and even in those moments when one or the other feared that it might not work, the fire between them refused to be extinguished.

She was going to be Zachary Barrett's wife. She was going to be the mother of his children, his partner in business, his companion in old age. She was suddenly overwhelmed by the magnitude of that responsibility. And then she thought about the flip side of that. Zachary Barrett was going to be her husband! She hoped he was up for the task because she knew that it wasn't going to be easy for him or any man!

She gently eased her cell phone from the palm of his hands. He snorted as he rolled from her, his body easing to the other side of the bed. Rising, she draped a warm blanket over his torso. Then she moved into the other room, excited to call her friend Stephanie and share her good news.

Chapter Sixteen

When Zachary woke up, it was dark outside, only the faintest light peeking in from the other room. For a brief moment he didn't know where he was, a wave of hesitation washing over him as his head snapped from side to side trying to recognize something or someone. He sat upright in the bed and then remembered that he was in the Bronx, in his baby's bed.

He threw his legs off the side of the mattress. Kenzie had removed his shoes and his socks, and he winced when his bare feet hit the wood floors. The air was cooler than he was accustomed to, and he was suddenly longing for the heat of Thailand. He took a deep breath and then a second as he stretched his arms high over his head.

He stood up and moved into the bathroom to empty his bladder and wash the sludge from his eyes. When he finally felt fully awake, he headed toward the living area, calling out her name. "Kenzie?"

"In here!" she called back. She turned to meet his gaze as he moved into the room. She was sitting in front of her computer, her fingers flying across the keyboard. "You're awake!"

He nodded. "How long have I been asleep?"

She turned to look at the clock. "About six hours. You were exhausted!"

He shook his head in disbelief. "I need to call Alexander. He didn't answer when I called him earlier."

"He called you. He said to tell you that he already grabbed dinner and was headed in for the night. The change in temperature has him feeling a little under the weather. He said he would meet us in the morning for breakfast."

Zachary nodded. "Have you eaten?"

"I wanted to wait for you. I picked up some groceries before I came back in. It's so cold out I figured I'd cook something for the two of us."

"You cook?"

Kenzie laughed. "Yes, I cook . . . sort of!"

He grinned. "I really need to take a shower." He lifted his arm and sniffed. "Yeah, I can definitely use some soap and water."

She shook her head. "Well, why don't you go use the last of the hot water while I put the roast beef on."

"We're having roast beef?"

"My version of a Philly cheesesteak. I'm going to sauté an onion and a green pepper, warm up the roast beef, and layer it on a hoagie roll with Swiss cheese. A few seconds under the broiler and we'll have dinner. I already made a salad."

"It sounds good." He turned then hesitated. "What do you do for exercise around here?"

Kenzie chuckled softly. "We have a gym here in the building. When the roads are clear, you can always run. And if push comes to shove, you can always get a membership at 24-Hour Fitness, which is about three blocks from here."

He nodded. "I am so glad you want to go back to Phuket," he said matter-of-factly. "There's no way I can train for my fight here."

"That's not true. Baby, this is New York. If it exists, it can be found here somewhere!"

"I've already looked. The one gym that would best meet my needs is the home court of the one and only Antonio Barrera. I can't train where my opponent trains."

"When we're home, you train wherever,

whenever. You make it work, and you do a great job of that. You could easily do the same thing here. I know you can."

He thought about her comment for a moment. He slowly nodded his head in understanding. He turned back toward the bathroom. "I really like it when you refer to Phuket as *our home*!"

"Me, too," she quipped as she tossed him a look over her shoulder.

Zachary gave her a wink of his eye as he hummed his way back to the bathroom and she began to prep their evening meal. He'd been standing beneath the spray of warm water for a good few minutes when the sliding glass shower door slid open and Kenzie stepped inside.

He grinned as she pressed her naked body against his, easing up on her toes to kiss his mouth.

"What about dinner?" he muttered softly as her kisses moved from his lips, across his jawline, into the warmth of his neck. Her mouth was warm and wet and teasing, and his whole body quivered in anticipation.

Kenzie shrugged. "I want dessert first!"

Hours later they sat naked atop her bed, sharing a bowl of orange sorbet. It was almost three in the morning, and sleep was eluding them both. There was too much to talk about, and the conversation was flowing smoothly.

Kenzie lifted the spoon to his lips, and Zachary sucked the chilled sweetness into his mouth.

"I am not supposed to be eating this," he said as he licked a drop of sorbet from her fingers. "My brother will have a fit if he finds out."

"I won't tell," she said as she took the next bite of the icy goodness.

"I really need to be good, though. I do have a title fight coming up."

"I'm still not comfortable with you and this fight, Zachary. I've been watching some of Barrera's fights on YouTube, and he's vicious. Are you really certain about being ready?"

"I have the best team in the business who will help me get ready. It's going to be fine."

She nodded. "What do you have planned after this fight? What's next for you?"

He hesitated for a moment. He'd given that question a lot of thought since signing his name to the contract that would put him back into the fight ring. He knew that this would more than likely be the last fight of his career, and he was more than ready for that. It was getting harder to get his body to cooperate, and he'd gotten to a point where he just didn't want to do it anymore. His answering her question was actually easier than she probably imagined it would be.

"I'm done after this, Kenzie. This is going to be my swan song. I hope to retire still holding the title belt, but if that doesn't happen, I'm okay with it."

"If you're ready to quit, why bother to fight this fight and take the risks you're taking?

He exhaled, a heavy breath blowing against her face. "One, this will be the biggest payday of my career, and two, I just want to prove to myself and everyone else that I still have it. There's this little voice in the back of my head telling me to go for it."

"It's probably my father's ghost!" She chuckled softly.

Zachary laughed heartily. "I was thinking the same thing!"

Kenzie said, "You know I'll support whatever you want to do, but please be careful."

"Always."

"Have you ironed out all the details?"

He nodded. "We're fighting in Vegas. In six weeks."

"Six weeks! Are you kidding?" Anxiety washed over her expression as she suddenly realized how much time had passed since he'd first told her about the fight.

"Actually I'm very serious."

"Six weeks doesn't seem like enough time for you to get ready. That really scares me!"

"I'm in pretty good shape, Kenzie. It's not like I'm starting from scratch to get ready. You just need to trust me to do what I do."

She took a deep breath. She leaned forward to kiss the sugar from his lips. "So when do you plan to marry me. Before the fight or after?"

"Whenever you're ready, I'm ready. Do you want a big wedding or something smaller?"

"Could we just go to the courthouse? I don't need anything fancy. I just want to say *I do* and be done."

"A woman who doesn't want a wedding?"

"I never believed in marriage, remember? I think we've both made some serious progress to even be thinking about tying the knot!"

He smiled. "We can do it in Vegas or Colorado."

"Colorado?"

"When we leave here I'm going to my brother's gym in Boulder to get ready for the fight. I don't know what the rules are there, but if you choose Vegas, there are no rules. No blood tests, no waiting period, no hassle."

"If we pick Vegas, Elvis could marry us," she said teasingly.

He laughed. "There are no limits in Vegas, but I don't know if I can work with an Elvis impersonator. I don't want to feel like my marriage is pretend. We'll need a real minister."

"Well," Kenzie said as she set the spoon and empty bowl against the nightstand, "whatever we decide to do, let's commit to doing it before we go back to Thailand. I hear the marriage ceremony there is even longer than the funeral ceremony. I don't think either one of us could take all that chanting from the monks again."

He nodded. "You'll get no argument from me there!"

There was a brief moment of pause.

"How did your interview go this afternoon?" Zachary asked, changing the subject.

"It was good. In fact, I'm actually done with the story. This meeting was more about my fact-checking than anything else. I'd like to submit it before we leave, but if that's not possible, it won't be a problem."

"If you need to spend a few more days here, I understand, but I need to go. I need to get to work."

She nodded. "Let me talk to Stephanie tomorrow, and we can decide then. I want you to meet her before you leave, though."

"I look forward to getting to know her. What about your mother? I'd like to meet the woman who stole Kai Tamura's heart."

"And I'm sure you will. One day. It just won't be anytime soon. She is on a cruise ship in the Greek isles right now. Something about finding herself a tycoon to be my stepdaddy."

Zachary laughed. "That sounds like the woman Kai told me about. What about our wedding? Do you want her there?"

Kenzie chuckled. "You're going to discover that my mother really isn't the maternal type. I'll send her a message, but if there's nothing in it for her, she's not going to go out of her way to be there."

"Are you okay with that?"

Kenzie smiled. "She's my mother. It's nothing that I'm not used to. I'm good. I swear."

Zachary nodded, leaning to kiss her cheek.

Kenzie yawned, sleep beginning to sneak in and lay claim to her body. She lay back against the pillows, propping them beneath her head and torso. She opened her legs. Wide. Exposing the best of her most intimate place. The seductive look she gave him was taunting, her eyes voicing nothing but need. She teased a finger across her clit and then past her lips, sucking it in like a lollipop.

Zachary felt his dick go rock hard with no hint of hesitation. Kenzie was totally naked, her knees spread apart as her right hand began to rub at her crotch. He leaned forward to eye her private spot, her fingers moving up and down and side to side. He bit down against his bottom lip, desire seeping with a vengeance from his eyes. Kenzie moaned softly, the sound exquisite to his ears as her knees came together to clamp her hand in the tight recess between her legs. Her body shivered and she closed her eyes, her movements intent on getting them both heated.

She brought her hand to her mouth a second time, tasting her own juices, and his cock twitched as he eyed her, feeling like an electrical impulse had surged from somewhere deep in his midsection. Despite his best efforts, he could barely contain his excitement, or his erection, but he tried to keep his expression calm and cool as he watched her.

"You are such a tease!" he exclaimed, his voice dropping an octave. He clenched his fists together, determined to hold off touching her and himself.

Kenzie smiled, her eyes still closed as she continued pleasuring herself. She shifted her feet and knees apart even further, practically doing a split against the mattress. Zachary lifted himself up, pushing her shoulders back as he moved above her. He knelt down between her parted legs and ran his index finger along the length of her folds. She was moist and sticky, the evidence of her arousal coating the tip of his finger.

He eased himself forward, his head dropping as he inhaled her aroma. Blood surged through his cock, his member practically pulsating. He fought the urge to touch himself, instead leaning forward to lick her in long strokes across the hood of her clit. Kenzie shuddered as he focused his attention on the hardened button. He shifted his mouth from side to side as he sucked her in. Her body moved beneath him, her buttocks sliding over the cotton sheets. Her belly quivered and her breath caught in her throat as she gave into the pleasure. She rested her hands on her breasts, grabbing her erect nipples as she began to rub them between her open fingers.

Zachary pushed her open even further, guiding one knee toward her shoulder as he draped her other leg across his back. She was soon moaning on every exhalation, and then he pressed his middle finger past her opening, sliding it easily inside. He wiggled it, the sensation almost too much for Kenzie to handle.

She began to vibrate against the bed, her hips lifting upward as she pushed against his palm. He kept his mouth suctioned to her clit, his tongue lapping at her rapidly. Her moans had become a low whimper, and then she orgasmed, her body going rigid as her legs pinned his head in place. Her torso arched upward, her head thrown backward. Her neck was elongated, the veins pulsing as if they too were ready to pop.

Dropping down from the intensity of the explosion, her body slowly stopped convulsing, beginning to fall limp. Her breathing was still heavy, coming down slowly as she loosened the grip she had on the bedclothes clasped tightly between her clenched fists. Her face was flushed, and a thin sheen of perspiration dripped between her breasts.

Zachary's dick was still hard as a rock and jutting from his body in need of some attention. He shifted himself up and forward until his knees were on either side of her head, his buttocks hovering over her breasts. He grabbed the base of his thick shaft and then he fed it to her, easing his member past her lips.

Kenzie latched on, her mouth enveloping his manhood like a warm blanket. He closed his eyes, momentarily sliding into the sensations that were bombarding his cock. Kenzie reached her hand up to stroke him while she worked her mouth up and down against him. Unable to contain himself, Zachary began to rhythmically match her thrusts as she slid him over her tongue again and again.

Zachary was giddy, lost in a reverie of sensations. He suddenly pushed himself from her body, moving to stand by the side of the bed. He pulled Kenzie to him, sliding her buttocks to the edge of the mattress and over the edge of the bed. He grabbed an ankle in each hand and pushed her legs apart.

Kenzie eyed him with anticipation, the excitement seeping past her thick lashes. And then he thrust himself into her, the tip of his cock pushing into her as far as he could go. He thrust himself in, hard and fast, until he was firmly embedded in the depths of her core, the sound of his thighs slapping against hers echoing around the small space.

Kenzie gasped, loudly, as Zachary pounded himself against her, withdrawing his body just enough to slam back into her. He released her legs and clasped her around the waist, thrusting with the velocity of a piston gone awry. He lasted no time at all before he screamed her name, burying his cock deep inside her one last time. His seed spilled deep inside her. He could feel himself pulsing in the warm, wet cavity as she clenched and tightened her muscles, determined to take all of him in. And then he fell against her, both completely lost in the intensity of their desire for each other.

They fell asleep wrapped tightly around each other. Kenzie was curled in a fetal position on her side, while Zachary held her in his arms, his thick limbs wrapped vice-like around her torso. Their breathing was synced nicely, each inhale and exhale of breath like the beat of the drumline pulsing in their chests.

They slept well, comfort coming after too many days of restlessness. Nightmares no longer plagued the duo, both settling into the sweetest dreams.

Stephanie had given the two brothers the once-over when they entered the restaurant. Their breakfast meeting with her agent and his twin had turned to brunch when their late-night frolics had caused Zachary and

Kenzie to oversleep.

The young woman hummed her appreciation as her eyes widened. "Lord, have mercy!" she exclaimed, muttering under her breath.

Kenzie giggled. "Down girl," she muttered back. "They are both taken."

"Is there a triplet somewhere?" Stephanie asked, her voice a low whisper.

"Sorry, girl, no triplet. Just the pair."

Stephanie shook her head.

Across the room, the two men stood in conversation with a sports fan. The excited young man and his sister had them cornered, wanting autographs and pictures. The two had been on selfie overload since they'd walked into the building and had been recognized.

When they were finally able to head toward the table, Kenzie grinned brightly, amused by her good friend's sudden case of nerves.

"Stop shaking, stop shaking, stop shaking!" Stephanie muttered under her breath.

Kenzie laughed. 'You are such a fool!"

"It is a sin and a crime for two men to be that pretty! Damn, those two brothers are *foine*!"

"We'll take that as a compliment," Zachary said as he extended his hand in greeting.

"It's very nice to meet you, Stephanie."

The young woman rose from her seat to hug one brother and then the other. "It's so nice to meet you both," she said.

Zachary kissed Kenzie on her lips and settled in the seat beside her. Alexander kissed her on the cheek, hugging her shoulders.

"So, how are you ladies doing this afternoon?" Alexander asked as he pulled out the chair beside her friend.

"We're good," Kenzie said. "How are you doing?"

The man nodded. "I'm ready to head back to warmer weather. It's just too cold here for me."

Both women laughed.

"This isn't cold," Stephanie said. "We're supposed to get cold weather later in the week. And it's a fluke. By now we should be getting more seasonal temperatures. Mother Nature is pissed about something."

"I'm glad that we'll be back in Colorado by then," Zachary said. "It might be chilly, but nothing like this."

Their waiter paused at the table to take their order. When everyone had selected something from the menu, including a round of white wine for the table, they all sat back in their seats, the conversation comfortable and easy.

"You know you're not supposed to be drinking, right?" Alexander shot his brother a look.

Zachary shrugged. "Last one!"

Stephanie looked from one to the other, her gaze stopping on Zachary's face. "You're not an alcoholic, are you?"

Kenzie laughed. "No, he is not. He's supposed to be in training."

"Oh, you're fighting again?"

Zachary nodded. "I'm defending my title in Vegas in a few weeks."

"Five weeks, to be exact!" Alexander added.

Kenzie bristled. "Five? I thought it was six?"

The two brothers exchanged a look. "Five weeks, six, it's soon," Alexander noted, trying to clean up his faux pas.

Kenzie turned to stare at her man. "Do not start our marriage off by making me mad at you, Zachary Barrett!"

Alexander sat forward in his seat. Excitement washed over his face. "Marriage? You two are getting married? When did this happen?" He shook his brother's hand, pumping his arm excitedly.

"I asked her last night, and Kenzie said yes!"

Kenzie held up her hand and wriggled her fingers.

"It's about time!" Alexander exclaimed. He stood and moved to the other side of the table to give Kenzie a big bear hug. "I am so happy for you two. Sarai is going to be thrilled."

Kenzie grinned. "Thank you!" She squeezed Zachary's hand.

"Have you set a date yet?" Stephanie asked.

The couple exchanged a look. "It's going to be a very short engagement," Kenzie said.

Her friend nodded. "Well, I'm ecstatic for you. It means I won our bet!"

Kenzie rolled her eyes. "We did not have a bet!"

"I'm sure we did. I'm sure we put some kind of money on you getting that fairy-tale ending we talked about."

Kenzie shook her head. "We didn't!" she said, laughing warmly.

"Knowing you," Stephanie said, "I'm sure it's going to be a non-traditional ceremony!"

"She wants a Vegas ceremony with Elvis officiating," Zachary laughed.

"That's definitely non-traditional," Alexander said, laughing with his brother.

"It won't be all that!" Kenzie noted with a shake of her head.

The conversation moved from their future plans to Zachary's training regime. They talked about Alexander's wife, a former Miss Thailand, the two training facilities that the two men owned, and their thoughts on pending political elections, ending with the duo recapping their favorite old-school television programs. Somewhere in the midst of it all, there had been stories about Kenzie and Stephanie's friendship, their college antics, and the many impossible situations the dynamic duo had gotten themselves into since befriending each other. It was a good time, and by dessert, the laughter was abundant, the bonds of friendship solidified, and plans made for them to definitely get together again.

Both men recognized that the relationship between the two women was more family than friend. Each was the sister the other had never known. The two bantered much like any pairing that had been through some thick and thin with each other. Together, Kenzie and Stephanie were fun and funny and extremely protective of each other.

When Kenzie excused herself to go to the restroom, Stephanie leaned across the table toward Zachary. The gesture was almost conspiratorial. Zachary leaned in to meet her.

"Kenzie has never trusted any man before you. And she trusts you. So if you hurt her, I will come for you," she said, her tone as casual as if she were talking about the weather. "I just want to give you fair warning."

Zachary smiled. "I love her. I will do everything in my power to make Kenzie happy. I'm not going to hurt her, and I'm not going to let anyone else hurt her either."

Stephanie sat back in her seat. She looked toward Alexander. "How do you feel about the two of them?"

Alexander smiled. "Those two were meant to be together. My brother loves her. And if he does anything to break her heart, I'll help you come for him. You have my word on that."

The young woman nodded. "I'm going to trust you both then."

The midday meal lasted a good two hours. As they rose from their seats to leave, Kenzie and Stephanie hugged each other tightly.

"My article is done. I emailed it earlier this morning."

Stephanie gave her a thumbs-up. "I haven't checked my messages yet, but I will the minute I get back to the office."

"I'm going to take a few weeks off. I'm

going with Zachary to Colorado, and then I'll be in Vegas with him. I know I'll have too much going on to take on any new assignments."

"No worries. I'll only query something if it's super spectacular and I know you're the only writer that it would be perfect for."

"There's something I've been thinking about that I might pitch to you in a few weeks. After that, we'll go from there."

Stephanie nodded. "The minute you have a date, let me know. I can't miss your wedding. That would be sacrilegious!"

"You just want to make sure I go through with it!"

"That too!"

Kenzie smiled. "Can you go by my apartment and water my plants for me, please? I don't know yet if I'm going to rent it out or sell it, but as soon as Zachary and I figure it out, I'll let you know."

Stephanie hugged her a second time. "If you change your mind about him," she gestured with her thumb toward Zachary, "I'll be here for you."

Zachary lifted his hands as if he were surrendering. He chuckled warmly.

Kenzie laughed, then shot him a wink. "Thanks, but I think I'm going to keep him!"

Chapter Seventeen

Boulder, Colorado, had to be one of the prettiest places Kenzie had ever seen. From the moment they'd left the airport, she'd felt as if she'd been dropped into the center of a picture-perfect postcard. Surrounded by stunning mountains called the Flatirons and with crystal clear Boulder Creek within a stone's throw of the downtown area, it was all simply extraordinary.

Neither of the twins had prepared her for what to expect. So when Sarai picked them up from the airport and drove straight to Alexander's gym, she was completely awed. Champs was a new, 120,000-square-foot athletic facility. The high-tech glass building sat on twenty-six acres of prime Boulder real estate with a panoramic view of the mountains in the distance.

When Kenzie had been writing her article about the two brothers, she'd read all their promotional brochures and knew that the marketing material deemed it the premier destination for health and fitness enthusiasts. Alexander and Sarai both had explained how it had been designed to give their members an unparalleled gym experience that supported all of their health and fitness aspirations. And despite the many photos she had studied and everything good that had been written about it, she really hadn't known what to expect. She was delighted to share that it exceeded her expectations and then some.

Alexander was extolling about everything good at the facility as they stepped out of the minivan and headed inside. "It really is my dream come true. We offer indoor and outdoor pools, nationally renowned group-fitness instructors and personal trainers, an indoor cycling studio, and cutting-edge fitness equipment. Our programming includes multiple weight-loss options, yoga, dance, and Pilates classes, indoor-cycling classes, outdoor-cycling rides, and so much more! If you *like* a gym you will *love* Champs!" he exclaimed.

Kenzie pointed to the sign on the door that shared the operating hours and contact information. "You don't ever close?" she asked.

Zachary laughed. "Good health doesn't

take a holiday, baby!"

Inside, they were inundated with fans and employees greeting the two brothers. It was quickly apparent that their star status knew no boundaries. There was a bright light shining on their notoriety, and with Zachary there to prepare for his title fight, it didn't look like it was going to dim anytime soon.

Kenzie stood off to the side as he was surrounded from all directions, the excitement surrounding his arrival enough to have her second-guessing if following him might have been a bad idea. Suddenly he was slightly boastful, with just the faintest hint of arrogance. It was that side of Zachary that she'd first gotten to know when he'd been in full champion mode. Sarai seemed to read her mind as she eased to her side.

Sarai slipped her arm through Kenzie's. "Zachary is very good with his public persona. He switches it on. He switches it off! The fans love the man that is a champion!"

Kenzie smiled. "I love that man."

"It makes my heart sing that you two were able to work things out. He needed you in his life, and I can tell by the way he looks at you that you make him very happy!"

"I hope that I make him as happy as he makes me."

Sarai smiled. "Come, let me give you a tour. We can catch up with our men later. Plus, I want to hear everything! I'm so excited that we are going to be sisters! It will be so nice to have another woman around who isn't trying to get with my man!"

Out of the corner of his eye, Zachary spied Kenzie as the two women walked off arm in arm. He smiled, something like joy washing over his spirit as his two favorite women in the whole wide world bonded. He tossed a quick look in his brother's direction.

Alexander nodded and smiled. "She's so happy for the two of you," he said, referring to his wife. "She predicted you and Kenzie were going to hook up before everyone else did!"

"You know I need Sarai to really like Kenzie, right?"

His brother nodded. "Yeah, I do, and I can say with reasonable certainty that you don't have anything to worry about."

The robust woman in the private office leapt from her seat, rushing to Zachary's side as he and Kenzie entered the room. Lynn Barrett hugged her son tightly, tears raining down over her cheeks. She pulled back to stare at him, then leaned in to hug him tightly a second time.

"Hey, Mama Lynn!" Zachary exclaimed as he kissed his mother's round cheek and hugged her back. "I swear you've gotten prettier since I've been gone!"

Kenzie didn't need to be told that the woman was Zachary and Alexander's stepmother. Lynn Barrett had raised them after their biological mother, Carolyn Barrett, had passed away from breast cancer when they'd been four years old. Zachary had fond memories of the time his Mama Lynn had spent bonding with the two of them by way of her gas oven. She had come into their lives, cooking and cleaning for them and loving them wholeheartedly as if they were her own.

She ran a shaky hand down the front of her blouse, then she tugged on the lavender-colored wig she wore on her head. Mama Lynn fanned that hand at him, words caught in her throat as she fought the urge to cry.

Behind her, Zachary's father moved from the leather executive's chair onto his feet. He stood as tall as his sons, but his coloring was all Alexander, the same burnt-umber complexion. There was no missing where the two younger men had gotten their good looks; the twins were his spitting image.

Even with his snow-white curls and a slightly rounded beer belly, Westley Barrett still turned a few heads.

Zachary introduced Kenzie to his family. "Dad, Mama Lynn, this is Kenzie Monroe. Kenzie, these are my parents, Lynn and Westley Barrett!" Zachary wrapped his arms around her shoulders and pulled her close. The gesture was possessive, and it didn't go unnoticed.

"It's a pleasure to meet you both," Kenzie said. She extended her hand. "We actually spoke on the phone a few months ago when I was doing the magazine article about your sons."

Mama Lynn wrapped Kenzie in a warm hug. "Kenzie, welcome to Boulder. We've heard so much about you."

"Not from me," Zachary teased, his head waving. "I haven't told them anything about you!"

Westley narrowed his gaze, fanning his own hand at his son. "Don't pay him no mind. It's a pleasure to meet you, too, Kenzie."

She smiled sweetly.

"Did you come right from the airport?" Mama Lynn asked.

Zachary nodded. "We were just about to head to the house and get settled in."

"Are you two staying with Sarai and your brother?"

Zachary shook his head. "No. I rented the house on West Coach Road again."

Mama Lynn shook her head, her brow furrowed. "I don't know why you waste good money. You know you two could have stayed with us or your brother. It would not have been a problem."

"I know," Zachary said, "but Kenzie's a nudist, and she doesn't wear clothes when she's at home. I didn't want anyone to be embarrassed by her body parts!" He grinned.

Kenzie rolled her eyes skyward. "Really, Zachary?"

He laughed as he leaned to kiss her lips. "You didn't find that funny?"

His father laughed with him. "Nothing wrong with being naked. Folks need to get a sense of humor!" the patriarch said with a deep chuckle. "Your mama likes to run around in her birthday suit when there's no one around too!"

Mama Lynn swatted at the two men. "You both play too much. Ain't nobody got time for your nonsense," she chastised. She moved to give Kenzie another hug. "I'm cooking on Sunday, Kenzie. Plan to come for family dinner. I can't wait to sit down to talk with you more."

"Thank you. I really appreciate that."

The matriarch reached up to squeeze her son's cheek. "Stay out of trouble, please."

"Yes, ma'am."

She gestured for her husband. "Let's go, Daddy. We have our ballroom dancing class in ten minutes."

When the door was closed behind them, Zachary pulled Kenzie into his arms and kissed her. He kissed her like he hadn't kissed her for days, missing the feel of her mouth beneath his. The moment sent a chill up her spine, and for a brief second, she almost fell into the sensation, forgetting that they were still in a very public place. The moment might have proven embarrassing if anyone had walked in unannounced.

She pulled herself from his grasp. "Mmm," she purred. "That was very nice, but we need to take it someplace else, I think."

Zachary hummed into her ear. "I'm ready to take you right on that desk right there!" he said as he slipped a hand beneath the hem of her blouse, his palm caressing her breast.

She giggled softly. "You need to stop. What if your parents come back?"

He nuzzled his face into her hair. "They're not coming back."

"Well, your brother might want his office back," she muttered, beginning to pant slightly.

"He doesn't. He and Sarai are making out in their corner on the second floor." He tugged gently at her nipple, the protrusion suddenly hard as a piece of sugar candy. He nibbled that spot behind her ear that always made her purr.

Kenzie wrapped her arms around his neck and plunged her mouth back on his. The kiss was frantic and heated and would definitely have gone further if there hadn't been a knock on the office door.

Zachary cussed. "Damn!" he snapped as he stepped back, moving his hands in front of himself to adjust the bulge that had risen in his slacks. Kenzie eased around him, pulling the door open. Sarai stood smirking on the other side.

"Hi!" Kenzie said.

Sarai's gaze swept between the two of them. "I didn't mean to interrupt, but Alexander wanted you to have the keys to the company car. You're going to need some transportation while you're here." She extended the key ring, meeting the look Zachary was giving her.

Kenzie laughed as Zachary took the keys from his friend's hand. "Thank you," she said as she ran her hand against his broad back. "We were just headed to the house."

Sarai nodded. "We will see you tomorrow then." She was about to turn, and she hesitated. She took a step closer instead, leaning to whisper into Kenzie's ear. "There's a key in the top drawer on the left. You can lock the door from the inside, and no one can disturb you," she said as she turned, tossing Zachary one last glance.

He shook his head. "Thank you, Sarai!"

Sarai grinned, and then she closed the door behind herself.

"Are you ready to go?" Kenzie asked, turning her attention toward Zachary.

He grinned. "Hell no!" he said as he rounded the desk and pulled open the top drawer. He pulled the door key from its hiding spot. "I have a personal problem that I need a little help with!" he said as he moved back around to lock the door.

Kenzie laughed. "Well, I guess I need to see what I can do about that!"

The home on West Coach Road was also a pleasant surprise for Kenzie. The entire family had warned her that Zachary had previously rented the private property for him and Sarai when he had come to train for his last title fight. Sarai had come with him from Thailand, the timing prior to her and Alexander, when family and friends still had questions about her relationship with the two brothers.

The custom-built contemporary sat on thirty-four secluded acres in a private, gated community. The open design featured a spacious kitchen and family room, formal living and dining rooms, two master bedroom suites, and three additional bedrooms. There was also a lower level with a great room, an office, and an in-home gym with a walkout patio.

Zachary had rented the space fully furnished, and the home looked like an interior designer's showcase. With the incredible views and sweeping landscape that surrounded the property, it bordered on extravagant, and was bigger than her New York apartment and his bungalow in Phuket put together.

Kenzie moved from room to room, in awe that the expanse of pine trees and the mountains that sat in the distance could be seen from every window. Zachary led her to the master bedroom. When they'd deposited their luggage, he pulled her further down the hall to a second master bedroom at the opposite end.

"That's where Sarai used to stay," he said,

sensing that the question was on the tip of her tongue to ask.

She blew a soft sigh. "This place is stunning!" she said. "And it's so big!"

He nodded in agreement. "It's a very cool place," he said. "But I'm going to have a much better time here this visit!"

"Why is that?"

He pulled her down onto the bed, settling her in his lap as he cradled her close. "Because this time I get to christen all of the rooms with you!"

Days later Kenzie sat at a corner table in Starbucks, her computer, a notepad, pens, and a stack of loose-leaf paper strewn across the table. She rose from her seat to get a refill on the coffee she was drinking.

She had just pushed the SEND button on a thirty-page proposal that she'd been working on. The project was well out of her comfort zone, but she was excited about it and anxious to hear what Stephanie thought about the pitch.

The idea had come to her the night she'd had her moment with her father, when he'd had a burst of lucidity and had known who she was. The memory of that experience had left her thinking about other families and other children who'd gone through what she'd gone through. It had her wondering about other parents with Alzheimer's who'd lost touch with the children who loved them, who couldn't remember the friends and family that had been a part of their past and were desperate to be a part of their future. And from there the story she wanted to write had come.

The prospect of putting so much emotion into words actually scared Kenzie. She was a journalist, and she dealt in facts and figures. Checking and rechecking, then regurgitating what was already known and spinning it in a different direction required only an investment of time and energy. This project would require so much more. It would be something else entirely.

Kenzie had proposed a full-fledged book about the trauma of the disease and its impact on loved ones. She was proposing four-hundred-plus pages about Kai and his story and the story of others who knew what her hurt felt like. Writing about her experience with her father would leave her vulnerable and open to scrutiny. She didn't know if she was prepared for what that might mean, but she knew to not write the story would always leave her wondering what might have been.

Knowing that she would have to find others who were willing to share their stories had set the tone for the research that would need to be accomplished. Her proposal had included a plan to make that happen as well. And now she was beyond excited about the work she needed to do. She was motivated to write and excited about how easily the words flowed when she sat back and just let them do their own thing.

The young man behind the counter leered at her. He looked sixteen and pimply, so wet behind the ears that you could still smell his mother's milk on his breath. He'd been winking and trying to flirt since the first day she'd visited and found the seat in the corner.

"Have you tried the chocolate crunch cookies?" he asked as he refilled her cup with hot coffee. "They're really good! I'm Leo, by the way!"

"It's nice to meet you, Leo, and no, I haven't tried them," Kenzie said smiling. "But it will have to wait until after my wedding. A girl really needs to be able to get into her wedding dress!"

"Oh," he said, his disappointment acute. "You're engaged?"

She nodded. "I am."

"I didn't see no ring on your finger," he said as he gestured toward her right hand.

Kenzie smiled as she wriggled the fingers on her left hand. "It's there," she said. She gestured with her plastic cup. "Thanks, Leo," she said as she moved back to her seat and settled down with the fresh cup of brew. She took a sip and then a second, and then she went back to her writing, allowing the words to consume her.

An hour later, her telephone rang. Stephanie's face popped across the screen. Kenzie plugged her earphones into her ears and answered on the second ring.

"Hey!"

"Hey, yourself! How is that fine man of yours doing?"

"I'm doing just fine, thanks for asking."

"I know you're doing good. You're writing. Brilliantly, I might add! So I'm thinking that man must be working some magic on you. I need to make sure he can keep it up. So, how is my future best friend-in-law doing?"

Kenzie laughed. "Zachary is doing exceptionally well. He's in full-time training mode, so while he's working I'm trying to keep busy."

"I just want it known that I really like when you're trying to keep busy."

"So do you think it has potential?"

"I not only think that it has potential, I

already have a buyer!"

Excitement widened Kenzie's eyes. "Don't play with me. You don't. Who's interested?"

"I don't play, and yes, I do."

Stephanie spent the next few minutes updating Kenzie with the details of the potential sale of her book. From start to finish, it was everything that she wanted it to be. The advance was significant. The due dates were generous, and the publisher was one of the Big Five, with an impeccable reputation for being supportive of their authors.

"I can shop it around if you want me to, but I'll be honest, Kenzie, this is a very nice deal. I don't see us getting better."

"I agree. So I'm good with it."

"Congratulations! I'll call them back in a day or two. I don't want us to look too eager, plus I'd like to see if I can get you a little bit more on the back end."

"How did you pull that off so fast?"

"Big things happen when you're having lunch with the right people at the right time!"

"Well, I am seriously impressed."

"As you should be!"

Kenzie could sense her friend smiling into her telephone as she continued. "I have to run. I have a conference call in ten minutes.

I will catch up with you later in the week."

"Thanks, Stephanie!"

"You're welcome! And remind me when we talk to tell you about my date with the editor from Barker Books."

"You had a date!"

"Girl, he wore a skirt with Brogan work boots! But he gave the best damn head!"

Kenzie laughed out loud. "You are so wrong! How dare you give me a tease like that just before you have to hang up!" Her voice dropped to a loud whisper. "I cannot believe you gave him some!"

Stephanie laughed with her. "I'll call you! Go share your good news with my new favorite guy!"

Zachary was working out in the elevated competition cage. His hands were taped tightly as he sparred with someone Kenzie didn't know. From where she stood on the other side of the weight room, she could see that he was throwing good punches as he dominated his opponent. Alexander and Gamon stood side by side, watching him intently. Gamon and his fight team had flown in the day before, and they'd all been working like maniacs since.

Alexander crossed his arms over his chest as he assessed his brother's abilities. He was nodding his head approvingly, sometimes leaning forward to get a better view of the two men in a clinch. He would occasionally shout out a suggestion, but for the most part he was there as an observer, allowing his twin to do what he did best. He and Gamon put their heads together and whispered.

Kenzie suddenly flinched as Zachary took a hard hit, the blow knocking him off sides. She was waiting for him to recover, but it didn't look like that was going to happen. There was a scuttle of noise that filled the room, hushed whispers voicing surprise. Zachary stomped out of the enclosure, moving to talk to his twin. The conversation was done and finished as quickly as it had begun. Zachary gestured for one of the assistants to come help him get the gloves off, and after tossing them across the room, Zachary stormed into the locker rooms. There was no missing the frustration that painted Alexander's face, the sentiment echoing in Gamon's eyes.

Sarai suddenly appeared at Kenzie's elbow. "How are you today?"

"I'm good, Sarai," Kenzie answered. "Do you know if Zachary is okay?"

"His feelings are hurt. He's off his game, and he's not listening to what his training team is telling him to do."

"What is he not doing?"

Sarai hesitated. She was looking around the room, eyeing Gamon and Alexander, who were still standing in intense conversation. She cut her eyes at Kenzie, and the young woman got the impression that Sarai wanted to say something, but something was holding her back from it.

"Please. Tell me," Kenzie demanded. "Maybe I can help."

"The men say that a fighter can have no distractions before a fight. He cannot do anything while he is training that will keep him from staying focused on his end goal. Many times I have heard my father warn the fighters that there are things they should give up if they want to be their very best on fight day. There are some things Zachary needs to give up and he . . . well . . . he is being Zachary."

Kenzie hung her head in reflection, thinking about Sarai's comments. She suddenly remembered her father's last warning to Zachary. *Women are a distraction. And they are trouble. You do not need trouble. You are going to be the champion one day. You don't need trouble, and this one looks like trouble.*

When she lifted her eyes to meet the look Sarai was giving her, the woman smiled. "It would only be until after the fight. Now, though, he needs to conserve his energy, and he needs to throw all that frustration into his match. After, it will be like makeup sex, and he will be very happy again! You will both be very happy!"

Kenzie shifted her gaze to the other side of the room. Gamon and Alexander were both staring intently. They stared for a brief moment, and then the two men headed into the locker room, following after Zachary. She returned her gaze to Sarai's face. "Tell your father and Alexander that I'll take care of him. He won't have any distractions, and there will definitely be no trouble!"

Inside the locker room, Zachary was pacing like a wild man. His frustration level was at an all-time high, and he was suddenly second-guessing if committing to a title bout had been a good idea. Not one of his sparring sessions had him looking like a champion. Junior athletes with little to no experience were landing punches they had no business landing. He was so far off his game he looked like an amateur.

His brother and Gamon suddenly moved into the room. Both men were eyeing him with reservation.

Alexander spoke first. "Where's your head at, Z?" Because you're not focused."

"I know. I don't know. I just . . ."

"You are not fighting like a champion," Gamon said. "You are not fighting like you want this."

"I don't know if I do, Gamon." Zachary suddenly looked dejected.

The other two men exchanged a look.

Alexander nodded his head. "Go home. Get some rest. Be ready to do better in the morning. But I'm going to need you to give me one hundred percent. If you can't do that, then don't bother coming back."

"And if I come back, give you hundred percent or more, and I still don't get any better, then what?"

"Then you have two choices. We cancel, or you get in the ring and get your ass kicked."

Standing in the spray of hot water, Zachary couldn't begin to understand or explain why he couldn't focus and why his training was so off-kilter. But there was absolutely nothing going right, and he needed to get his act together. Gamon and Alexander had both given him their opinion, and although he knew that he wasn't following their directives to the letter, he wasn't doing much wrong.

He was glad the day was over. He needed

another opinion to help him work through the concerns and questions he had, and he hoped Kenzie would be waiting for him when he was ready to leave. He thought he'd seen her briefly right before he had started sparring, and then she wasn't anywhere to be found. But he trusted her, and he knew that she wouldn't lead him in the wrong direction. He looked forward to hearing her thoughts, to learn what she thought his problem might be.

Standing there Zachary had to admit that he had reached a point of no return. He was ready to be officially retired. He had no problems passing the game over to the younger boys rising behind him. Personally, if he were honest with himself, he was past the point of being ready to say good-bye to the sport and to try his hand at something new.

On one hand, he wanted to believe that he needed this fight. One more rally under his belt to go out on top. That was his vanity speaking. He thought of the endorsement deals that were contingent on him winning. There was a men's clothing line with a champion's label. They weren't looking for the face of that deal to be a former champion. Second place wasn't going to make the cut.

On the other hand, he really didn't need this fight. He didn't need to put his body through the brutal beating he would have to endure. Everyone knew his opponent punched with an iron fist. They didn't call him Undertaker because he was good at flower arranging. The man hit hard and getting hit hard actually hurt.

He was financially solvent, so it really wasn't about the payday. The eight-figure payout for the winner wasn't anything to spit on, but he already had eight figures in his bank account. Revolution was a profitable venture, and his investments were paying off nicely. His issues with the other gyms that surrounded him had been resolved, their owners smart enough to not cross him again. And he and Kenzie both had been blessed by Kai's love and shared a substantial inheritance bequeathed to them.

He was on that thirty-year-old uphill climb, and he wanted children and a family. He needed to be healthy in order to be fully engaged and active in their lives, most especially since he was in a relationship with the woman he actually saw bearing his children. Zachary suddenly realized his list for *not* fighting was far longer than his list for going through with it was.

He swiped a bar of Ivory soap across his

skin. The lather bubbled nicely. Using an oversized washcloth, he washed his body until he felt clean. He finally turned off the water when it started to chill, and the last of the suds disappeared down the drain.

Stepping out of the shower, Zachary wrapped himself in a towel, drying the moisture from his skin. When he was dry, he stepped into a clean pair of sweats. After gathering his personal possessions, he exited the locker room. He looked around the gym for a familiar face.

Sarai stood off to the side, training a client. He saw her excuse herself, moving toward him. "Hi," she said softly.

"Hi! Have you seen Kenzie?"

Sarai nodded. "She said to tell you that she'll meet you at the house."

He nodded, and then he leaned to kiss her cheek. "Have a good evening," he said, and then he was gone.

Kenzie knew that Zachary wasn't going to take all of her news well. She also knew that doing whatever was necessary to insure his success would always be front and center on her to-do list. She heard him when he came through the front door. He called out her name before he'd gotten the entrance closed and locked behind him. She took a deep breath before moving out of the bedroom toward the living space.

"Honey, I'm home!" He laughed, lifting his eyebrows up and down.

She laughed with him. "Hi," she said as she returned the greeting. She wrapped her arms around his neck as he lifted her in his arms and kissed her mouth. "How was your day?"

He shook his head. "I have definitely had better. How about you?"

"I had a good day!"

"I'm glad to hear it."

"Are you hungry?"

He nodded. "Yeah, I actually am. Do you want to run out and get something to eat?"

She shook her head. "No. Sarai arranged for food to be delivered. You're supposed to be watching your diet, remember?"

He shrugged. "What are you eating?"

"I'm eating what you eat. I need to clean up my diet with you."

She hugged him, nuzzling her nose against his skin. "You smell good!"

"Bath day today. I used soap and water."

She laughed. "It must be Tuesday!"

He tapped her backside as she led the way toward the kitchen.

Kenzie had already set the dinner table, and the food rested on the stovetop. They were eating an oversized salad with grilled chicken breasts. It was simple and filling. She prepared both of their plates and sat down to join him.

Zachary took two bites before he spoke again. "So what made your day so good?"

She grinned, her smile canyon wide. "I sold a book today," she said as she filled him in on her proposal and book deal.

He stood, moving to her side to kiss her. "I am so proud of you! Congratulations, baby!"

"Thank you! So what happened that you *didn't* have a good day?"

Zachary told her about his training session gone bad, adding the details of his pros and cons list for even participating in this fight. She listened intently, allowing him to rant and get past the frustration. When he was done, he looked to her for her opinion.

"You have to fight," she said. "You don't have a choice."

Her answer surprised him. "Why would you say that?"

"First, you signed a binding contract, so you are legally obligated to proceed with this fight. You are a man of great integrity, so you would never just break a contractual agreement."

"I'm sure there's an out clause."

"There's a reschedule clause, and you can only drag it out so long. Too long and you definitely won't be ready to fight."

"Point taken."

"And second, there's a part of you that has something to prove. It's why you signed in the first place. You want this last hurrah!"

He didn't bother to respond to that comment, something about it striking a nerve. He nodded, his eyes locking with hers.

"Why do you think you're distracted? What's on your mind?" she asked.

Zachary leaned back in his seat. "Honest?"

"Why would you lie to me?"

"I wouldn't. I don't have any reason to lie to you," he said shaking his head. "I think part of my problem is I'm thinking about how this fight is going to impact *our* future. If it's not going to benefit the two of *us,* then I can't think of any reason to do it. So I think my problem is I can't get you out of my head. I want to make you proud. I'm worried about being a good husband. You seem to be the only thing I can focus on."

She nodded. "Well, that's not good. My father told you about letting a woman get in the way of what you need to be doing. And I have no doubts your brother and Gamon are still telling you the same thing."

"They've had some things to say, I'm sure."

"So, we need to figure out how to get you back on track because you can't lose this fight, Zachary. That's not even an option!"

He blew a heavy sigh, as Kenzie was not saying anything he hadn't already known. "You're right. I was much more disciplined for my last fight. I need to get back to that."

"Which brings me to my next issue."

Zachary's eyes widened. "And that is?"

"I think we should practice celibacy and refrain from sexual activity until our wedding night."

"You're kidding, right?"

"No, I'm very serious. It will serve two purposes. It will help get you back on track with your training and guarantee us a really great honeymoon."

Zachary sat staring at her, his eyes blinking rapidly. "You're serious? You're really serious?"

Kenzie laughed. "Why would you think I'm kidding?"

"It'll never work. There's no way we can share the same bed and I not make love to you at least once a day. Hell, we couldn't even share the same house and different bedrooms. It's not going to happen, I promise you."

"I thought about that. That's why I'm moving in with your brother and Sarai. Gamon is going to move in here with you."

Zachary tossed his hands up in frustration. "I can't believe you're conspiring against me. This was my brother's idea, wasn't it?"

"You're being dramatic. I'm not conspiring against you. I'm conspiring *for* us."

He shook his head. "So when do you plan to marry me?"

She smiled. "Fight day. You handle your business, and I promise that night I will handle mine."

Zachary groaned. "So do I get to make love to you one last time before we do this? Bust one last nut for the road?"

Kenzie giggled. "Get your mind right, Zachary! Because I swear, if you lose this fight you're not getting any *that* night either!"

Zachary hadn't taken Kenzie seriously, and now she was gone, having actually moved out of the house where they had been staying and into the house with Sarai and his brother. He sat in the family room, Gamon eyeing him intently. *Gamon was not the roommate he'd been hoping for,* he thought as he tossed the man a look.

Gamon laughed. "She is coming back. After fight you will not be able to get rid of her!"

"Promises, promises," Zachary said.

Sarai laughed. "So what else can we do for you?"

"I think you've done more than enough."

"I don't know why you are mad with me. I had nothing at all to do with this. It was all Kenzie's idea."

Zachary rolled his eyes skyward, "You didn't say anything at all to Kenzie? Not one word or suggestion?"

"Oh, I said something, but I didn't tell her to move out. She just knows how you are."

"How I am?"

"You have no self-control."

"Excuse you! I have great self-control!"

Alexander interjected. "No, you really don't. Kenzie may have single-handedly figured out how we need to help and support you."

Zachary mumbled something under his breath.

"What did you say?" Sarai asked.

Zachary stood up, heading toward the room's exit. "I said I'm going running. I need to burn some energy off."

Alexander laughed. "Oh, yeah! We are on the right track now."

Chapter Eighteen

Zachary threw a left-right combo with a round-house kick. His technique was picture-perfect. The people on his team all nodded their approval. He repeated the exchange, kicking with his other leg the second time. He was down a good twenty pounds since Kenzie had moved out, and he'd gotten focused, nothing but lean muscle clinging to his bones. Now they were days away from fight night, and he was as ready as he would ever be.

Alexander jumped into the ring with his twin. His hands were covered with boxing pads, and he held up his palms in a defensive stance. Zachary threw a chain of punches. *One, two, two, one.* And then another. *Two, two, one, one.*

"Good job," Alexander said. "Have you watched the tapes on Barrera?"

Zachary nodded. "He's short on foot work and deadly in the clutches. I'm going to need to stay off the ropes or he will hurt me. And I can't afford to get hurt."

His twin nodded in agreement. "You need to take him out early. Don't try to go the full twenty-five minutes. He just gets better the longer he's in the ring. Don't dance with him if you don't have to."

The brothers both relaxed. Alexander tossed the pads over the side of the ring. Zachary held out his hands as his twin began to untie his gloves. The two men exited the ring together.

"Do you want to run with me?" Zachary asked.

Alexander shook his head. "No, and I really don't want you running. You did the treadmill earlier, right?"

"I did."

"Hold off on doing any further cardio today. And until the fight, just keep it light and easy. Conserve your energy."

"Yes, boss!"

"The girls are at Starbucks. Do you want to head over and join them?"

"You mean you're going to actually let me spend some time with my woman?"

Alexander laughed. "I'm even going to let you spend some time with my woman!"

"Let me grab a quick shower, and I'll be right there!"

■ ■ ■ ■

Zachary was excited about spending some time with Kenzie. Since she'd moved into his brother's home, their time together was perfectly planned by everyone else except them. That first week had been the hardest. The second had been as challenging, and then suddenly things had just clicked for the two of them. Her determination had fueled his. Kenzie was rock solid when she wanted to accomplish something. Her strength and fortitude were impressive, and it made him proud.

While he'd been focused on pulling his training regime together, she'd thrown herself into her research. Every night they spoke on the telephone, and she always had a new Alzheimer's story to share. The project had her connecting with people from around the world, and she'd been writing furiously. Her energy and enthusiasm had fueled his.

The excitement registered across Kenzie's face when he and his brother entered the coffee shop. She waved excitedly. Zachary eased into the booth beside her. He pressed his mouth to hers just as she drew her hands to his face, cupping his cheeks in her palms.

The kisses were quick pecks; both were mindful not to start something they wouldn't be able to finish. The chemistry between them was thick and abundant.

"Hi," Zachary whispered, kissing her again.

"How are you?" Kenzie asked.

He nodded. "I'm really good." He shot a look across table, his eyes connecting with his sister-in-law, who was watching them intently. "Sarai!"

"Zachary!"

Alexander leaned over to kiss his wife, who kissed him back. "Hey, sweetheart!"

Sarai wrapped her arms around the man's neck and hugged him. "Are you boys good today?"

"Very good!" Alexander answered.

The women had already ordered a round of coffee for the table. The family fell into easy conversation. Zachary was particularly grateful for the opportunity to catch up on talk that had nothing to do with the upcoming fight. And any chance to be near Kenzie had him doing a quiet happy dance.

"So have you two made any wedding plans?" Sarai asked. Her eyes skated from one to the other.

Kenzie nodded. "We have planned to not make any plans."

Zachary nodded his agreement. "Sometime during the day, we're going to find a little chapel and a justice of the peace. It's going to be short and sweet, and then I'm going to win my fight and forget how you all have been conspiring against me."

Kenzie grinned. "What he said."

"Well, your brother and I would love to host your reception," Sarai said.

Kenzie shrugged. "We appreciate that, but the after-party for the fight will be reception enough. We don't want a lot of fanfare."

Zachary gave Kenzie a squeeze. "Kenzie doesn't want anyone going overboard. She wants simple and private, and I plan to honor that. Whatever my baby wants she can have."

The other woman nodded.

Alexander shook his head. "I thought every woman dreamt of having a lavish wedding. Isn't that what all little girls aspire to?"

Sarai laughed. "I aspired to falling in love with the perfect guy."

"Me too!" Kenzie echoed.

Zachary laughed. "You two sure got lucky! It's a good thing you found me and A before we got gone!"

Alexander laughed. "I know that's right!"

The laughter rang easily through the

room. The abundance of love around the table was endearing. The hour was well spent as they made plans for the weekend and double-checked that they were all on the same page with whatever Zachary might need to insure things ran smoothly while they were in Las Vegas.

Alexander was the first to shut down their little program, rising from his seat. He pulled Sarai by the hand. "I'll be in the car. Kiss your woman goodbye and meet me out there in the parking lot when you're done," he said, his eyes focused on his brother's face.

Zachary nodded. When the other couple had stepped through the entrance door, moving out of their eyesight, Kenzie kissed him again, her tongue darting back and forth.

He pressed his cheek to hers and held on. "Are you sure everything is okay?" he asked. "You don't need anything, do you?"

"I need for this fight to be over so things can go back to the way they were. I miss you!" Kenzie's jaw was tight, and her brow creased in frustration. The faintest smile pulled at her lips.

"I miss you too! But it won't be much longer now."

"Are you feeling better about the fight?"

Zachary grinned. “I feel really good. I’m confident that I’ve got this.”

She smiled. “So am I. You looked good when I saw you sparring the other day.”

“You were checking up on me?”

“I needed to make sure you’d found your groove.”

“It took me a minute, but it’s all good! I really am very happy with how the training has gone. My brother has been working the snot out of me!”

“What do you have planned for later?” Kenzie asked.

“What I do every night. Keep my fingers crossed that you’ll sneak over and give me some.”

Kenzie laughed. “Just a few more days, baby!”

“I might not want it then.”

“That’ll be fine too!”

Zachary chuckled. “You know I’m lying!”

Chapter Nineteen

Zachary stood toe to toe with his brother as Alexander wrapped his hands in gauze tape. Alexander was painstakingly meticulous with the over-and-under, round-and-round covering that would afford his twin a semblance of protection from the elements in the fight ring. Zachary's eyes skipped from his sibling's face to the crowd beginning to gather in the room.

The space wasn't large, and it was filling quickly. Their parents were holding court in a corner on the other side as Mama Lynn regaled anyone who would bother to listen with stories about the two of them. There was Gamon, Zachary's personal physician, his cut man, two of his sparring partners, his corner guy, UFC officials, a representative from the MGM Grand, which was hosting the event, and a handful of media personalities hoping to score an exclusive interview. Sarai and Kenzie were the only important people missing from the bunch, and no one seemed to know where either was.

Zachary began pacing back and forth, his hands resting against the line of his hips. He jumped an imaginary jump rope, rising up and down on his toes to stretch the tightness out of his legs. He tilted his head left and then right, popping the tension out of the muscles in his neck. His stomach was doing flips, and he realized that in his whole career, this was the first fight that truly had him nervous. He clenched his fists and threw some easy punches.

"We need to get you in your gloves," Gamon said, gesturing him toward the table that sat in the center of the room.

Zachary looked toward the door, glanced at his brother, then nodded his assent. Though he was trying not to panic, his usual pre-fight regime was shot to hell. With the lacings finally tied on his gloves, Zachary stood in the center of the room, continuing to warm up. Gamon held up cushioned sparring pads for him to throw light punches and kicks at. He needed to work up a sweat to get his muscles warm and loose, and his team was insuring that happened.

An hour later, arena officials announced fight time. Panic suddenly washed over

Zachary's expression. He turned to his brother. "Where the hell are they?"

Alexander shook his head. He grabbed his cell phone and dialed, but neither woman answered her line. He and his twin exchanged a look, and he could see the anxiety rising in Zachary's eyes. "They'll get here," Alexander said, hoping to ease his brother's angst.

Before either man could respond, the room door flung open, and the two women rushed inside. Relief flooded Zachary's face.

"We are so sorry," Kenzie exclaimed. "We were literally stuck in traffic!"

Zachary kissed her mouth. "You're here. That's all that matters."

"We need to pray," Sarai said. The room went quiet as she grabbed the two brothers by the hand.

Kenzie closed their small circle, bowing her head as she laced her fingers through Alexander's and pressed her warm palm against Zachary's forearm.

Sarai whispered a Buddhist chant of protection over them all, and then Zachary asked God for guidance and clarity. A collective *amen* rang throughout the room when they were done.

Kenzie kissed his mouth. "Kick ass!" she admonished, a bright smile on face.

The official handler who had been assigned to the team cleared his throat for their attention. "I'm sorry, but we really need to head to the ring," he said, listening to something being said into his earpiece.

With his clipboard and ink pen in hand, the man verified everyone's passes, then gestured for them to follow. At the door, Zachary took the lead. Alexander, Gamon, and his father, Westley, fell in after him. The rest of the team followed, and Kenzie, Sarai, and Mama Lynn brought up the rear. Everyone wore their Revolution T-shirts, the bright blue emblem on the lime-green shirts showcasing the gym's logo.

The trek to the ring wove through a chamber of back tunnels to the outdoor arena. The event had closed down the Las Vegas Strip, and the crowds were massive. It looked like a parting of the seas as people moved aside to let the reigning champion through. Zachary's name was being chanted over and over again. Repetitions of "Hammer! Hammer! Hammer!" resounded through the air. Their guide lifted up his hand and held them in place for a brief second, awaiting the signal to have the current world champion step into view. And then the sound system blasted Zachary's theme song to announce his entrance.

When the 1990s rap song “U Can’t Touch This,” by MC Hammer, sounded out of the speakers, Zachary turned to give Kenzie one last look. She was laughing, her hands held high over her head as she clapped in time to the music. She blew him a kiss, and he grinned, every ounce of his earlier anxiety dissipating. He tossed his brother a look. Alexander’s smile was wide, and he patted his twin on the back, sending him forward.

Zachary stepped past the cordoned area and moved out into view. The crowd erupted, their loud cheers vibrating through the late-night air. Cameras snapped photographs, fans screamed, and people standing near the path they took reached out to try and touch him. As they neared the infamous octagon cage that the fighters would be locked in, Zachary threw up his arm, pushing his gold championship belt into the air, and he screamed with the music. *Hammer time!*

Tears streamed down Kenzie’s face, and she didn’t even know she was crying. The emotional overload from watching Zachary in the ring had her screaming and shaking and ready to throw her own punches.

In the first minutes of the first round, Zachary had taken Barrera down to the ground easily. Some thought the head crank was going to be the end of the challenger, and then he'd come back with a triangle choke. In the second round, the two men were exchanging blow for blow, one right after the other. Zachary was taking each punch without faltering, and the harsh dull thuds of Barrera's gloves slamming into his body had Kenzie cringing.

On several occasions, it looked as if the fight could have gone either way, most especially when the two went from submission attempt to submission attempt as they rolled back and forth on the ground. The sheer technical beauty of the submissions and escapes would be replayed over and over again for all aspiring fighters, the trend going down as some of the best play-by-play in history.

Time seemed to stand still as the two men went from the clenches back to pummeling each other like they were each punching bread dough and not human flesh. And then the crowd went wild! Barrera had Zachary in a deep choke hold. Kenzie watched as he began to turn a deep shade of beet red and then eggplant purple. She screamed and yelled with the crowd, which was shouting his name, "Hammer! Hammer! Hammer!" over and over again. For a brief moment, it looked as if the champion's reign was about to come to an abrupt end, but they didn't know Zachary the way Kenzie and his family knew him.

She screamed. Alexander screamed. His friends and family all screamed, telling Zachary to get up and finish the fight. Escaping the choke, he nailed Barrera with a back kick that knocked the wind from the fighter's sails. Zachary grabbed him by the throat, literally picking him up off his feet and then slamming him down to the ground. Applying his own rear choke hold around the other man's neck, his muscles bulged as he applied pressure, steadied his footing, and held on.

For three minutes and ten seconds, he refused to let go until Barrera tapped out, unable to take the pain a second longer. For three minutes and ten seconds, Kenzie would have sworn on everything she held sacred that she had held her breath, refusing to release it until the moment Zachary threw his fists in the air and screamed, "Hammer time," proclaiming his win.

The noise level throughout the open-air arena hit a whole new decibel level. Kenzie and Sarai grabbed each other, jumping up and down as if they were twelve years old and at the concert of their favorite boy band. But through the noise, Kenzie suddenly heard Zachary call her name. Lifting her eyes back to the cage, she saw that he was clutching the bars, calling for her.

Gamon helped her push her way to the entrance, and as she threw herself inside, Zachary caught her, sweeping her into his arms. He hugged her tightly as she hugged him back.

"Are you going to marry me now?" he asked, whispering in her ear.

Kenzie grinned. "Hell, yeah!"

Sneaking out of the MGM Grand Hotel after the fight had actually been easier to accomplish than any of them had imagined. The after-party, a UFC-sponsored celebration, which had featured two live bands and a lengthy high-profile guest list, was loud and overcrowded, everyone focused on the abundance of food and the free booze. Only the media personalities wanting a sound bite from Zachary realized he was gone, and by then it was too late.

With everyone's permission, Kenzie had given a rising sports journalist named Cheryl Duncan exclusive access to Zachary and his post-fight story. Cheryl was talented and determined and, since she was competing in a field dominated by aggressive and arrogant men, appreciative of the opportunity. Once she'd gotten her fan girl moment out of her system, she'd been the consummate professional, asking Zachary and Alexander a series of questions that had actually given Kenzie reason to pause.

"You've said that this would be your last fight, but there's a long list of heavyweights who believe you should give them a chance, including Mendes and Robert Gracie. What do you say to that?"

Zachary smiled sweetly. "Mendes and Gracie couldn't beat Barrera. I put Barrera on his ass twice. I don't have anything else to prove. I'm proud of the professional career that I've had. I've accomplished what many said I couldn't do. I've held the heavyweight championship title for over ten years. It's mine. No one's been able to take it from me. I don't need to fight again."

Cheryl Duncan shifted the digital recorder in her hand. "Is it true that you're in negotiations with NBC to join their sportscasting team?"

Zachary cut an eye toward Kenzie, who gave him a slight wink of her eye. He shrugged his broad shoulders. "I'm in negotiations with a number of organizations to do a lot of things. I'll be excited to make those announcements when the time's appropriate."

The limousine they were all riding in suddenly came to a stop. Sarai looked out the window, then shot them all a look. "We're here!" she exclaimed, her excitement rising.

Cheryl looked confused.

Kenzie tapped her hand. "We have to make a quick pit stop before we head back to the party. Do you have any more questions?"

"I just wanted to ask both men what's next for them." She looked from Alexander to Zachary, her eyebrows lifted curiously.

The limo driver swung the side door open, extending a hand to help the women exit the vehicle. Zachary crooked his index finger at Cheryl, gesturing for her to follow. "I'm about to close the biggest negotiation of my life," he said. "Come join us!"

The Little White Wedding Chapel was a Las Vegas staple. Known worldwide, the venue had been the go-to spot for thousands of love-struck couples. The list of stars who'd gotten hitched there was lengthy and diverse. Sarai had arranged for them to have the Romance Package, which included the chapel, thirty-six digital photos, music, and fresh flowers. It was everything Kenzie and Zachary had wanted.

Mama Lynn, Westley, Gamon, and Stephanie were there waiting for them when they arrived. The women pulled Kenzie into a back room to slip on her wedding dress, the only traditional thing she'd agreed to after much prodding from her two friends. The beaded lace and crepe gown was a Rose Clare design. It was ivory, off the shoulder with a simple back bow, and it fit her like a custom-made glove. Like a magician with hairpins, Sarai pulled Kenzie's thick curls into a stunning up do and showcased her pageant girl makeup skills with perfection. It had taken less than thirty minutes, and Kenzie was a stunning bride.

Stephanie brushed a tear from her eye. "Damn, girl! You look hot!"

Kenzie laughed as she studied her reflection in the mirror. "I do look good, if I say so myself."

Sarai looked at her watch. "You guys are up next. Are you ready?"

Kenzie took a deep breath. "I've been ready!"

"Stop!" Stephanie suddenly shouted. "Lord, we are about to send you to marriage hell with nothing but bad luck!"

Kenzie looked confused. "Excuse me?"

"Something borrowed, something blue?"

They all laughed.

Sarai unsnapped the Pandora bracelet on her wrist. "Wear this. It's your borrowed."

Kenzie twirled the beautiful charms that adorned the piece. "It's so pretty. Do I have to give it back?"

"I will hunt you down if you don't," her new sister-in-law said. "My Alexander gave me that."

Stephanie raced from the room, rushing back in a few minutes later. She was pulling a blue lace garter belt from its packaging. "They sell everything here. I added it to your bill!" she said.

Kenzie laughed as she stepped into the garment and slid it up the length of her leg. "Something blue. Check!"

Mama Lynn stepped forward as she dug into her handbag, finally pulling out a lace handkerchief. "When Mr. Barrett and I first got married, I found this in a drawer of things that had belonged to his late wife. I started carrying it when I would take the boys someplace and they'd start crying for their mama. I would wipe their tears with it and tell them she was watching over them from heaven. It always made me feel good, so I've never taken it out of my purse. Here's your something old."

Tears misted Kenzie's eyes as she clutched the hanky in her hand. Mama Lynn kissed her cheek and squeezed her arm.

"So all we need is the something new, right?" Sarai asked

Kenzie nodded. She lifted her foot, the price tag still stuck on the bottom of her satin shoe. "I think we're good!"

They laughed, and then they pointed Kenzie to the door, leading her toward her future.

Cheryl sat in a front pew. She'd already posted a photo of Zachary on her social media accounts, announcing her exclusive interview. It had been an image of him seeing his bride for the first time, as Kenzie glided down the aisle toward him. Tears had rained over his cheeks, and joy had been the bright light in his gray eyes.

She would later profess to one of her journalism mentors that this had been one of the highlights of her blossoming career. Witnessing the marriage ceremony of the world's heavyweight MMA champion just moments after his career-ending win had truly been an honor.

Kenzie and Zachary stood hand in hand as the officiant, an older man with a really bad toupee and a gold lamé tuxedo stood between them. He held a bible in his hands, and a million-dollar smile filled his face.

The wedding party was small enough that Kenzie asked for everyone to stand with the two of them, enveloping them in a semicircle. As she looked from one to the other, she was suddenly struck by the abundance of love that filled the room. And then she thought about her father, wishing for a brief moment that they could have had more time together and that he could have been there to walk her down the aisle. She thought about her mother and the well wishes that had come over an international call. The older woman's exuberance had made her smile, her only advice being that Kenzie make sure they had joint bank accounts and promising to come see them the first chance she could.

Reading her mind, Zachary squeezed her hands, her fingers entwined with his. Having his family there to celebrate the moment brought him immense joy. He knew Kenzie was missing hers, even if she tried to pretend otherwise. He knew how much she was missing Kai because so was he, never fathoming that the old man would not have been there to celebrate the moment with them.

Out of the blue, a gust of wind blew the door to the chapel open. On the other side of the door, someone's sound system was playing, an exotic tune of drums and woodwinds resounding in the distance. The couple locked gazes, eyebrows lifted, and then they laughed, taking it as a sign that maybe Kai Tamura was still watching over them both and somewhere the monks were chanting prayers for them all.

The gold-clad minister cleared his throat as he stole a quick glance down at the postcard printed with their names. "Dearly beloved, we are gathered here today, in the presence of these witnesses, to join Zachary Barrett and Kenzie Monroe in matrimony, which is commended to be honorable among all and therefore is not to be entered into lightly but reverently, passionately, lovingly, and solemnly. Into this union, these two persons present now come to be joined. If any person can show just cause why they may not be joined together, let them speak now or forever hold their peace."

Stephanie suddenly coughed as if she were clearing her throat, and Sarai giggled.

Mama Lynn shook her bright red wig. "You all need to stop," she said as they all laughed.

The minister continued. "Zachary Barrett, do you take this woman to be your lawfully wedded wife?"

Zachary grinned. "I do."

"And Kenzie Monroe, do you take this man to be your lawfully wedded husband?"

Kenzie smiled. "Of course I do. Nobody else is going to get him!"

The minister nodded. "Then by the power vested in me by the state of Nevada, I now pronounce you husband and wife. Mr. Barrett, you may now kiss your bride."

The ceremony was over in less than ten minutes. The happy couple declared it the most perfect moment in both their lives. The last question Cheryl asked before they dropped her off at her hotel was what they would have changed, if anything, and both had said absolutely nothing!

CHAPTER TWENTY

Staring out at the scene below, it felt as if they were floating twenty-nine stories over the city. The panoramic views of the glittering Las Vegas skyline were unparalleled from the Skyloft suites at the MGM Grand Hotel.

After dropping their family and friends off at the post-fight celebration, the newlyweds had one thing on their minds, wanting to spend a few quiet moments in each other's company. It had been weeks since they'd last been behind closed doors with each other and left to their own devices.

Zachary had swept her into his arms and carried her over the threshold, his mouth latched to hers as he kissed her. And then they'd both laughed, marveling at how magnificent the entire day had been.

"You are the most beautiful woman!" Zachary had said, with Kenzie still clutched in his arms. "You really clean up nice," he'd teased.

Kenzie had laughed. "You're not so bad yourself. I love the tux. We must do this more often."

"What? Get married?"

"You're stuck with me forever. You will never be getting married again, so don't get any ideas!"

Zachary laughed.

"No," she continued. "We need to make a point of getting dressed up and going out more often."

"I agree. We look pretty dressed up!" he teased as he set her back on her feet. She'd leaned to give him another kiss, their mouths dancing sweetly together.

She pressed a palm to his chest, and he winced, a hint of hurt wrinkling his brow.

"You need to soak," she said as she pushed his jacket off his shoulders. She unbuttoned the bright white shirt, allowing her fingers to lightly graze his skin. There was a huge bruise blossoming across his chest, the black and blue coloration spreading with a vengeance.

"How hard did he hit you?" Kenzie asked, her eyes widening.

Zachary shrugged. "Not as hard as I hit him back," he said matter-of-factly.

She shook her head. "I'm going to run a bath for you. Sarai left a bag that she said you'll need. It's got some Epsom salts, anti-inflammatory meds, and pain pills. We need to get you comfortable."

He grabbed her hand. "I'm with you. I am comfortable," he said as he recaptured her mouth one more time.

Kissing Zachary was a dream come true. Kenzie couldn't imagine any other man ever making her feel the way he made her feel. She knew that his kissing her was a distraction, and she allowed herself to give in to it for just a brief moment.

Pulling herself from him, she gasped, swiftly inhaling. He smiled, the look he gave her intense.

"You're taking a pain pill, Zachary," she said.

He laughed. "The pain pill will put me to sleep."

"You need to rest. You just won a championship fight. I know you're hurting, and I know you're trying to hide it."

"It's not that bad."

She shook her head. "Sarai ordered a ton of ice. The tub is full. She said you need to soak for a few minutes to keep the swelling down."

"Why is Sarai trying to ruin my wedding

night? I didn't bother her and Alexander when they got married!"

"She is not trying to ruin your wedding night."

"Do you know what ice water is going to do to my thang?" he asked, his eyebrows raised.

Kenzie laughed. "I'll warm your *thang* up. I promise!" She turned, moving into the bathroom, and he followed.

Zachary hated to admit it, but he did need to soak, every one of his muscles feeling like he'd been hit by a Mack truck. The few lucky shots Barrera had gotten in were swollen, the bruises beginning to shift color from flaming red to varying degrees of black and blue. As he stepped out of his clothes and stared at his reflection in the mirror, he looked like an accident victim. He knew that in that moment there was nothing sexy or romantic about his body.

Kenzie shook her head as she eyed him. It hurt to see him like that, so she could only imagine what he had to be feeling. "My poor baby!" she muttered softly as he stepped into the bathtub and the chilly water.

Zachary held his breath until his body was completely submerged. Then he cussed, a row of expletives falling out of his mouth.

"You cuss like a damn sailor!" Kenzie exclaimed. "You need to work on that!"

Zachary laughed.

Giving him a moment, Kenzie picked his clothes up off the floor, moving into the oversized bedroom to hang them in the closet. By the time she returned to his side, his teeth weren't chattering nearly as much as before. She passed him a glass of champagne.

"Don't tell. I don't think you're supposed to mix your medication with alcohol, but you look like you could use a drink."

Zachary grinned "God, I love you!"

"I love you too!" she said. She lifted her own glass to toast their union, and then they both took a sip.

He blew a soft sigh as they sat quietly together, falling into a comfortable silence. They didn't need words, the moment being exactly what the two needed it to be. A good few minutes passed as she sat on the tub's edge, watching him watch her.

"You about ready?" she asked.

He nodded. "I need to take a hot shower first."

"Do you need me to help you?"

He shook his head. "You can join me."

"I can do that," she said softly.

Zachary stood, stepping out of the porcelain tub. He moved to the shower and turned the water on hot. Stepping into the glass enclosure, he stood beneath the heated spray, allowing the warm, wet blanket to wash over his body.

Kenzie pushed her lace gown from her arms, the garment falling to the floor. As Zachary watched her, she did a slow, seductive striptease out of her lace panties and strapless bra. When she was naked, she strode slowly toward him. Zachary extended his hand, pulling her inside the spray of water with him.

Kenzie eased herself slowly against him, her gaze focused on his face. He winced slightly as her skin touched his. "Are you okay?" she whispered. "I don't want to hurt you."

He shook his head, his hands slowly skating the length of her back. "It's all good. Having you in my arms like this is the best bandage ever!" He smiled, and then he leaned in to kiss her.

In that moment, everything was perfect, and good, and right. They traded easy, gentle caresses, reveling in the warmth of each other's touch. Zachary was in awe of just how deeply he had missed her, how much he needed her, and the intensity of the emotions that were billowing like the sweetest breeze between them. He was feeling just a bit toasty from the champagne and the pain pills, and slowly but surely nothing hurt, everything tingling with pure desire. The look in Kenzie's eyes had melted every sinewy muscle into putty, and he was overjoyed at being able to lose himself in her gaze.

Reaching behind him, he shut off the water; then he lifted her into his arms, carrying her into the bedroom. He laid her gently on the bed, then dropped his body down against hers. Lying side by side, they held onto each other, settling into the heat and the warmth of one another. They stared into each other's eyes and lost themselves in the love that gleamed from their stares. Staring at him, as his hands traced seductive patterns across her skin, Kenzie wanted to scream with joy, the kind of elation that was like winning the raffle or the biggest prize at the state fair. She was happier than she had ever been before, and as he kissed her, he was feeling the exact same way.

She placed her palms against his chest and pushed him gently back against the mountain of pillows. "Relax," she whispered. Her smile was teasing as she kissed him again, her lips brushing ever so gently against his. Her smile widened when Zachary closed his eyes, savoring the moment, finally allowing himself to let go.

Kenzie kissed him down the length of his torso, to his abdomen. She dipped her tongue into the well of his belly button, gently licking him in a slow, easy circle. He squirmed, and his male member twitched. Her fingers gently brushed his bruised skin, and where her hands trailed, her mouth followed, her tongue gliding slowly back and forth.

Zachary pulled her back to him, reclaiming her mouth. He kissed her over and over again as he wrapped his arms around her and held her tightly against him. "Like this," he whispered. "I just want to hold you like this," he repeated as he pressed one palm against her buttocks, pulling her tightly against him. His other hand pulled her leg over his legs; he wanted to feel her body draped sweetly over his.

As she settled herself against him, it was a moment of ecstasy. She thought of every whispered word they'd ever shared, every touch, all the goose bumps, the sensations of tongue on flesh, all the squeals and groans and mumbled utterings, the twitches and chills and shakes. The memories were sweet and decadent, and both relished the future that would bring them more and bigger and better. Then Zachary drifted off into a deep and restful sleep, with Kenzie following in kind.

Hours later Kenzie stood on the patio, leaning on the glass rails as she stared out at the shimmering lights that magnified the best of the city. Her thoughts drifted back to the past as she reflected on everything that had gotten her to this moment. She thought about her father and Thailand and the home she and Zachary would make there. She thought about the babies she suddenly wanted to hold in her heart because they would be his babies. She was Mrs. Kenzie Barrett, Zachary's wife, the woman he'd chosen to take his name and share in his life

From the doorway, Zachary stood watching her. She was exquisite and easily the most beautiful woman in the whole world. She looked content and happy, and in that moment he promised her, himself, and God that he would do whatever was necessary to ensure she never lost that glow.

Zachary was suddenly consumed with emotion. Every dream he'd ever had had come true. Winning the title didn't compare to the prize that now carried his name, the woman who'd promised to love him through sickness and health. Everything about his future seemed bigger and brighter, and Kenzie would be there by his side, encouraging, motivating, and supporting him with everything in her.

He called her name softly. "Mrs. Barrett," he said as he came up behind her, wrapping her in his arms.

Kenzie smiled. She relaxed her body against his, sliding into the heat that was rising between them. "You're awake!"

He nodded. "Come back to bed," he said, and then he pressed his bare skin against hers. It was an indescribable perfect pleasure.

The employees of Thorndike Press hope you have enjoyed this Large Print book. All our Thorndike, Wheeler, and Kennebec Large Print titles are designed for easy reading, and all our books are made to last. Other Thorndike Press Large Print books are available at your library, through selected bookstores, or directly from us.

For information about titles, please call:
(800) 223-1244

or visit our Web site at:
http://gale.cengage.com/thorndike

To share your comments, please write:
Publisher
Thorndike Press
10 Water St., Suite 310
Waterville, ME 04901